# Río Chama

# OTHER FIVE STAR WESTERNS BY JOHNNY D. BOGGS:

*The Lonesome Chisholm Trail* (2000)
*Once They Wore the Gray* (2001)
*Lonely Trumpet* (2002)
*The Despoilers* (2002)
*The Big Fifty* (2003)
*Purgatoire* (2003)
*Dark Voyage of the* Mittie Stephens (2004)
*East of the Border* (2004)
*Camp Ford* (2005)
*Ghost Legion* (2005)
*Walk Proud, Stand Tall* (2006)
*The Hart Brand* (2006)
*Northfield* (2007)
*Doubtful Cañon* (2007)
*Killstraight* (2008)
*Soldier's Farewell* (2008)

# Río Chama

## A Western Story

## Johnny D. Boggs

**FIVE STAR**
*A part of Gale, Cengage Learning*

Detroit • New York • San Francisco • New Haven, Conn • Waterville, Maine • London

Five Star Publishing, a part of Gale, Cengage Learning.



Set in 11 pt. Plantin.

Printed on permanent paper.

**LIBRARY OF CONGRESS CATALOGING-IN-PUBLICATION DATA**

Boggs, Johnny D.
Río Chama : a western story / by Johnny D. Boggs. — 1st ed.
p. cm.
"A Five Star western" —T.p. verso
ISBN-13: 978-1-59414-737-1 (alk. paper)
ISBN-10: 1-59414-737-X (alk. paper)
I. Title.
PS3552.O437R56 2009
813′.54—dc22 2009005172

First Edition. First Printing: June 2009.
Published in 2009 in conjunction with Golden West Literary Agency.

Printed in the United States of America
1 2 3 4 5 6 7 13 12 11 10 09

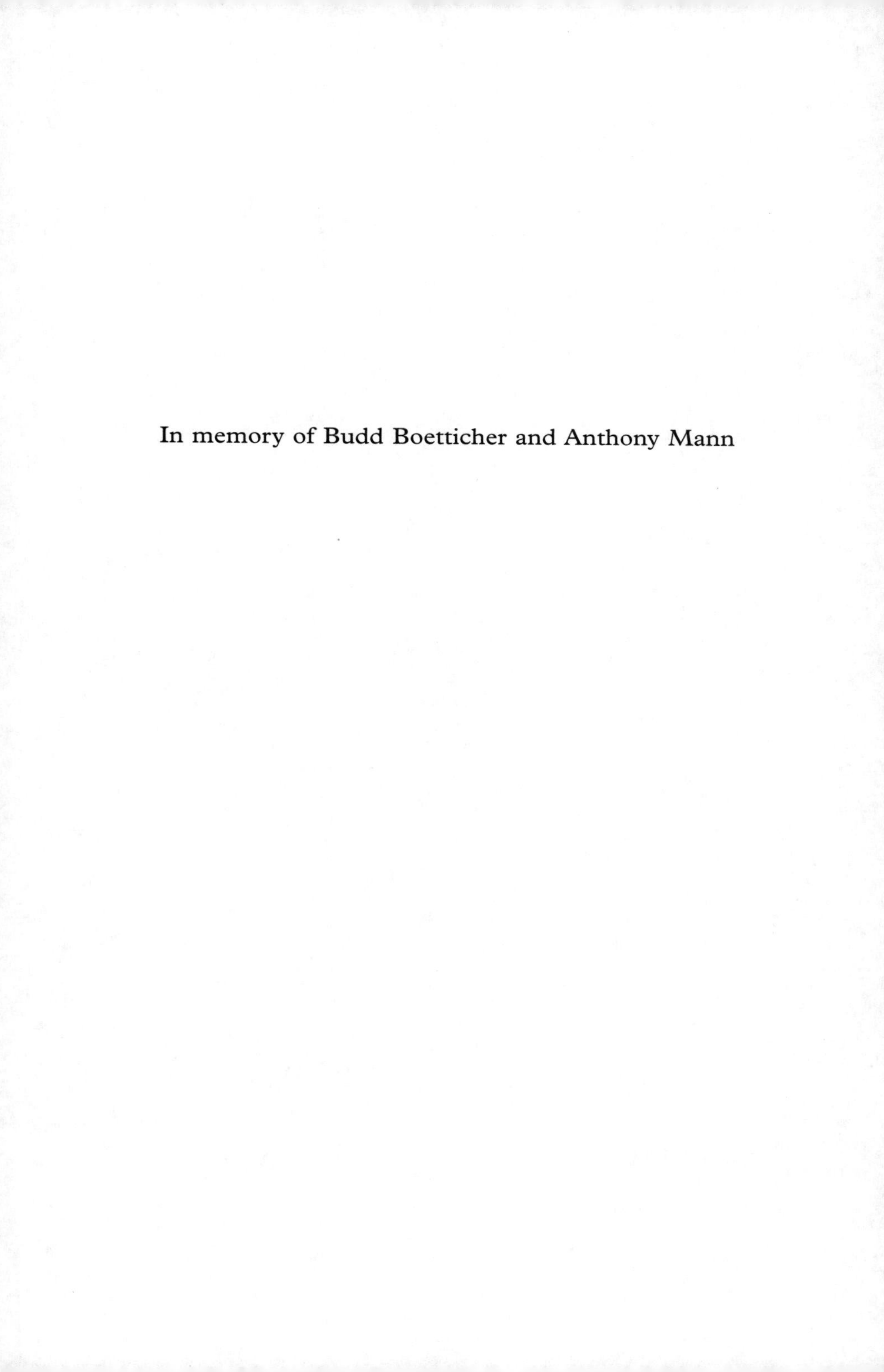

In memory of Budd Boetticher and Anthony Mann

# PROLOGUE
# FROM THE DIARY OF JAMES R. GAGE

*Friday, April 29, 1898*

The Northwest New Mexican published an interesting bit this past week. I quote part of it here: *Tramps and sneak thieves will probably in the future give Chama a wide berth. The rope is a desperate but sure remedy.*

While I wouldn't bet a plug nickel on the veracity of such a statement, I'd wager even less on the chance that carpet-bagging newspaper editor has of staying in business once Senator Cole reads that highfalutin editorial.

The editor's a newcomer, so she must not know the way things work in the Chama valley. The hanging is set two weeks from today, but nobody in the territory believes that Jeremiah Cole will ever swing. Why, I dare say, the case never would have come to trial if that Mex had not been appointed territorial governor, and Jeremiah most certainly never would have been convicted if not for the man who young Cole helped lynch.

Appeals have run their course, so now everything rests on the will of God, or rather, the will of Senator Roman Cole.

# CHAPTER ONE

Fear stopped him.

He had stepped onto Water Street, having cut down the long, narrow alley from San Francisco, and now he clearly saw his destination, just across the deserted road lined with adobe and dust. Walk, he ordered, but did not move. Could not move.

Fear.

When was the last time he had been scared? It felt like a lifetime ago, on the morning that bald-headed sawbones in Baltimore had handed him his death sentence. Or a time or two since then, after he had shunned the damp cities for the West, back when those early coughing spells had him fearing death. Certainly he had not been frightened in more than a dozen years, surprising doctors by still living, if he could call what he did living. Yet here he stood, hands trembling, just a few rods from the Santa Fe City Jail. Why now?

What could they do to him? Throw him in jail? Prison? He had spent time in jails, probably should have been sent to prison a time or two. That didn't frighten him. Kill him? On the streets of Chloride, he had faced down two men for no other reason than the fact they had insulted him. He had been shot at more times than he could remember, wore a slight scar across his forehead left by a card player who had not taken kindly to losing. That man he had left dead on a poker table in Mogollon. He had arrested murderers and bank robbers, and never once been afraid. A few people had whispered that he had wanted to die, and maybe he did. He was a dead man anyway, had been one for sixteen years.

A white-haired Mexican in dingy cotton led a burro up Bridge Street, giving him only a passing glance before disappearing inside the livery next to the alley. He should move now, before the city sprang to life, and the streets filled with people.

Suddenly Britton Wade knew the reason behind his fear, and he grinned. He wasn't scared of death, or of jail, or of anything they could do to him, if he failed. He feared only shame. What if his scheme failed? Newspaper editors would ridicule him, all across New Mexico Territory, maybe throughout the United States. Jeer him. Make him the butt of their jokes, their mocking editorials. They'd spit on his life, although he had pretty much spat on his own life. Yet, somehow, he had never shucked his pride.

"Let them laugh," he said in a dry whisper, summoning his courage, and crossed the street, pausing only for a moment at the door to set down his Gladstone bag, suppressing a cough. Then, looking up and down Water Street, he picked up his grip, and stepped inside.

"What is this?"

With cold eyes boring hard through Wade, the old jailer held the paper Wade had handed him for inspection, and repeated his question, his voice heavy with a Mexican accent although his eyes looked Irish.

Wade wet his lips, wondered if he were sweating heavily—he certainly felt hot despite the chill of the spring morning outside—and took the paper, gave it a glance, suddenly laughing at his stupidity. He had given the jailer the wrong paper, his membership card, diploma, whatever one felt like calling it, that he had been carrying for years.

*Lungers Club*

*Cure all maladies, we tuberculars unite*
*Coughing and wheezing, we continue the fight.*
*For rest and recuperation in hot springs we soak.*
*At the adobe hotel, we laugh and joke.*
*We might be sick and crazy, too,*
*As we form a club with members so few.*
*Some have not as others have wealth,*
*But we bask in a warm sun and return to good*
*health.*
*So join us now, if you will and very soon,*
*Better you will feel.*
*Lungers ever retreating never.*

He thought: *Keep this up, and they will laugh at you, all right!*

"My mistake," Wade said. "Foolish of me." He opened the catch on the Gladstone, folded his Lungers Club membership card, and put it inside *A Tale of Two Cities,* then rummaged until he found the letter from the Río Arriba County sheriff. He also discovered the tattered commission as a deputy United States marshal, brought it out as well. For added credibility. He might have need of it, plus a great deal of luck, if he kept acting so nervous.

With a flash of a smile, Wade handed letter and commission to the jailer. The old man, giving Wade a look of disgust, wiped his hands with a bandanna that he kept in his trousers pocket before taking the new papers.

*"Un momento, por favor,"* the jailer said, after inspecting the documents, and disappeared into the tombs.

When the jailer returned five minutes later, he had not fetched the prisoner, but a tall, muscular man in a broadcloth suit with a sheriff's badge pinned to the coat's lapel. The man kept slapping the papers against his thigh while staring at Wade without speaking.

Since consumption began to destroy his lungs, Wade had played poker, and won fairly often, just the way he had won with a .44-caliber Merwin & Hulbert when facing men who by all rights should have easily killed him. He won because, one way or the other, he didn't give a damn. *This is just a poker game,* he told himself. *What can they do to you?*

"You bring no deputies?" the lawman finally asked. "You are all *Señor* Murphey sent?"

"I'm alone," Wade said, waiting.

The lawman frowned, but stopped rattling the letter and commission. He was Mexican, dark-haired, thick mustache, bronze face. Looked pretty tough, and certainly strong enough to thrash a five-foot-six lunger that a spring wind could blow away.

"I asked *Señor* Murphey to send many deputies," the lawman said. "I asked him to request an Army escort to meet his men at the Chamita station. That is what the previous sheriff did when those two killers were hanged in 'Ninety-Six. The sheriff ignores all that I ask of him. Instead, he sends you."

*I should have thought to have stolen a badge,* Wade thought, up in Chama. *Yeah, a badge might have helped.*

Wade had never looked distinguished, certainly not in the past few years. His dark hair was short, thinning, flecked with gray, and he wore a mustache and long under-lip beard that stretched from lip to chin, both mustache and beard desperately needing a trim. His black hair, blacker eyelashes, and granite eyes seemed to make his gaunt face look even paler. He had left the Exchange Hotel dressed for the trail, wearing a Mackinaw over frayed vest, and lace-up shirt of heavy red flannel, a stained silk bandanna, battered Stetson. Blue and black striped britches were stuffed inside trail-worn, scuffed boots. All he had to his name he wore or carried in the Gladstone, and the grip was practically empty except for Dickens, Dumas, and what had become his bible, the "improved edition" of *Hoyle's Games.* Shaving kit, folding comb, two decks of cards, a bottle of laudanum, flask of rye whiskey, and $43.17 in coin and greenbacks. Plus the battered watch in his vest pocket.

Not much to show for forty-one years.

Nothing about him stood out, except the Merwin & Hulbert holstered on his shell belt, so he took a moment to push back the Mackinaw, and hook both thumbs near the belt's brass buckle, straightening.

"I reckon Murphey figured I was up to the job," he said.

"Murphey instructed me that he would deputize Dan Augustine," the lawman said, "and send him with Augustine's *asesinos.*"

A smile flashed across Wade's face. "Dan found himself indisposed." Wade spoke with confidence. "So here I am."

When the sheriff glanced again at the papers, his face changed, and he stared back at Wade, considering him with renewed interest, pursing his lips, then asking, his voice lacking the thunder it had displayed moments earlier: "You are Britton Wade?"

"What's left of him."

"I thought they had buried you by now."

"Some tried."

The lawman handed back the papers, which Wade dropped inside the Gladstone, snapping the grip shut. Thinking now: *I might just pull this off.*

"Bring Cole," the lawman told the jailer, barking the order in Spanish when the old man didn't move fast enough. Once they were alone, the lawman leaned against the adobe wall.

"It is this way, Wade. I am sheriff here, and you know why that boy you are taking to Tierra Amarilla is to hang. This country is about to blow up, what with the war, and with what the Cole boy did. Many people . . . my people, that is, maybe not you *norteamericanos* . . . do not want the Cole boy to disappear, yet that is what they expect will happen. They will read in the newspaper how Jeremiah Cole escaped, has disappeared, fled the country, that there is no justice in Río Arriba County, or wherever Roman Cole can reach. His arm is stronger and longer than the arm of the law. They know Senator Cole's power. And after all these years, they know the power of the Santa Fe Ring."

Metal chains *rattled* behind him, and the sheriff looked down the darkened hallway, then quickly back at Wade. "Whatever happens, *Señor* Wade, *por favor,* make sure it does not happen in Santa Fe County."

"It won't," Wade assured him.

"Please sit down." The sheriff pointed at a vacant chair. "You have papers to sign."

Relaxing now, Wade accepted a cigar from the sheriff, hearing the jailer bring in Jeremiah Cole, but not looking up, making the kid wait. The sheriff said the cigar was of excellent tobacco, but to Wade it tasted like the dirt of the jail. When he had signed the last paper, he rose slowly from his chair, and looked at Jeremiah Cole.

"You ain't Dan Augustine," Cole said.

Thought Wade: *You're not what I expected, either.*

He looked no older than twenty, his blond hair curly, though matted with sweat, the black and gray striped woolen prison clothes carrying the stink of months of confinement, brogans without laces that looked as if they would cripple a man if he wore them too long. His eyes were bright blue, no beard stubble on cheeks or chin, his skin showing more color than Wade's, like he had been riding his father's range rather than rotting in a jail cell, waiting to die. Pleasant-looking, if not for the filth of the tombs, the dirt under his fingernails. Taller than Wade, his shoulders broad. Didn't look like someone capable of murdering a *padre,* lynching him, leaving that Mexican hanging from the limb of a cottonwood outside his *santuario.* Nor did he resemble Senator Cole, but had inherited his father's cock-of-the-walk attitude.

"This is Britton Wade," the sheriff said, and Jeremiah Cole grinned.

"Well. That's something, ain't it." He held his manacled hands in front of the sheriff, waiting, still smiling, confident, and the lawman set his cigar in an ashtray to produce a key from his vest pocket.

"Leave the bracelets," Wade said, and the kid's jovial expression died. "But take off his leg irons."

While the old jailer removed the manacles, Jeremiah Cole stared at Wade, lips tight.

"You will want the key, *sí?*" the sheriff asked him. "To these?" Pointing his smoking cigar at the iron cuffs.

Wade's head shook. "You keep it. Less chance of the boy getting loose if there's no key. He can wear them to the gallows, for all I care."

Both the sheriff and the old jailer stared at Wade curiously. Cole's eyes darkened. Still not sure what was happening.

"If you will permit a word of advice, *señor,*" the sheriff said. "Anyone can escape the territorial prison with little more than a spoon and a pulse. That is why we house the prisoners doomed to die on the gallows in our humble jail. I have heard that the jail in Chama is much stronger than the one in Tierra Amarilla. If you seek justice, I suggest that you take this boy to Chama, and let him wait there until he is to die."

"I've heard the same thing about the Chama jail." Wade couldn't fight down his smile.

"The train leaves at ten-oh-eight," the sheriff said. "If it pleases you, you may wait here."

"We'll mosey on."

He couldn't wait. Dan Augustine was likely to show up at any moment. He thanked the sheriff and jailer, shook their hands, and, after the old man opened the door, he picked up his grip, and shoved Jeremiah Cole toward the dirty street, still empty. Cathedral bells sang out near the plaza. 8 A.M.

Filling his lungs with fresh air, the boy spread his legs, and hooked a thumb down the street. "I'd like a bath, buy some new duds. We can get a room at the Claire Hotel. Pa stays there when business brings him to Santa Fe."

"You smell fine to me, kid." Actually he stank like a hog pen.

Wade pointed at the livery.

The kid just stared, confused. Used to having things go his way, at least, until he had been tried, convicted, and forced to wait in the city's jail until all appeals had been denied.

"The depot's. . . ."

"Move!"

Now, Wade understood how this nice-looking kid could be guilty of such a brutal murder. Screaming, Cole charged, swinging his manacled hands, but Wade ducked underneath him, spitting out his cigar, tossing the Gladstone at the boy's feet. Cole tripped over the bag, sprawled in the dirt. Before Cole could regain his feet, Wade kicked him in his forehead, a glancing blow that flattened the youth. Suddenly Wade held the Merwin & Hulbert, cocked, aiming the seven-inch barrel at Jeremiah Cole's forehead.

"High time you savvy this." Wade crushed out the cigar with his boot heel. His lungs ached, but he didn't cough. In fact, he felt pretty good. That surprised him. "I ain't Dan Augustine. That Río Arriba County sheriff your daddy has in his back pocket didn't send me. Nor did your daddy hire me to fetch you, and turn you loose so you could hang some other poor priest. We're not going to the Claire for some eighteen-bits-a-night room where all your daddy's powerful friends can help you. We're not going to take the train to Chamita where Dan Augustine, and any of your daddy's guns, will be waiting to set you loose . . . and kill me. I'm working for *Padre* Virgilio, for Father Amado, for all those Mexicans you left without a man of God. I'm working for the law, my law. I'm taking you to Chama, boy. You're going to hang. Or you can make another fool play, only the next time, I'll blow your brains out. Makes no never mind to me."

# Chapter Two

Northwest of Santa Fe, arroyos criss-crossed the drying landscape, dotted with piñons and junipers that swept from the Sangre de Cristo range to the Jemez Mountains. The air remained crisp, winter fighting off spring, heavy clouds threatening some sort of moisture, probably already dumping snow higher up in the mountains, which still showed patches of white on pine- and aspen-covered slopes.

They had covered maybe ten miles—not the distance Britton Wade had hoped to have traveled, but he had picked paths off the main road, hiding, more or less playing it safe, keeping a sharp eye for dust. With night falling, Wade had decided to make camp behind two conical mounds just west of the trail, one of hills sprouting a wind-carved yellow formation that gave the landmark its name, Camel Rock.

"How about a fire?" Jeremiah Cole said as he swung from the dun mule. "We can get some coffee boiling."

"No fire," Wade said. He had drawn the Merwin & Hulbert before dismounting his piebald mare, and motioned with the barrel for his prisoner to sit beside a gnarled juniper. When the kid finally sat down, sighing heavily, Wade unsaddled horse and mule, hobbled them at the base of the hill, and lugged up two canteens and his Gladstone. He'd fetch the bedrolls later.

He tossed a canteen to Jeremiah Cole.

"Coffee would taste better than this," Cole said.

"No coffee."

"It'll get cold tonight. Think I just spied me a snowflake."

"It'll warm up where you're going."

"You, too, Wade." Jeremiah Cole unscrewed the canteen and took a sip. "You know this ain't gonna eventuate well for you."

"You'll fare worse."

The kid laughed. "As my pa would say . . . 'You beat the Dutch, old man.' You could be enjoying a mighty good whiskey, maybe even a fine-looking whore, at the Claire Hotel, eating green chile stew, and sopping up honey with tortillas. If you had taken the train, we could be in Chamita by now. I know a girl. . . ."

"You haven't shut up since Santa Fe," Wade said.

"Just trying to get to know you. That's all. It's a long ride to the valley." Cole's eyes narrowed, but he kept smiling. "If you make it that far."

"We'll make it."

The kid laughed. "I wouldn't make that wager. I mean, on the both of us living to see the gallows. You do know who my father is?"

"You've told me ten times."

"You're crazy!" Panic now in the kid's voice. "Why are you taking me in?"

"You killed a priest."

"Was he your *padre?*" Jeremiah Cole put both hands behind his head, and leaned back against the tree, tried to sound light-hearted again. "No, you ain't got to answer that. I've heard stories about Britton Wade. The gambling parlor or saloon is your church. 'Britton Wade, he's a blood brother of the devil.' I seem to recall reading that in some newspaper, maybe a penny dreadful. You probably killed a dozen priests in your day."

"Shut up."

"All you got to do is let me go. Make things easier on the both of us."

Slaking his own thirst, Wade said nothing.

"You might not even live to see Española."

He looked back at the horses. The sun had dipped behind the mountains. The Jemez range loomed before him, the Santa Fe Mountains behind him. A long way to go. He'd kill for a cup of coffee right about now, or a good taste of whiskey. The kid was right, too. It would turn mighty cold before morning, and the wind sure felt like snow. His flask was three-quarters full of a smooth Irish whiskey, but he didn't want to drink anything, not whiskey, certainly not the laudanum, anything that would dull his senses. Jeremiah Cole seemed harmless enough, chatting like they were old pals, smiling, trying to charm Britton Wade, but he had seen the kid's temper back outside the jail, and knew the young murderer must be waiting for a chance to jump him, kill him.

The kid sighed again. "You're a dead man, Wade."

He looked back at Jeremiah Cole, and surprised the kid with a wry grin. "Yeah," he said. "I know."

Too dark to read, he sat several rods from Jeremiah Cole, listening to the kid's heavy breathing. Five days, he figured, to reach Chama, and he'd have to sleep at some point. Not tonight, he told himself, fighting weariness. Dan Augustine would be after him by now, but where would the gunman go? What would he do? How much time did Wade have?

At first, Augustine and the Santa Fe sheriff would be confused. They'd blame each other, blame the Río Arriba County law, blame Senator Roman Cole. Augustine would send one of his boys to the Santa Fe depot, and when the train left, they'd search the town. Eventually they'd learn that Wade had bought a horse, mule, and rigs at the livery. Then what would Augustine decide? Take the trail from Santa Fe? No, not Augustine. He was too lazy to do that much work. Augustine would get back on the train, head to Chamita, and wait. Or, come morning, he'd send some of his boys south. Some would guard the road to Abiquiu.

That made sense. Unless, of course, the livery man, suspicious, immediately reported the purchase of a horse and mule. Perhaps, right now, the Santa Fe sheriff was leading a posse after Britton Wade and his abducted prisoner. How much time did Wade have before the senator started on the trail? How long before everyone in the territory knew Wade was alone with Jeremiah Cole? The senator would post his own reward, paying handsomely to whoever freed his son from this crazy gambler with a foolish scheme and odd sense of justice.

Even if he managed, through some sort of miracle, to bring Jeremiah Cole to Chama or Tierra Amarilla, no one could guarantee that the killer would hang. The senator could bust his son out of jail. What was it the priest back in Chama had told him? "I fear you are embarking on a mission that is noble but forlorn."

He felt suddenly tired, gave a slight cough, and shivered in the chill. The first mistake happened when he didn't take the key to the prisoner's handcuffs. It had sounded pretty good at the time, made the Cole kid fear him, fear what might really happen to him, but Wade's act had been just stupid. Had he kept the key, he could have shackled Jeremiah Cole to that juniper, then slept with some peace, although not enough.

The livestock and tack had set him back $35, and he didn't know which was more worn, horse and mule or saddles and bridles. Next, he had dropped another $4.72 on Lion coffee, hardtack, jerky, and tortillas. That left him a grand total of $3.45.

"Is it worth it?" he asked himself.

The *rattling* of metal saved his life. That, and his gambler's luck.

His eyes shot open, and, against his instinct, he rolled to his left. Iron whistled in the wind, the metal cuff bit into his ear, a glancing but searing blow that could have brained him good. Above him, in the darkness, came Jeremiah Cole's grunt, and then his surprised yelp as Wade kept rolling, tripping his prisoner in his path. Had Wade gone right, instead of left, the kid would have been on top of him, beating him into unconsciousness, most likely death, with the iron manacles.

A heavy cloud moved past the moon, two days past full, bathing the camp in white light, and Wade scrambled to his feet, thumbing back the .44's hammer, cursing himself for falling asleep. Blood gushed from his earlobe, down his neck.

"Drop it," he ordered as Jeremiah climbed to his feet, turning, wielding the handcuffs like a knight's mace. The kid measured his chances.

"Father Amado doesn't give a damn whether I bring you in alive or draped over that saddle," Wade said. "It's your call."

The metal bracelets dropped at Cole's feet, and the kid laughed, holding up his wrists, revealing bloody, raw skin, just before another cloud blanketed the moon.

"They say my wrists are big, but my hands are lady-like," Jeremiah Cole said. "Real dainty and small. Takes a bit of work, but I'm pretty good at getting rid of them things. They tell me Billy the Kid was the same way, could slip out of iron bracelets just like me."

"Lot of good it did him," Wade said.

He felt the cough coming, savage, tried to suppress it, knew he couldn't, then almost doubled over, hacking, coughing, forcing himself to straighten, backing away, almost blinded by the pain, waiting for Jeremiah Cole to make his play, but the kid just stood there, grinning in the darkness, as the moon reappeared, shaking his head slowly, mocking him.

The pain eased, the coughing ceased, and Wade glanced at

his hand, wiping the bloody froth on his pants leg.

"You try something like that again," Wade said, "and I'll kill you."

"You told me that back in town."

"I won't tell you again."

Cole started making his way back to the juniper, settled underneath the tree, and shook his head, his grin widening. "Oh, you ain't got to worry about me, old man. I'll just bide my time. I ain't worried about you, no, sir, not one bit. You'll cough yourself to hell long before we ever see the Chama valley."

They made even worse time the following day, the clouds thickening, the wind blowing harder, flakes of snow falling every now and then. The desert lost much of its color, and the hills lost much of their juniper. Again, Wade rode off the trail, keeping out of sight.

His ear stopped bleeding, his lungs no longer ached. Even Jeremiah Cole stopped his incessant chatter, resigned, Wade figured, to the fact that he'd have to travel north one way or the other. At noon, Wade opened a pack of Lion coffee, and they rested in the brown hills, filled their stomachs with black coffee and hardtack, and a good dose of blowing sand, while letting the livestock graze and drink from a pool of water. All the while, Wade looked from his perch and watched the road off to the east.

Biding his time. That was another mistake. A man on a good horse could easily travel the twenty-five miles from Santa Fe to Española in one day, yet it had taken Wade and his prisoner two. He had given Dan Augustine and the senator two days, let the word spread that Britton Wade was bringing in Jeremiah Cole to hang.

Mistakes, and bad luck.

In the middle part of the afternoon, Cole's mule lost a shoe.

Maybe the kid had helped things along, but it didn't matter. Wade had wanted to skirt around Española, but he was no farrier, couldn't risk a lame mount, so they waited in the hills a few hours, then made their way into the greening valley and the village of Española.

It was a dirty little place, but it had water as three rivers—the Grande, Chama, and Santa Cruz—met, and it had a livery stable. Española had grown out of the dirt and cottonwood trees when the Denver and Río Grande Railroad's Chile Line laid tracks back in 1880, a popular spot among the railroad men because of the food served at a restaurant run by a Mexican lady named Josefita Lucero. Britton Wade's stomach grumbled at the thought of food, but, as light as his purse was, he could not visit any café.

The livery man's face soured when Wade swung off the piebald, pointing at the mule's left hind foot, and asking in broken Spanish if the jack could be shod this evening. "*Muy pronto, por favor.*"

Sucking on a corncob pipe, the man grunted, refused to commit, until Wade flashed a greenback, then another. Wade couldn't blame him for being suspicious. Although he had taken time to shave at the noon camp—much to Cole's dismay—trail dust darkened his face, and his jacket remained caked with dried blood. Nor did Cole look presentable. Neither looked to be a promising, paying customer. The man set the pipe aside, and tugged on his thick, long, graying beard, mumbled something in Spanish underneath his breath, and at last nodded slightly.

Cole quickly dismounted, handed the reins to the burly Mexican, and hooked his thumb across the street.

"*La cantina*'s mighty inviting. Let's take a smile."

Wade's head shook.

"Hell, I'll buy."

"With what?"

"Senator Roman Cole's credit runs far and wide, Britton. You ought to know that. Why, my pa would be honored to buy you a drink. And folks here would be glad to stand us to a whiskey or three. The senator's a right popular man in these parts."

"Sit down over yonder, and shut up." Wade moved to the trough, cupped his hands, splashed water over his face. When he looked up, he saw them. Slowly straightening, he wiped his face with his bandanna, pushed his coattail away from the .44, and shot a quick glance at the livery man, busy filing the mule's hoof, his back to the street.

Three Mexicans stood in front of a hitching rail across the street, one pointing at the livery, whispering. Not looking at Wade, not even considering him, but staring at Jeremiah Cole. The youngest of the three, a boy in his teens, sprouting the beginnings of a mustache, nodded and took off running in his sandals, disappearing down an alley. The other two—older men, one hatless, the other wearing a bowler—spread apart. One held a shovel, and the man in the bowler tugged on a small-caliber revolver tucked in his sash.

Yet another bit of bad judgment, Wade figured. He had more, much more to fear than just Dan Augustine, and the powerful senator. The words of the Mexican sheriff echoed inside his weary head: *Many people . . . my people, that is, maybe not you* norteamericanos *. . . do not want the Cole boy to disappear, yet that is what they expect will happen. They will read in the newspaper how Jeremiah Cole escaped, has disappeared, fled the country, that there is no justice in Río Arriba County, or wherever Roman Cole can reach.*

They'd be after him, wanting to kill the Cole boy, and Wade if he got in the way, to prevent some obstruction of justice.

Hoofs sounded, and the man with the pistol waved his hat, bringing the rider, a tall *vaquero* on a palomino mare, to a stop. More talking, more pointing, and the *vaquero* dismounted, tethered his horse, oddly enough, in front of the rail next to an out-of-place-looking bicycle. When the *vaquero* gathered his lariat and a battered Winchester rifle from the saddle, Wade cursed his luck.

"Cole," he said. "Come here."

The kid looked up, shook his head, and stretched his legs and arms. "I'm comfortable right here. Unless you've a mind now to have that whiskey."

Easily Wade walked to his horse, gathered the reins, and pretended to be looking for something in his Gladstone. "Don't look across the street, Cole," he said—and, damn him all the hell, the boy did exactly that, shot to his feet, his face masked in wonder.

"I don't think they give a damn about your pa, kid," Wade said just above a whisper, "and care even less for you."

The kid's bluster evaporated. He wet his lips, looked to Wade for help.

Across the street, the batwing doors to the *cantina* opened, and a man in a blue bib-front shirt stepped out—the first *gringo* Wade had seen in town—followed by two other white men. The one in a blue shirt reached for the bicycle, but stopped when he heard shouts down the street. A church bell suddenly pealed. The livery man looked up, walked away from the mule toward the street in wonderment, tugging on his beard.

"When I jump into the saddle, you leap on right behind me," Wade told Cole. "Hold on tight. And before you think about trying to beat my brains out like you did last night, you take another gander at that mob." He made himself smile. "I'm the only chance you got, kid."

*What chance?* he thought as he mounted the piebald.

# Chapter Three

Whenever Roman Cole crested the ridge overlooking the valley, he would stop his horse, dismount, and smoke an El Pervenir from Havana that he had bought in Santa Fe solely for this purpose. For the rest of the day, whether he reached the spot shortly after breakfast or in the gloaming, no matter the season, no matter the weather, he would stare, admire, and relax his weary legs and backside from sitting so long in the saddle. Those who rode for the Triangle C called it his ritual—so did just about everyone from the Jemez to the San Juans—but Roman Cole considered it much more than just liturgy, although he wasn't quite sure what he'd call it.

It gave him pleasure, looking across the land, his land.

A stagecoach ran twice a week from Abiquiu to Chama, a mud wagon carried passengers from Abiquiu to the railroad in Chamita, where travelers could take the train to Santa Fe, but Roman Cole had been riding this route on horseback for three decades. He didn't care much for coaches, tolerated railroads only by necessity and for money, but loved the feel of a saddle, although, at sixty-two years old, the forty-pound C.P. Shipley slick-fork rig didn't seem so damned comfortable over a two hundred-mile journey, roundtrip—not that he'd ever admit the aches in his joints or the chaffing of his thighs and hindquarters to anybody.

The cold wind blew a strong scent of wet pine, and he forgot all about the yellow dust he had been eating along the trail. He called himself a cattleman, but he had always admired trees. He was a man who liked shade, who liked the strength of the Ponderosa pines. Thirty years ago, when he had first come to this country, and built his home, he had left many trees standing at his ranch headquarters. More than a handful of his riders felt closed in by the forests, but not Roman Cole. Most Western men wanted a view, needed to see where they were going, but Roman Cole could not have cared less. Farther off to the east and north, higher in the mountains, he logged his land, even owned two of the four sawmills in the Chama valley, yet that was for profit, and Roman Cole was a man who knew about profit. Within reason, he told himself. A heartless man could have, would have destroyed much of the forest years ago.

Cole dismounted the buckskin, loosening the cinch and hobbling the stallion before unbuckling a saddlebag and withdrawing a cigar and a flask of Tennessee sour mash. Here, he had that view his cowhands so admired. After clipping his cigar with his pocket knife, he walked to the edge of the hill, settling his back against an old pine that had served as his resting place for a number of years. Below him the valley stretched on, grasslands, wanting to green up although drifts of snow remained in the shade, creeks already swelling, filling the *aquecias* that led from the rivers and streams to the Mexican farms, watering the crops that he, Roman Cole, let them grow. Shorthorns wearing the Cole brand grazed in pastures that reached from Sawmill and Tecolote mesas, past Willow Creek to gorges and mountains full of elk and bear. Behind him lay the forested pike from Abiquiu, and that desert country that reached down to Española and toward Santa Fe.

Most of his friends—well, business acquaintances, for Roman Cole had met few men worthy of being called his friend—from Washington City and St. Louis, even some of those from Denver, all pictured New Mexico as some vast wasteland, a scorching desert of cacti and Apaches that they might find down toward Las Cruces, but the country here looked beautiful, chilly today, downright frigid in the winter, but a verdant Eden in spring and summer, and, God, so beautiful in the fall when the oaks turn red and the aspens gold.

The road forked, the right trail leading into Tierra Amarilla—T.A. for short—the left heading north to Chama and the railroad. He had helped bring the railroad to Chama. History might remember him for that. He could make out the Brazos Cliffs, could picture the Canones Box and Sugarloaf Mountain, thought that maybe he'd disappear in those hills after the spring run-off, take his son and catch browns and rainbows until they were sick of trout. Yes, that would be a great way to celebrate. He hadn't taken his sons—no, son—fishing in how many years? Hell, he'd never taken Jeremiah fishing.

This was Cole land, as far as he could see. Inspiring. Satisfying. By Jehovah, it would take him another full day's ride before he even reached ranch headquarters.

Stretching his legs out before him, he struck a lucifer, and lit the cigar. Then he just sat there, the only noise the rustling of the pines in the wind, and the stallion using one of those big tree trunks to scratch an itch. Roman Cole smoked, and watched.

He was halfway through his El Pervenir when he saw the riders, loping across the pasture between the forks, mounted on horseflesh too good to belong to some Mexican peasant or any of the smaller ranches south and west of Cole land. His riders. Looking for him.

Cole wasn't sure how he knew that, but he felt certain they were coming for him. Joints popping, he stood, stepped out of the shade, and waited, still smoking his Havana. Anyone who rode for the Cole brand would know where to find him. He'd let them come.

The Chama valley seemed cut off from most of New Mexico. Some folks said it should belong to Colorado, for the border was just a few miles north. The trains, part of the Denver & Río Grande Railroad's San Juan Extension, ran from Antonito, Colorado, as did the telegraph line, when it was operating. Most of the news came from Colorado. Denver might be some three hundred miles away, and Santa Fe only one hundred, but, to those who lived in the valley, it often felt that Santa Fe was as far removed from Chama as the gold fields in the Yukon.

Roman Cole really didn't care one way or the other, but he understood the way New Mexico worked, knew all too well of *la mordida,* the bribes one paid to those in power to get things done. Sometimes, such payments went to Senator Roman Cole. Other times, he paid whoever he needed to pay. It was considered part of the business of doing business here. He had learned to accept it, had learned to use it. He had used it again on this latest trip.

A good trip, he thought. He had lined up Dan Augustine, and paid *la mordida,* and now had to wait. Wait for this whole insignificant affair to blow over like an afternoon monsoon in late July.

A rider on a dun horse veered from the rest, waving his massive cream-colored sombrero, yelling back to the other five riders.

Cole crushed the cigar with his boot heel. They'd seen him, and now made a beeline for the hill. He had never been much for worrying, but his gut felt odd, and he spat out the taste of tobacco, tried washing it down with sour mash. Something had gone wrong. He could feel it, knew it, and he suddenly cursed.

Matt Denton, the Triangle C rider with the big Mexican hat, led the others up the hill and was the first to dismount, glancing back hopefully at his companions, as if wishing someone else would take charge.

He turned back, pushed up the brim of the stupid hat, said—"Mister Cole."—and waited.

*Idiot!* Cole tossed the flask underneath the pine. "You've rode for me nigh four years, Denton," Cole said. "You know damned well who I am."

"Yes, sir." The kid stared at his scuffed boots.

Denton and Jeremiah were pals. The young rider with the sombrero had even acted like Jeremiah's brother since Billy, Cole's oldest, had died. Cole regretted speaking sharply to him, but he refused to soften. "Then spit out what you got to say, Denton."

Matt Denton took a deep breath, exhaled, and made himself look into Roman Cole's cold eyes. "Well, it's Jeremiah, sir. He got took."

"Took?"

"Yes, sir. Took right out of jail. The jail in Santa Fe. By Britton Wade."

"What do you mean took? Busted out? What?"

"Dan Augustine come down, just as you ordered him to, only, by the time he got there Monday morn, the sheriff said somebody else had done come and fetched Jeremiah. He had a letter from Sheriff Murphey, had a commission as a federal deputy . . . so the sheriff down there didn't think nothing of it. Bought a couple of horses at the livery across the street, and lit a shuck. Augustine's gone after them. Says he'll earn his pay."

Cole looked around behind him, wished he had not tossed away that flask. He could use a snort. Nothing made sense. Taken from jail by Britton Wade?

"Britton Wade, that gunman and cardsharp?"

"Yes, sir."

Cole blinked. He hated to be like this, confused, uncertain, downright taken aback. He had steeled himself to hear that Augustine's plan had not worked, that some bean-eater seeking vengeance had shot Jeremiah Cole dead on the streets of Santa Fe. He could have handled that, easily. He would have fetched Jeremiah home, buried him beside his brother and mother, then taken vengeance himself. But this. . . .

"This just beats the Dutch," he said. "Britton Wade?"

"Yes, sir."

"I never done no bad turn on Wade, never even met the man. Why would a killer like him . . . a damned lunger . . . why would he take Jeremiah out of jail?"

Denton wet his lips, looked back at the other riders, and once again found no help.

"Where's Murphey?" Cole demanded.

"Back in Chama, I reckon. Maybe T.A. He brung word to the ranch, said he had to get back to town."

"Like hell." That fool sheriff would rue the day. Coward. Numbskull. Oh, Luke Murphey was fine beating up drunks and old men with those giant fists of his, but the sheriff was anything but a man. Hiding either at the courthouse in Tierra Amarilla or at the jail in Chama. Hiding from Roman Cole's wrath. Twenty years ago, Roman Cole would have stomped Sheriff Murphey into the ground with a boot heel. Thirty years ago, he would have shot him dead on the streets. Even ten years ago, Roman Cole could have picked ten men better suited to wear a badge. Times had changed, though. Look what he had for a sheriff. Look what he had for men—mere boys—riding for the Triangle C.

"Archie Preston told us to not quit riding till we found you," Denton said.

Archie Preston was his foreman, one of the few good men Cole had these days. Just knowing Archie was up to snuff made Cole breathe a little easier.

"Archie said to tell you he'd ride up to Jawbone Mountain and fetch Zechariah Stone. They say old Zech can track a fly across the Tusas Mountains."

"What else did that jackleg Murphey say?"

"He just brung the telegram." Suddenly remembering that, Denton fetched the slip of yellow paper from his vest pocket, handed it to Cole, who read it quickly. It said nothing other than what Matt Denton had told him.

"Britton Wade," Cole said again, just to say something. After balling the telegram in his hand, he tossed it in the wind.

"Well, there's one thing you ought to hear, Mister Cole," Denton offered reluctantly.

"Go on," Cole snapped.

"Murphey didn't say none of this, but Tom Oliver. . . ." He craned his neck toward a lanky cowhand with the thick brown mustache, who sat gripping his saddle horn and looking mighty uncomfortable at having been drawn into the conversation. "Tom and me heard that Murphey up and locked up Britton Wade for . . . for. . . ."

"Vagrancy," Tom Oliver said, now even more annoyed.

"Turned him loose first of last week," Denton finished.

"That still doesn't explain why Wade would take my son out of jail."

"Well, maybe it does, sir, because that was about the time them Mex preachers was begging that Murphey do right by the law. This is what those *padres* was saying, Mister Cole, not us. But we heard that that old Father Virg-something-or-another was offering a reward of two hundred dollars to the man who got Jeremiah up here for the hanging."

Cole sighed. Oddly enough, he felt better now that he understood how things were working. The priests, Virgilio and Amado, were stirring up trouble again. That he had expected. He just hadn't counted on Britton Wade's gumption.

"Wade could have stole the papers," Tom Oliver said. "Stole 'em right off Murphey's desk. The papers that allowed the law in Santa Fe to turn loose of Jeremiah. That's just a guess, though. That was what Luke Murphey was guessin'."

Probably more words than Tom Oliver had spoken in three months, but Cole nodded at his rider, even thanked him.

"I think you're right, Tom. Money. That's what all of this is about."

"Yes, sir," Denton said.

Cole couldn't help himself. He simply laughed, shook his head, and walked back to pick up his flask. A lunger, a damned saddle bum, planned on bringing his son to Río Arriba County. And for what? Two hundred dollars. Cole took a drink, laughed again, and shoved the flask into his saddlebag. Two hundred dollars? He had spent more than that on *la mordida,* slipping a donation to the attorney general, to Sheriff Murphey, to some Army commanders, the warden at the territorial prison, the editor and publisher at the *Santa Fe New Mexican,* even the archbishop. He had paid everyone except that greaser sheriff in Santa Fe, who had shown all along how much he sided with all those other Mexicans who wanted Jeremiah to die. They didn't want Jeremiah Cole to hang for what he had done, though. Oh, no. Roman Cole knew those sons-of-bitches better than that. They wanted to punish Roman Cole for all of his crimes, for taking their land, for running Río Arriba County the way it needed to be run, for bringing progress to the Chama valley, for getting richer while they remained poor.

"To hell with them." He hadn't realized he had said that aloud until he looked at his riders again. Ignoring them, he stared across the valley, and shook his head.

"Mister Cole?"

With a sigh, Roman Cole shot a glance at Matt Denton and the other riders.

"What do you want us to do, sir?"

"Cut dirt, boys." A quarter mile off, a mule deer drank from an *aquecia.* Silence. He stared at the sky. Clearing up. Might even warm up come tomorrow. He hadn't heard the *creaking* of saddle leather, knew those young riders were just waiting, staring at him blankly, wondering just what in hell he wanted them to do. Finally he heard Matt Denton's drawl.

"Well, sir, where is it that you want us to go?"

Cole turned, glaring. "It took me three days to ride from Santa Fe," he said, "but I ride mighty hard. Wade's taking Jeremiah to Tierra Amarilla or Chama, and there's only one road that leads up here. Ride south."

"What about the stagecoach?" another rider—Cole couldn't recall the name—began. "That gunman might bring. . . ."

"He won't take the stage. Wade's too smart for that."

"What about Zechariah Stone?" Denton asked.

"I'll send Zech after you. And Dan Augustine, too. Cut dirt, boys. Time's wasting. Fetch Jeremiah back to me, and bring me Britton Wade's head in a gunny sack."

Denton's face paled. His Adam's apple bobbed. "Well, sir, I mean, Archie Preston, he says that Wade might not be doing this for that reward the *padre* posted. I mean, sir, well, two hundred dollars ain't that much money when you figure things. Archie warrants that Wade might plan on delivering Jeremiah to you, and not the Mexicans."

"I know that." Unless Britton Wade was a complete fool. Roman Cole would gladly pay more for his son's safety. *But I'll be damned if I'll pay* la mordida *to a greedy lunger son-of-a-bitch,* Cole thought.

"I said bring me his head," he said. "Now, ride out."

# Chapter Four

They were gone in an instant, the quickness of the paint horse surprising Wade. Maybe the piebald wasn't so worthless a mount. Whirling, the startled livery man leaped out of the way with a Spanish curse, barely missing being trampled. Equally surprised were the men in front of the *cantina*. To keep them that way, Wade fired a round over the flat-crowned hat worn by the *vaquero*.

The mare thundered across a little wooden bridge. Wade tugged the reins, turned east, kicked the horse's ribs, wishing he wore spurs. He wanted to look back, but didn't. Shouts. A bullet *zipped* past his ear. Jeremiah Cole's grip tightened around Wade's stomach. Curses. The *clanging* of the bell grew louder, and moments later they passed a square adobe church on the right, a white cross barely visible on the pitched tin roof, door wide open, a white-haired man pulling the bell rope urgently. Into the gloaming, they rode, faster, down a narrow trail lined with thick cottonwoods. Suddenly the bells from the church ceased, replaced by the sound of a running horse. The *vaquero*.

*Another mistake,* Wade thought. *I should have shot his damned horse.*

A dog barked. They galloped past a frightened woman, hiding behind a cottonwood, eyes wide, mouth open, small hand clutching the throat of her dress.

He didn't know where he was going, knew little about this part of the territory. More horses had joined pursuit, and, as hard as this piebald ran, Wade realized the small horse couldn't carry the weight of two, not for long. He had covered perhaps two miles when he spotted flaring yellow lamps ahead of him. Although still game, the piebald was faltering, already lathered in sweat.

Another shot. Then another. The pursuing hoofs sounded closer. A voice called out in Spanish. The *vaquero.* Seemed to be telling the men riding with him not to shoot.

The trail narrowed. A *jacal* on the right. Stone wall surrounding what appeared to be a small vegetable garden. Coyote fence on the left, hiding a small adobe, white smoke pouring from the chimney. They were coming into another village. No wonder the *vaquero* with a conscience wanted his comrades to hold their fire. A door slammed. Another dog barked, and was answered by hordes of mongrels. Wade turned the piebald left. His lungs fought for air. Jeremiah Cole squeezed harder. They entered a small plaza.

"*¡Vete al carajo!*" came a curse from behind, and the *vaquero*'s response was lost to a gunshot.

Squealing, the piebald stumbled, and Wade knew the mare had been hit. He tried to kick free of the stirrups, tried to tell Cole to jump. Too late. Gunfire ripped through the growing darkness again. He hit the cobblestones, hard, saw a blinding flash of orange as his head struck. Coughed. Opened his eyes. Tried to stand. Couldn't.

Hoofs. He had to move. "God," Cole moaned.

Somehow, he still held the pistol in his right hand, but his left shoulder felt numb. Coughing slightly, he cocked the .44, aimed over the dead mare pinning his right leg, and fired. Once. Twice. Worried, the riders quickly reined up. A bullet whined off a rock, and the *vaquero* cursed. Wade's head throbbed, his ears rang, and he could catch only pieces of the *vaquero*'s commands. Something about a priest, sacred land, children, women, the

Blessed Mother. With a grunt, Wade pressed his left leg against the saddle, pushing, dragged himself from underneath the piebald.

A door flung open, casting light briefly from a coal-oil lantern, just long enough for Wade to spot the Gladstone a few rods from the dead horse. Many of its contents, *Hoyle's,* the laudanum, had spilled onto the plaza. He heard a woman's gasp before the door slammed, shutting off the light and the woman's prayer.

"God," Cole muttered somewhere behind Wade.

Wade had also seen something else, just ahead of him, could still make it out as the skies darkened.

He fired again, heard the bullet's ricochet, and shoved the .44 into his holster, stood, weaving, looked back. His left arm wouldn't work.

"Cole," he said. "Get up." He didn't wait, just moved to the kid, jerked him to his feet with his right hand. "That way," he said, shaking his head, trying to clear it, then pushed Cole forward. "Through the gate!" he yelled, ducking to pick up the Gladstone, stumbling, staggering more than running.

A rifle *boomed,* immediately followed by a shotgun blast, and an instant later the pursuers from Española were shouting at each other. Across the plaza raced Cole and Wade, underneath the adobe archway, down a shrub-lined path. Wade could just make out the adobe building, pitched roof, the twin pointed bell towers on either side. He hoped he had guessed right—for once.

More shouts.

Cole reached the door first, pushed, grunted, cursed, turned back to yell: "It's bolted shut!" He started to run, but Wade grabbed him, threw him back against the door, surprised at his own strength.

His head was bleeding. He jerked on the iron pull.

"It's locked, I tell you!" Cole screamed at him. "Let's get the hell out of here!"

Wade's strength was quickly ebbing. He didn't know why. He felt himself slipping, sliding down the door. Yet he drew the Merwin & Hulbert, grabbed the barrel, twisted, pounded the walnut butt against the heavy oaken door that was adorned with carved wood painted white, eight-point stars and fancy crosses. He yelled words he long thought lost to him, somehow seeing, although he was probably imagining it, Jeremiah Cole's shocked face, his mouth agape, as Wade beat on the door, shouting: "Sanctuary! Sanctuary!" He cried out something in Latin, thought better of it, tried again in Spanish. The last thing he heard was his own weak voice pleading, *"¡Pido santuario! ¡Pido santuario!"*

# Chapter Five

It all had begun in the Chama jail.

Britton Wade had stood behind some impressive bars in the past decade, like that rotary jail in Gallatin, Missouri, which folks said resembled a squirrel cage with its pie-shaped cells on a well-greased axis turned by the jailer's crank. Once, years ago, he had found himself chained to a large mesquite—The Jail Tree—in the blistering summer sun in Wickenburg, Arizona Territory. Down in Chloride, back in 1889, he vividly recalled joking to the beer-jerker who worked at The Gem Saloon about how he often felt an urge to write a book about all the jails he had struck. Although he had thrown more than his share of men into such confines, lately he found himself locked away for hours, sometimes months.

There was nothing special about the log building that housed him on that dark spring morning in Chama. Stone floor. No windows. Iron bars sunk deeply into earth and timber. More like a dungeon. He lay on cold flagstone, close to the bars, trying to breathe, watching a stream of water crossing the dark hallway toward him, hoping it was water, but the pungent smell reached him first, and he rolled away, groaning, to escape the urine.

From the opposite cell came laughter, followed by a conversation in Spanish.

Using the bars, Britton Wade pulled himself up, head still pounding, his dry mouth tasting of forty-rod whiskey and perhaps his own vomit. Whatever had landed him in this unholy place had been blacked from his memory, but he didn't need to remember. He could guess. No, it wasn't a guess. He knew. He had gotten drunk, again, started a fight, again. Wade felt the knot over his left ear. Had lost the fight. . . .

Again.

He recalled something else. When he stepped off the train, he had been broke. Either he had pawned something of value for money, had gotten lucky and won some poker hands early, or had stolen the whiskey. It didn't matter. Here he was.

Brushing the dirt off his trousers, Wade stared at the two Mexicans across the hall, then at his companions in the cramped cell: an Irish railroader, his head between his knees; a man in buckskin trousers with a face purple with bruises, eyes swollen shut; and a snoring cowboy with a black eye and busted lip. Wade knew none of them, and they didn't give a fip about him.

The hall door opened, forcing Wade to close his eyes tightly against the light, which really wasn't that bright. Footsteps sounded like an elephant stomping, and then a sharp voice barked out: "You! Come on!"

After forcing his eyes open, he found a pockmarked man wearing a deputy sheriff's badge.

"I said come on," the deputy said, stuck a key in the lock, grinding, jerking open the heavy door.

Wade grabbed his hat off the floor, thankful the urine had missed it, started to put it on his head, thought better, and stepped into the hall. The deputy slammed the door shut, causing Wade to flinch, locked it, and motioned Wade to walk ahead of him.

"Careful where you step," the lawman said.

The Mexicans in the opposite cell, lying on their cots or on the floor, sniggered.

★ ★ ★ ★ ★

They stepped into the jailer's office, warmed by a coal-burning Windsor stove, just as a burly man in a brown coat kicked some poor fellow on the floor.

"I made room, Sheriff," the deputy behind Wade said. "This feller was the only one standin' up."

The man in the brown coat whirled, considering Wade with a moment's glance. "He'll do as good as any," he told the deputy. Then to Wade: "Sit down. I'm almost finished here."

A broad-shouldered man with a thick red mustache flecked with silver, the sheriff spoke in a heavy Irish brogue. His fists resembled anvils, knuckles like rocks, scarred, flecked with blood. He looked big enough to have inflicted all the pain Wade had seen through bloodshot eyes back in the jail, and if that railroader and cowhand had not been able to whip the sheriff in a drunken brawl, the tiny, silver-haired man in the black robes, balled up on the floor could do nothing against the big lawman's wrath.

"Feel like giving me any other orders, you damned greaser?" The sheriff drew back, kicked the man in the ribs with square-toed stovepipe boots. "You think I don't know me job?" He lifted his leg, tried to stomp the old man's head, but the man had enough awareness, enough sense, to roll from the boot heel. Then the sheriff spit on the groaning man, spun around, pointing a thick finger at the deputy. "Greg, haul this Mex's carcass inside."

Wade found himself staring at the old man on the floor, and grimaced when the man rolled over, his lips split, hands clutching his gut, but black eyes open, still defiant. He wore a reversed collar of white. A crude wooden cross attached to a rawhide thong that hung around his neck was now on the floor, stained with the priest's blood.

The next thing Wade knew, he had forgotten his hangover,

his own decrepit condition, had filled a ladle with water from an oaken keg in the corner, and knelt beside the Mexican priest, lifting his head, letting him drink.

Most of the water dribbled down the old man's chin, but he still managed to say—*"Gracias."*—although the effort alone caused pain.

"Gambler," the sheriff said to Wade's back, "you're out of me hoosegow because we need room for this troublemaker. But I can just as easily let some other dumb bastard go free."

Ignoring the lawman, Wade helped the priest to his feet, eased him to a chair, and heard the sheriff moving up behind him, heard the leather *creak* as the big plug-ugly drew a Schofield revolver from the holster, and Wade knew he was about to be buffaloed.

The outside door swung open, letting in a sharp blast of icy wind, and another deputy stepped inside, pounding muddy boots on the floor, pulling out an envelope from inside his canvas coat, and telling the sheriff: "Murphey, I got them papers you need from the judge to fetch young Cole from Santa Fe."

"Throw them on me desk, you blathering idiot, and close the damned door!" The sheriff holstered his revolver, and Wade straightened, turning to face the lawman.

"Seems like I missed quite the doin's," the new deputy, grinning, said after he set the envelope down and warmed his hands by the stove.

"Virgilio was raisin' Cain again," the first deputy said.

"All I ask of *Señor* Murphey is for justice," the priest said through tight lips. At first, Wade thought the old Mexican was talking to him, but the priest kept those dark eyes trained on the Río Arriba County lawman. "That you do as the judge has decreed. That you do not bend to the demon Cole's ire."

"You mean Senator Cole," the first deputy said with a chuckle.

"Jeremiah Cole has been sentenced to hang." The priest crossed himself. "God have mercy on his soul. All I ask. . . ."

"You do more than ask, greaser." Murphey placed both hands on his hips. "You and that shadow of yours been preaching up quite a sermon of fire and brimstone for your chile-loving churchgoers, ain't you? Oh, don't think I haven't heard about that bounty you offered. Two hundred dollars for the gent who brings you Jeremiah's head. That's mighty Christian of you." The sheriff surprised Wade when he looked at him and smiled. "Does that sound Christian to you, Mister Gambler? You ever met a man of God like this old *padre* here who wants to see some young man get his neck stretched? Is that what God himself would wish? Is that what Christ would preach?"

"I'm no theologian," Wade said.

The sheriff stared at him blankly. Theologian wasn't in his vocabulary.

"Judas money, iffen you ask me," the first deputy said. "It stinks of Judas money."

"And now this little man of God tries to bribe me," Murphey said, his thick head bobbing, "with thirty pieces of silver."

Speaking in Spanish, the priest gasped, and clutched his ribs. Wade took the ladle and walked back to the bucket to bring the old man more water.

"It is not true," Father Virgilio said, switching to English. "We offer money for justice, to see Jeremiah Cole brought here to face his crime, and to face his Redeemer. We pray for his soul." Now the priest stared at Wade, as if he were staring into Britton Wade's own lost soul, continuing: "Yet we also must do this for the souls of those who attend our parish." Fighting pain, he crossed himself. "We do not want the young Cole lad murdered. We do not want his blood to stain the hands of those poor men and women who live in this valley, but they cry for vengeance. This is the only way to bring peace to the Río Chama."

The sheriff laughed. Wade knelt beside the priest, handed him the ladle.

"I ain't that up on Scripture," the first deputy said, "but don't the Good Book say somethin' 'bout 'Vengeance is mine, sayeth the Lord'? Don't it?"

Ignoring the question, the priest drank. He thanked Wade, who stood, placing the ladle on the lawman's desk near the envelope.

He had heard about Jeremiah Cole on the train down from Antonito, Colorado, playing poker in the smoking car with Dan Augustine. "I could use a man like you, Wade," Augustine had said, after emptying Wade's meager purse before they had reached Osier Station. "Could use your gun. Pay's good. Roman Cole's no skinflint, not when it comes to saving his boy's neck."

Senator Roman Cole ruled the Chama valley. There were those that said he ran New Mexico, at least its northern ranges, and some said he, along with lawyer Tom Catron, controlled the notorious Santa Fe Ring, which, in turn, governed, through force, power and bribery, the business and politics of the territory. One son had died—hanged himself, if the stories were to be believed—three years earlier, and now the only other child, twenty-year-old Jeremiah Cole, had been sentenced to the gallows for one of the grisliest crimes imaginable.

Jeremiah Cole, with parties unknown, had ridden up to a little Catholic church in the Chama valley, beaten the priest senseless, then strung him up by the neck, leaving him kicking, choking to death from a cottonwood branch. Cole had been found guilty of murder, the appeals denied, and Governor Miguel Antonio Otero had signed his death warrant. There were those across New Mexico and Colorado who said the only reason Cole's son was even brought to trial was because Republican President McKinley had appointed a Mexican as territorial governor in 1897, and the murdered priest had also been Mexican.

The execution had been scheduled for Friday, May 13, 1898, outside the Río Arriba County Courthouse in Tierra Amarilla.

Wade had declined Augustine's invitation. He couldn't say exactly why. Maybe he hadn't cared for Dan Augustine's reputation. Maybe he didn't want to work for another hired gunman. Maybe he didn't want to work for a man who had beaten him soundly, busted him, at jacks or better. Maybe it had something to do with Britton Wade's own forgotten past.

Whatever the reason, Wade had not given the story of Jeremiah Cole another moment's thought . . . until now.

"I'm done pampering this greaser," Sheriff Murphey said. "He's a bad egg. Threatening the peace of me valley, trying to bribe a duly elected officer of the court, preaching death instead of love. You're under arrest, Virgilio. And you. . . ." His eyes burned with fury, but Wade didn't look away, recalling something else Dan Augustine had told him: *The county sheriff's all bluster, acts like a big man, but Roman Cole butters his bread, and that mick law dog would piss his pants if the senator looked at him long enough.*

"You was too drunk last night to tell us anything," Sheriff Murphey was saying. "I'd fine you, but your wallet was empty. I'm turning you loose, Mister Gambler, but I don't like vagrants in me town or me county. Greg, fetch his possibles."

"He didn't have nothin' much but an ratty old grip with some books and such in it." The deputy pulled the Gladstone from a pie safe, snapped his fingers, remembered something else. "Though this might fetch a few dollars." He opened a desk drawer, and a moment later dropped the grip and gun belt on top of the desk.

The sheriff's eyes brightened at sight of the gun rig. "Well, on second thought, that pretty pistol and leather ought to cover the fine. Reckon we'll just confiscate that in lieu of thirty dollars or thirty days."

"I reckon you won't," Wade said. He wondered if he had overplayed his hand.

"Like I said." Murphey cracked his knuckles. "I can lock you back up with *el padre* and set some other rascal free. I'll be keeping the gun."

"Read the name stamped in the belt, Greg," Wade said, and waited.

"I'll be hanged." The deputy looked up in shock, pointing a bony finger at the gun belt. "It says that this here is. . . ." He turned to stare at Wade. "It says he's Britton Wade."

His hangover had vanished, and he stood a little straighter, felt a bit prouder, as he walked to the desk, grabbed the gun belt, buckled it on. No one said a thing, but Sheriff Murphey nodded at the priest, and the two deputies moved, pulling Father Virgilio to his feet, half dragging him toward the cells.

"Father?" Wade asked quietly, right hand on the Merwin & Hulbert's butt.

The deputies stopped. The priest lifted his aching head.

"Is there anything I can do for you, Father?"

*"Por favor,"* the old man said, "if you will tell Father Amado in Parkview what has happened here today."

"Consider it done."

*"Vaya con dios."*

The door shut behind the priest, leaving Wade alone with the sheriff.

"I still want you out of me county, Wade," the sheriff said. "Next time, I'll have Roman Cole's men with me." He nodded for emphasis before fleeing to the jail cells himself, frightened at being alone with a man with Britton Wade's reputation.

Wade took a deep breath, checked the Gladstone, saw his books, his flask, his laudanum, other sundries. He hadn't planned on doing anything else, other than telling this Father Amado that the old priest was in jail, likely had some busted ribs, could stand to see a doctor. Then Britton Wade would be on his way, find some other town, farther south, likely wind up in some other jail. Yes, that's what he figured would happen.

Then, his eyes landed on the envelope.

# Chapter Six

Jesus Christ looked down at him from the cross.

Britton Wade didn't know how long he had been staring back at the ornately carved wooden crucifix hanging on the mud-colored adobe wall. Didn't know how long he had even been awake. Wasn't exactly sure where he was.

He lay on his back, on a straw bed on the floor, shirtless, bootless, left shoulder bandaged, no longer numb but hurting like a son-of-a-bitch. The room was Spartan, with only the crucifix, the bed, a wooden bowl, and old towel by his side, a small brown jug within reach, two tallow candles flittering light through tin sconces on the wall over his head. He smelled the sweet fragrance of piñon burning in the small fireplace across the room. His boots leaned against the wall, but he couldn't find his gun belt, his grip, or the Merwin & Hulbert .44.

With his right arm, he pushed himself up, sitting, waiting for the room to quit spinning, and gently tested his left arm. He could move it, but the shoulder flamed with pain. He saw blood-stains on the cotton bandages, knew he had been shot. His eyes narrowed. *Where's Cole?*

Before he could muster enough strength to stand, he heard footsteps behind the adobe wall, and a moment later he had a visitor.

"Ah, you are awake." A young priest, black hair, black eyes, brown robe of coarse wool, knelt beside him, placed the back of his right hand against Wade's forehead, and smiled. "No fever.

*Muy bien.* Forgive me. I am Father Marcelino Eusebio de Quesada y Azcárranga." He bowed and shrugged. "A long name for such a short man."

"I'm. . . ." Wade stopped. The room had started spinning again. He felt the priest ease him back on the straw bed. When he opened his eyes, the small Mexican man nodded.

"I know who you are, *señor.* You are Britton Wade, the killer."

Wade swallowed. His mouth was dry as dirt. Realizing this, the priest handed him the small jug, lifted his head, helped him drink, much as Britton Wade had assisted Father Virgilio in Chama. The water tasted so good.

"*Señor* Cole is with your friends," Father Marcelino said gently.

"You know who we are." Wade closed his eyes again, took a deep breath, slowly let it out. "Yet you. . . ."

"You come to this house of God asking for sanctuary. Thus you shall have it as long as it is His will. Perhaps, my will."

Suddenly Wade's eyes opened, serious, concerned. "You said . . . my friends?"

"Bienvenido a La Iglesia de Santa Cruz de la Cañada. Known to you *norteamericanos* as the Holy Cross Church. The village, or colony as it was called in the time of Diego de Vargas, is officially La Villa Nueva de Santa Cruz de Los Españoles Mejicanos del Rey Nuestro *Señor* Carlos Segundo. Again, a big name for but a small place. It is the way of our people. But most call it Santa Cruz." The priest looked at the dark walls, humbly. "It has a long history in New Mexico. For more than one hundred and sixty years, this house of God has stood here, although the . . . how do you say . . . parapets? . . . sí, that is the word . . . they are new." He looked back at Wade. "*Lo siento.* I talk too much, but my heart is full of love for history, this history of my people, the history of my village, the history of this *santuario.* You asked of your friends?"

"Yeah. Who?"

"You should thank your three companions perhaps more than me for keeping you from harm's way. I grant you and *Señor* Cole sanctuary, *sí.* But they keep it. Wait. I will bring them here. They will be most pleased to learn that you are awake. *Un momento, por favor.*"

Wooden sandals tapped across the floor, and Wade tried to call out for the priest to wait, that he had more questions, but the windy little man was gone, and Wade forced himself up again, looking for his pistol, his Gladstone, anything. Briefly he thought about the crucifix on the wall. Could he use that as a weapon? Then, exhausted, he just gave up, still sitting, and waited. If those three men, whoever they were, wanted him dead, they could have killed him already.

Five minutes later, Father Marcelino returned to the room, followed by a tall, slender man wearing a blue bib-front shirt. Wade remembered him, back in Española, coming out of the *cantina,* the one with the bicycle. Wade hadn't studied the man's face back then. It was too dark, and he hadn't had a whole lot of time, but it didn't take him long now to remember.

"Clint Paden," Wade said.

A boyish grin spread across Paden's handsome face.

"God bless you, Brit." The Southern drawl hadn't lessened any over the past decade. "I can't tell you how happy I am that you remember me after all these years."

He was a young man, maybe not yet thirty, with bright green eyes, and long, sandy hair. Hadn't shaved in a day or two. Wore brick-colored britches stuck in shiny black boots, red silk scarf around his neck, a London-made Webley revolver was holstered on his left hip, butt forward, and he carried an 1881 lever-action Marlin in his left hand.

"How long have you been out?" Wade asked.

Still smiling, Paden shook his head. "Oh"—he waved off the

question like it was a joke—"they didn't give me but two years. On account that I was just a kid sowing his oats. You ought to remember that, Brit."

"I meant for killing that drummer down in Eddy."

Briefly the smile vanished, then reappeared. "You still read the newspapers, I see." Paden shrugged. "But you don't read enough. Yeah, I rode down to Eddy where they was building that flume, stopped in at Wolf Town, this little watering hole. Had a big old wolf, stuffed, showing off 'em yellow teeth, yellow eyes. I think they use marbles for eyes when they're stuffing a wolf like that. I sure admired that wolf. Anyhow, I figured on just passing the time dealing a few hands of twenty-one, but there was this law . . . nobody told me, mind you . . . that says no gambling, no petticoats." The grin flashed wider. "Don't that beat all, Brit? So this drummer takes exception, starts arguing with me. But he had a pepperbox pistol on him, so the grand jury give me what they call a no-bill. Self-defense. No, sir, I haven't seen the inside of a jail in a long, long time." The smile was gone. This time it did not come back. "Not like you, Brit. You see, I read the newspapers, too."

The priest said something about bringing Wade stew and coffee, and left. Wade remembered the bicycle.

"You stealing bicycles now, Clint?"

The gunman shook his head, and knelt beside Wade.

"The boys and me figured on riding up to Las Vegas and joining up to fight the Spanish and free the Cubans. Sounds like a mighty fine adventure. Give me a chance to see something other than juniper and dust. I read this advertisement in the *New Mexican,* and it said something like . . . 'Cuba Libre and Our Bicycles Go Well Together' . . . and that looked so damned patriotic I had to buy one. *Buy* one, Brit. Not steal it. I was going to ride it, and the boys would trot their horses, all the way to Las Vegas. That was the plan. But Randy, well, he mentioned that he knew this little *señorita* in Española, so we lit a shuck there first. Lucky, ain't it? Fate? Meeting up with you like it all played out?" He bent over, laughing until tears formed in his eyes. His breath smelled of wine. "I mean to tell you, Brit, that was the funniest-looking posse ever I did ride with."

"That's because most times," Wade said, "the posses were chasing you."

Clint Paden wiped his eyes, and slapped his thigh. "That's certain sure. But this was different. Mexicans runnin', most of 'em barefoot or in sandals, and my boys on their horses they had left at the livery across the street. And that big, tall Mexican ridin' that palomino. And me on my brand new bicycle. All chasin' you, and Jeremiah Cole."

Shaking his head, Paden continued. "That's all you read about in the newspapers of late. The war in Cuba. The gold in the Klondike." His eyes bore into Wade's. "And Senator Cole's son." His head nodded in approval. "That was a smart move you made, Brit. Askin' for sanctuary. I never would have thought of it."

"Father Marcelino says I should thank you."

He shook his head. "Maybe. But I'd say that little *padre* kept the rest of 'em Mexicans out of here. He wasn't sure what to do at first, but he come through. Tiny as he is, and a Mexican to boot, that little feller's one to ride the river with." He tapped the Marlin's stock on the floor. "Although, me and the boys might have helped persuade those gents. Helped 'em get right with God."

"Who are the boys?" Wade inquired.

"You wouldn't know 'em," Paden replied. "Randy and Stew. We been ridin' together about six months. I left 'em in the church, to keep an eye on Jeremiah Cole." He made a sweeping motion with his free hand. "Tell you what. This is a mighty big spread. Church, boneyard, stable, some other buildings, and this here . . . where you're at . . . is what they call the rectory. All surrounded by a high adobe wall. Reminds me of the Alamo down in San Antonio, where Davy Crockett and all 'em Texicans got carved up by the Mexican army. But don't fret none, Brit. We'll fare better here than how Travis done in Texas. And it ain't likely Cole's got sand enough to sneak out of the church. The Mexicans would really like that. They want the boy dead. Ain't that somethin'?"

Silence.

Paden frowned. Tapped the Marlin on the floor again. Serious at last, and getting to the point. "I figure it this way, Wade. You aim to bring Jeremiah Cole to the senator. Maybe Senator Cole hired you to do the job. Yeah, I figure the senator would pay a right smart of money to get his boy away from that noose." He lifted the rifle, balancing it on his thigh, aiming the barrel slightly at Wade's shoulder. "I also figure, seein' as how shot up you are, seein' as how your coughin' is a damned lot worser than it was ten years ago, seein' as how every Mexican betwixt here and Chama would like to hang Jeremiah Cole hisself, I figure you'd be obliged to take on me and the boys as partners. Yes, sir. That's how I figure it."

"You've figured it wrong."

"How's that?"

"I'm not working for Roman Cole. I'm bringing the kid in to hang."

Paden stared at him incredulously. He cleared his throat. "What . . . what are they payin' you for that job?"

He made Paden wait before answering. "Nothing."

A longer silence.

"That's gritty," Paden said softly. After a while, the smile returned. "But I reckon, your shoulder like it is, and you without your armory, I guess me and the boys could just take Jeremiah Cole from you, and fetch him to his daddy. Yes, sir, I reckon we could collect a right handsome reward, and not have to split it with you."

"Maybe," Wade said. "But first you'd have to get past those angry men waiting just outside the church compound. If you somehow managed to do that, well, then you'd have to get past Dan Augustine and his boys."

A brief flash of fear shown in those bright green eyes. "Augustine?" Paden said. "What's he got to do with this?"

"Roman Cole paid him to fetch his son home."

Wetting his lips, Clint Paden considered this.

"Sixty, seventy miles to the courthouse in T.A.," Wade said. "Another dozen or so to the stronger jail in Chama. Even farther to the Cole Ranch. Against every man in the territory who wants to avenge a priest's murder. Against Dan Augustine and his thirty men." Wade had no idea how many men Augustine had hired, but would guess it to be hardly thirty, probably not even ten, although now, since Wade had changed the course of events, that number might have grown. "Against Roman Cole's men, who are probably eager to bring Jeremiah home, too."

"How was you gonna get that job done?"

"I have a plan," Wade said.

The priest's sandals *clopped* on the floor, closer, and Paden smiled his biggest grin yet. Leaning over, he slapped Wade's wounded shoulder. Wade gasped, bit back a curse. "Just like old times, Brit," Paden was saying. "Looks like you need me as much as I need you. Because you can't get Jeremiah Cole to Chama without me and the boys."

Using the Marlin, Paden pushed himself to his feet. "I ain't buyin' your story that you're doing this for nothin'. One way or the other, there's money involved, and I aim to collect." Passing the priest as he walked through the doorway, Paden said with a laugh: "*Padre,* take good care of *mi amigo.* We's pards."

★ ★ ★ ★ ★

"You are a learned man," Father Marcelino told him, handing him the Gladstone. "I myself prefer Balzac and Hugo over Dumas and Dickens, but. . . ." Eyes beaming, the priest shrugged.

They sat at an uneven table in the rectory, washing down their supper of cabrito and corn tortillas with black coffee. Wade set the tin cup on the table to take the grip. It felt too heavy. He placed it on the floor, unfastened the latches, found the .44 and gun belt inside. When he looked up, the priest flashed a curt smile.

"*Señor* Paden removed it when he brought you inside the church," the little man said. "The one called Randy had been wearing it, but I took it from him this morning before you awoke. They did not argue with me." He couldn't match Clint Paden's smile, but he tried. "Well, *un poco.*"

Wade checked the pistol, which had been reloaded, but not cleaned. He stood to buckle on the rig, then shut the Gladstone without checking for anything else. His left shoulder felt sore, stiff, but the bleeding had stopped—Paden had cauterized the wound with a hot knife after digging out the lead slug the night Wade had arrived at the church, pleading for asylum before passing out. He knew what the priest was doing now. Politely asking us to take our leave. Couldn't blame the man. Besides, he had stayed too long already. Two full days, with evening coming shortly. By now half of New Mexico Territory knew that Jeremiah Cole was holed up at an old Catholic mission in Santa Cruz. Including Dan Augustine.

"I can never repay you for your hospitality," Wade said.

*"Sí,"* the priest said. "You can." He sat at the table, staring out the window. "You can do this by leaving this place." His head shook with a heavy sadness. "My people are poor, but they are good men all. They are devout. They are simple." Shaking fingers found the cross hanging around his neck. "They are hu-

man. They want blood. They must not have it!" A tear rolled down the priest's cheek. "For their own souls, they must not have it. You, I beseech you, you must see that they do not spill the blood of *Señor* Cole."

A similar sermon to what Wade had heard in Chama, even in Santa Fe.

"You know what Cole did," Wade said. It wasn't a question.

*"Sí,"* the priest answered anyway. "As does everyone."

"You can't blame them for wanting to kill him."

It was snowing. A wet, driving snow, fueled by winter's last breath. From the window, Wade couldn't even see the adobe walls of the church compound.

"I confess to you, my friend," Father Marcelino said, "I wished for the death of *Señor* Cole myself, for what he did. It was so horrible, his crime. I also tell you this. Were it not for the guns of *Señor* Paden, your *compadre,* and his friends, I might have lost to the temptation of Satan. Once I opened the doors to the *santuario,* I might have . . . no . . . I would have, with pleasure, upon recognizing this mad killer, I would have denied you refuge, would have let those men take Jeremiah Cole with them." His voice rose as he continued, unaware that he was gripping the cross so tightly his knuckles whitened, his fist trembled. "Gladly would I have tightened a rope around his neck. Gladly would I have kicked a chair from underneath his feet. Gladly would I have denied him a burial in the consecrated land beyond these walls!" His head bowed. Letting go of the cross, he studied the imprint left in palm and fingers.

Wade had been holding his breath. He exhaled only when the priest looked up, trying to smile again.

"I am glad Our Father stayed with me on that night."

Wade wanted to speak, yet didn't know what to say.

"Word has reached Roman Cole," Father Marcelino said wearily. He looked through the window. "If he comes here, he or his men, Santa Cruz will flow with blood. This must not happen." With a heavy sigh, the small man turned back to Wade. "It takes a long time for the people in northern New Mexico to accept outsiders," he said softly. "No matter their blood, no matter the color of their skin, yet they are especially distrustful of . . ."—he forced a grin—". . . you *gringos.*" He tapped a finger against the frosted windowpane. "I come from the village of Santiago Papasquiaro in the Sierra Madre many, many kilometers from here in Mexico. During the first few years I was here, I longed to return to that village, but now I could not dream of leaving Santa Cruz, of leaving this church. My people have grown to trust me, love me, and I love and trust them. Nor could I leave New Mexico. There is a beauty to this place. You will not find it elsewhere." He tapped the glass again. "The snow is so whiter. The sky so bluer. The light as if it shines directly from heaven. The water flows clearer." Turning slowly, he shook his head. "Alas, the blood is redder. Forgive me, *mi amigo,* but you must leave. You and your friends. You must take your prisoner." He was staring out the window again. "And go."

Wade stood, put on his hat, picked up the Gladstone. He was already wearing his Mackinaw for the ancient adobe building did not hold heat very well.

"The storm will give you cover," the priest said without looking at him. "That, and the darkness. You will find five horses in the stable in the west corner, beyond the *santuario.* They are saddled. Do not ask from where these horses came. Just take them, and go."

Wade was at the door when the priest finished talking. Before he left the rectory, Wade said, not looking back: *"Vaya con dios."*

Before the door slammed shut behind him, Father Marcelino responded, but the bitter wind howled down the priest's blessing.

# Chapter Seven

*Affidavit of Juan Gregorio Callas,*
*Dated September 7, 1898*

United States of America,
Territory of New Mexico
1st Judicial District Court
of the United States

In the United States District Court for the County of Santa Fe in the 1st Judicial District of the Territory of New Mexico, August Term, A.D. 1898:

I, Juan Gregorio Callas, duly elected sheriff of the County of Santa Fe, Territory of New Mexico, and a citizen of aforementioned county and territory, and also commissioned as a deputy United States marshal for said territory, do hereby swear and affirm that on or near 5 May 1898, I was in my office, having just returned from dinner, when I received word that the fugitives Britton Wade and Jeremiah Cole (testimony regarding them attached hereto) had taken refuge in the Holy Cross Church in the village of Santa Cruz, County of Río Arriba. Using the authority vested in me as deputy marshal, I, and I alone, purchased a ticket on the Denver & Río Grande Railroad, and traveled by that railroad to the town of Española, Río Arriba County, where I there procured transportation by wagon to the town of Santa Cruz. Upon my return to Santa Fe, I filed a request for payment from the 1st Judicial District Court of the

United States to reimburse my expenses (to wit, round-trip train ticket of $3.35, round-trip wagon trip of 75 cents, *per diem* expenses of $6, $10.15 total). A check for that amount from the court was received by me on or near 17 June 1898.

When I arrived in the village of Santa Cruz, on the evening of 5 May 1898, I found the people in a state of great anxiety. Also, a late snowstorm had struck, reducing visibility to only a few meters. With no local constabulary in the vicinity, I took charge of the situation, discharging some of the men who had laid siege to the church, deputizing four men whose honor and courage I knew, from past experience, to be above reproach. I interviewed several citizens and learned that what had been reported to me in Santa Fe was true, that Britton Wade and Jeremiah Cole, or at least two men matching those descriptions, had been seen and recognized at a livery stable in Española and pursued to Santa Cruz.

Snow covered a horse that had been shot to death in the village plaza. It was later determined and affirmed that the dead animal was the same paint horse purchased by Britton Wade at Yakov Chavez's Livery Stable in Santa Fe. The horse, witnesses attested, had been shot and killed during the pursuit of Wade and Cole. The fugitives had been forced to leave a mule, also purchased from Yakov Chavez, in Española, thus the paint horse had been carrying both men, Wade and Cole, when it had been killed.

Cloaked by the darkness of the evening, Wade and Cole managed to run to the Holy Cross Church, where they asked the priest for asylum, which was granted. Three white men, names unknown, who had joined the pursuit of the fugitives in Española, then, brandishing weapons at the posse from Española, forced the men, using the threat of violence, back outside the gate surrounding the church property. Said wall is constructed of adobe, about two feet thick, circling the churchyard at a height that ranges from four to twelve feet.

Descriptions of the men as given to me are as follows:

1. White male, approximately twenty-five years old, round shoulders, approximately 140 pounds, about 5 feet, 5 inches tall, never looks you in the face while talking, light hair, brown eyes. Armed with a shotgun and large-caliber revolver, the latter reportedly either a Remington or a Colt. Was seen riding a black horse, but neither horse nor saddle was ever found. Likely stolen by one of the pursuers from Española that I discharged upon my arrival in Santa Cruz.

2. White male, approximately thirty years old, 6 feet tall, 170 pounds, armed with a repeating rifle and revolving pistol. No distinguishing marks. Was riding a bicycle, which was found leaning against the church wall. Subsequent investigations upon my return to Santa Fe revealed that the bicycle, a Monarch model, was purchased at City Cyclists, a shop on Sandoval Street, by a man matching the suspect's description. Shop owner, however, could not provide the name of the purchaser, who paid cash and is not believed to be a resident of the city.

3. White male, approximately twenty-five years old, 5 feet, 6 inches tall, about 150 pounds, long straight black hair, black eyes, light whiskers. Armed with a Colt Lightning pump rifle of small caliber and Colt revolving pistol. Was riding a sorrel gelding, branded on the left hip 3-Bar-Lazy-7. Subsequent investigations upon my return to Santa Fe revealed that the brand was registered to Milton Barstow, rancher, Lincoln County. Communicating by telegraph, the sheriff of Lincoln County informed me that the horse in question had been reported stolen in February. Sorrel horse, which was left behind in Santa Cruz by the suspect, was returned to its rightful owner in the latter part of May. Saddle and tack, if either belonged, legally, to the alleged thief, revealed nothing about the owner.

During a brief lull in the winter storm, I avowed to approach the church and parley with the priest with the intention of persuading the priest to turn over the fugitives under the promise that I would return them, unharmed, to Santa Fe. Leaving my Colt pistol and Winchester carbine with one of the men I had deputized, and, waving a white apron given to me by one of the ladies of Santa Cruz, I approached the church, and, to my surprise, found the front door unbolted.

Inside the church, I discovered, praying at the alter, a small priest, approximately 5 feet, 2 inches tall, perhaps thirty years old, who warmly greeted me and introduced himself as Father Marcelino Eusebio de Quesada y Azcárranga. I informed him that I was sheriff of Santa Fe County and a deputy United States marshal, and asked him to release into my custody the two men to whom he had granted sanctuary. I also said I would not arrest the three men who had assisted the fugitives, and would equally ensure their safety.

"This," he said to me, "I cannot grant you."

Hearing this, which I had expected, I told him that Jeremiah Cole had been sentenced to death for the most heinous murder on territorial record, and that Britton Wade had been charged with an assortment of crimes. I told him that I did not wish to see any more bloodshed. I also told him that if Senator Roman Cole, Jeremiah's father, or any of his men arrived in Santa Cruz, there was little I, alone, would be able to do to prevent escalating violence.

Smiling, the priest then began talking about something strange.

"Have you heard of the curse?" he asked me.

I shook my head in the negative.

"Forgive me," he said. "I read too much history."

He continued his story, or should I say a history lesson, on the Tierra Amarilla Land Grant, which was in the newspapers fifteen or so years ago when Senator Roman Cole purchased those 600,000 acres for $200,000. According to Father Marcelino, the Tierra Amarilla Land Grant was set aside by the Mexican government in 1832. The grant was to be a community grant, the father said, but after the United States gained control of New Mexico Territory and during the turmoil over several fraudulent land grants, documents were poorly translated, resulting in Congress confirming and declaring that Tierra Amarilla was a private, not community, grant, which allowed Senator Cole to purchase the land, which many believe to be worth millions of dollars, stripping many citizens of the Río Chama valley of land they then believed, and believe still, to be rightfully theirs.

It was at this time, Father Marcelino told me, that a *bruja* in the village of La Puente cast a curse on Roman Cole. The senator, or land-stealer as he was known among whom the priest called the heirs of the Tierra Amarilla Land Grant, would see all of his family die by the rope, and then would die by the rope himself.

"That is why Senator Cole does not want to see his young son hang," the priest said, "for then he knows that he will hang himself."

I did not know what to say to such a story, but I have heard that the senator's oldest son was discovered hanging in the ranch barn, and that the senator's wife also took her own life in such a manner. Are the stories true? *¿Quién sabe?* [Who knows?]

Upon my return to Santa Fe, I did not attempt to substantiate the story the priest told me, for it seemed to hold no legal bearing on the events I am recalling.

When the story was finished, I told Father Marcelino that the fate of Roman Cole, whether preordained by God or some Río Arriba County witch, did not concern me at the moment, but Britton Wade and Jeremiah Cole did. I told him the law of the territory and the law of the United States could force him to hand over those fugitives.

"I answer to a higher law," the priest said.

We talked for another half hour, and the priest, yawning, asked me to return in the morning for another discussion, that he must prepare his supper, read his Bible, and go to sleep.

The following morning, with snow falling lightly and the skies starting to reveal patches of blue, I was concerned tremendously at the arrival of Dan Augustine and a party of ten to twelve men. Augustine was known throughout the territories of New Mexico and Arizona and the states of Colorado and Texas as a ruthless shootist, but he produced to me a commission as a duly appointed deputy sheriff for Río Arriba County, and a letter of introduction from *Señor* Lucas Murphey, sheriff of said county. Augustine said his orders were to bring Jeremiah Cole to Tierra Amarilla for his scheduled execution, 13 May 1898.

Anger rose among the gathering population of Santa Cruz, some of whom shouted curses while at least one boy in his teens threw icy rocks at the mounted gunmen. Through the grace of God I managed to calm down both sides, and informed Augustine that I had been talking to the priest inside the church, and thought I might persuade him to hand over the fugitives to me.

"You've shown your colors," Dan Augustine told me. "I'll be the one who takes Jeremiah Cole out of that church."

Voices became more heated, but one of the newcomers, a man called Archie Preston, whose name I recognized as an employee of Senator Roman Cole, told Augustine to give the sheriff, meaning me, a chance. Finally, it was agreed by all parties that four of us, an Española man named Ernesto Luján and me representing the Mexican population, and Dan Augustine and another deputized rider named Zechariah Stone representing the Río Arriba County sheriff's posse, would enter the church and continue our parley with Father Marcelino.

Again, I located him praying at the alter, and, removing our hats—all except Augustine—and sitting on the pew at the back of the church, waited for him to approach us. He greeted me warmly, and shook hands with each of the other men—excepting, again, Augustine, who ignored the priest's proffered hand—as I made the introductions, but the pleasantness of the conversation soon ended.

"Hear me out, *padre,*" Dan Augustine said. "I got more than a dozen men outside, and we've come to fetch Jeremiah Cole. You give him up . . . I don't give a tinker's damn about Brit Wade . . . but you give me Jeremiah, or these walls will come tumbling down like Jericho. We'll kill everyone standing outside that tries to stop us, and you'll be saying mercy instead of Mass."

Ernesto Luján shot to his feet, shaking a finger and scolding Augustine for his insolence and sacrilege, but Father Marcelino, his face pleasant, told the good man to sit down, that everything was all right, that we are all God's children.

"You'll give up one of your children," Augustine said.

"I cannot surrender him," Father Marcelino said. "For he is not here."

Dan Augustine shoved the priest aside, and began searching the church. I followed him, soon joined by *Señor* Luján and *Señor* Stone. The four of us began a thorough investigation of all buildings in the church compound, finding only some bloodstained rags that led us to believe one of the party, possibly Britton Wade, had been wounded during or before the siege. Dan Augustine, in my presence, threatened to hurt the priest, but *Señor* Stone told him to "leave it go. We've been hornswoggled is all." Stone, a silver-haired, thick-bearded man in buckskins, laughed, and walked to the empty livery stable in the western corner of the premises. I followed, while Dan Augustine and *Señor* Luján raced back onto the plaza to report the departure of all the men who had been hiding at the Holy Cross Church. This also caused great excitement among all those gathered, white and Mexican. A search was organized, to no avail.

After Stone, Augustine, and Preston led their posse west, hunting the fugitives, and I disbanded the remaining men from Española and Santa Cruz, I returned to the church grounds and joined Father Marcelino inside the rectory.

"Do not ask me where those five horses came from," he immediately told me.

"Who said anything about horses?" was my response.

"I have heard of this man Zechariah Stone. He has been called the Kit Carson of our time, a noted tracker." The priest sighed. "I could not turn over anyone who asked for sanctuary," he said after a long while, "but nor could I watch men who come to me for confession die for someone like Jeremiah Cole."

"Was Britton Wade shot?" I asked.

He hesitated, but eventually confirmed my suspicions, pointing at his left shoulder.

"Badly?" I asked.

"The bullet is out. It is unlikely to cause his death. But his lungs. . . ." He bowed his head.

"Britton Wade took Cole out of my jail," I told him. "There are warrants for his arrest. Who were the other four men?"

He looked up. "There were only three. I did not learn their names. Friends of Wade, they said. But I doubt much of that, although Wade knew one of them."

"The fourth man brought the horses then?"

His face looked bewildered. "What is all this talk of a fourth man? I gathered the horses myself. Five horses, from a dear friend whose name I will never reveal. Five men. Wade, Cole, and the three others whose names I do not know."

"Father," I said, "it was you who told me that *Señor* Stone has been compared to Kit Carson. He is the great tracker, the famous scout. We found signs of six horses in the snow and in the stable. Not five! Six! Now who was with them?"

Shock replaced bewilderment. The priest crossed himself, whispered something I could not understand. At last he told me: "I do not know!" And he rushed outside, through the snow, to look at the tracks himself, although, by that time, most of the signs had been obliterated.

These are the events that I have recalled to the best of my memory. As to what happened later in the month involving the parties I have mentioned, I cannot testify, for I returned to my job as sheriff in Santa Fe and only heard secondhand or read of the great manhunt and subsequent events.

I will state for the record that I believe Marcelino Eusebio de Quesada y Azcárranga to have been a young man driven by what he believed to be in the best interest of his parishioners, his community, and his church. He was a devout Catholic, an exceptional priest, and I enjoyed very much the chance to meet him, and talk to him. I was saddened to learn that he had accidentally drowned in the flooding waters of the Río Santa Cruz in June of this year.

Signed,
Juan Gregorio Callas,
Sheriff, Santa Fe County

Witness the Hon. Robert Ellison, Chief Justice and presiding judge of the 1st Judicial District Court of the Territory of New Mexico and seal of said court at Santa Fe this Nineteenth day of October
A.D. 1898,
Danl [Daniel] Grant, clerk

# Chapter Eight

Snow, wet and heavy, blown by a driving wind, stung their faces as soon as Clint Paden opened the heavy door. Turning back toward Jeremiah Cole, the gunman drew his British Bulldog, and placed the barrel under Cole's chin. "Best remember this, boy . . . those Mexicans want you deader than I do. So don't cry out." It was a needless warning.

Paden holstered the revolver, then looked over Cole's shoulder at Wade. "Which way you say is the stable?"

"Northwestern corner."

"All right." His breath became frosty as he looked outside. "Can't hardly see a damned thing out there."

Paden took the point, leaning into the wind, head bowed, left hand pulling his jacket close against his throat, slugging through snow that reached halfway up his boots. Behind him came Jeremiah Cole, prodded along with the pump rifle held by Stew, a pockmarked man needing a shave, somewhere in his twenties, with dark, greasy hair touching his collar. Paden's other saddle partner, Randy, followed, a suspicious, light-haired gent, maybe a tad shorter and a few pounds lighter than Stew, clutching a double-barrel W.W. Greener near his chest, nervously glancing over his shoulder, as if he thought Britton Wade might shoot him in the back.

Stew had been the one, however, voicing his suspicions about the priest's motives, suggesting that an ambuscade awaited them in the stable.

*You've hit bottom, Clint Paden,* Wade thought, *and sank into the mud, if you're riding with these two.*

That impression surprised him, as if he held Clint Paden in some regard. Quickly closing the church's back door, he was thinking about nothing but following the four men, keeping them close, and keeping his hand on his own .44.

Inside the rock-walled stable, they stamped snow off their boots, shook their hats, and found, just as Father Marcelino had promised, five saddled horses, contentedly eating freshly forked hay. Another horse snorted in the far stall. A lantern hung on the wall, casting yellow light inside the stable, and Paden turned down the wick, so that there was just enough light to see. While the other men looked around, softly cursing the cold, Wade quickly picked the buckskin, the best mount of the lot, and secured his Gladstone behind the cantle.

Next to him, Clint Paden shoved the big Marlin into a scabbard, and tightened the cinch on a rangy sorrel. "Snowing mighty hard," he said casually.

"But it won't last." Wade checked his own cinch before shortening his stirrup.

"In case we get separated," Paden said, "what's your plan? How you thinking about getting all the way to the Chama valley without getting killed?"

Wade hesitated, but a quick glance at Jeremiah Cole made him realize Clint Paden had been right. He couldn't get the kid all the way to Chama, not working alone. A forlorn hope, just like Father Amado had told him. But how far could he trust a man like Clint Paden? Wade let out a mirthless laugh, knowing he had been forced to deal in the devil.

"Roman Cole's men will be watching the road." Gently stroking the buckskin, Wade eased around the horse to work on the other stirrup. "So will Dan Augustine. They'll also have to keep a sharp eye on the stagecoaches and the railroad. Thinking we could take the train to Colorado, come down from Antonito to Chama." He sniffed, wiped his nose. No, being seen in Española probably ruled out any train trips.

Paden blew on his hands, his eyes brightening at the thought of trains. He had an easy smile. "I like trains. Riding in those big cars, how those coaches sway, hearing the music of 'em iron wheels on 'em rails. Drinking a whiskey and warming myself by a stove. So why ain't we catching a train?"

"I didn't want to get caught inside a car. Not by Dan Augustine."

"I'll grant you that." Paden looked back, and barked at his men: "Stew, you was the one so jo-fired we was gonna get ambushed here. I figured you'd want to light a shuck. So quit lollygagging, and get on one of these horses. You, too, Randy. Put our friend Mister Cole on that sway-backed chestnut."

The man named Stew kept looking out the stable door into the snow and darkness, then down the stable toward the dark stalls. "Thought I heard somethin'," he said.

Ignoring Stew, Paden looked back at Wade. "So no train. No stagecoach. And there's only one road to Chama. Lessen you want to ride to Taos, and cut through the mountains up Tres Piedres way."

Wade shook his head. "Roman Cole will be watching that road, too."

"So . . . ?"

Wade swung into the saddle. "Ride through the gate," he said. "Down into the Santa Cruz. They won't be able to track us in the river. We'll follow that all the way down to Española, then hit the Río Chama. And follow the Chama all the way north."

"Are you crazy?" Paden mounted the sorrel.

"Maybe."

"Ride up the Chama River?"

"We won't be in the river the whole way. But we'll sure follow the river. It's kind of a natural road. . . ."

"If you're a trout," Paden interrupted.

"They won't be watching the river." Wade glanced over his shoulder. Randy kept the shotgun trained on Jeremiah Cole as the prisoner, his hands bound in front of him with rawhide, mounted the chestnut. Stew kept looking around, licking his lips, fingers nervously tapping his rifle.

"They won't be watching the Chama," Paden said, "because it can't be done. You ever seen Chama Cañon?"

"No." Wade tugged on the reins. "Have you?"

"Not exactly, but I heard about it. On one side of it is this place called Mesa del Las Viejas. And up on the other side are some mountains, one of which is known as Dead Man's Peak. It got that name for a reason, Brit." He shook his head, and spit. "That's a hell of a plan you got, pard."

"You're free to pull out," Wade fired back, smiling, but finding his pistol butt. Just in case.

With a grunt, Paden pulled his hat down low, and muttered something. Wade couldn't catch most of what the gunman said, but he did hear: "Reckon we'll give your plan a try, for now." Then Paden looked back at Stew, who still had not mounted his horse, and now had walked to the edge of the stable, looking in the stall.

"Stew, by grab, I. . . ."

The long-haired man aimed the Lightning rifle at the loft, and spoke easily: "I tell you I heard somethin'."

Only now, Wade heard it, too.

"This dun horse," Stew was saying, "rode in recent-like. Saddle's still on, wet, startin' to slip, and snow's melted in the stall. Come on down here, you back-shootin' bastard!" He was yelling at the loft, pumping a shell into the little .22 rimfire rifle.

Wade pulled himself up, standing on the saddle, reaching up, then climbing into the loft, hoping Stew wasn't so stupid as to shoot. The wind would drown out most of their conversation, but maybe not a gunshot, certainly not a gunfight.

Crouching, head bent to keep from hitting the ceiling, he peered over the straw. This close to the roof, he could hear and feel the wind, the cold night air. He reached into his Mackinaw, found the matches, and struck a lucifer on the rough-hewn cottonwood *viga* above him.

A knife slashed for his stomach.

Wade dropped the match, the flickering flame vanishing almost instantly, sucked in as much air as his worn-out lungs could hold, trying to avoid the knife, felt the blade tear at his coat, and suddenly he was falling onto the loft floor, watching the shadowy figure in a flat-brimmed black hat lunge at him. He rolled, trying to find his revolver, hearing the horses stomping below, found the shadow again, now drawing the Merwin & Hulbert from the holster.

A panther-like scream shattered the night. Then came Clint Paden's surprised shout. Still clutching the knife, the shadow leaped from the loft.

Hoofs stomped, Jeremiah Cole shrieked, Stew's rifle *popped,* and the horse in the far stall kicked the wall angrily. "Now there'll be hell," Wade said through clenched teeth. He was back on his feet, running, leaping from the left, landing away from the horses, toppling over, rolling, coming up with the .44, seeing the chestnut rearing, snorting. Randy and Paden fought to keep the horses under control. Stew pumped another round into the Lightning, tried to aim.

At what?

Wade scrambled to his feet, thumbing back the hammer, looking. Where was Cole? There. On the ground, rolling, desperate to avoid those crashing hoofs, blood gushing from his nose.

The shadow in black, knife raised, cursed. The knife struck at Cole's back.

"Don't!" Wade aimed the pistol.

Stew's back came into his sights. Wade cursed, moved to his left, heard Paden shout something, then saw the long-haired gunman swing the rifle hard, the octagonal blue barrel *thudding* wickedly against the shadow's head. The hat flew off. Long red hair spilled out, and the shadow collapsed, knife spinning through the air, bouncing off the stone wall.

Blinking, Wade gasped for breath. It had all happened in a matter of seconds, no more than half a minute.

On crawled Jeremiah Cole, a petrified rat, gasping, bleeding, eyes wide.

"Stop it!" Wade kicked him in his face, watched him roll over, grunting, falling still, yet conscious. Next Wade hurried to the door, peered into the darkness, heard the wind scream, waiting, watching.

Nothing.

For once, Britton Wade's luck hadn't turned bad. Or so he thought, until he turned around to discover Stew aiming his rifle at the red-headed shadow lying, face down, next to the chestnut.

"Hold it, you damned fool!"

Wade looked up, surprised to find Clint Paden pointing his revolver at Stew's face.

Stew looked up, his face bitter, the barrel still pressed into that flowing red hair, his finger tight against the trigger.

"It's a woman," Paden said.

"Yeah, and the bitch was tryin' to kill us all," Stew said.

"Not all of us," Jeremiah Cole said. "Just me."

Wade chanced another look outside, holstered his pistol. "Pull that trigger," he said, "and we'll all get killed. It's by God's own grace no one heard that first shot." When the long-haired weasel finally relented, cursing under his breath as he shoved the rifle into the saddle scabbard on one of the bay horses, Wade hoisted Jeremiah Cole to his feet, and shoved him toward the chestnut. "We best ride," Wade said. "Now!"

"Brit's right." Paden had holstered his revolver, and unsheathed the Marlin, backing the sorrel out, ducking to look out the door. "All 'em Mexicans must be drunker than Hooter's goat," he said. "If they didn't hear that ruction."

"The wind," Wade said, "carried the noise away." He kept looking at Stew, holding the bay's reins and saddle horn, but still glaring at the unconscious woman lying in the straw and manure.

Paden was talking to Wade. "Out the gate. To the river. Down the Santa Cruz to the Chama."

Wade nodded.

"I should slice her throat," Stew said in an icy whisper.

Paden's eyes blazed. "She's out cold, Stew. Now let's ride."

"She heard us!" Stew barked back. "Heard where this lunger's takin' us. Sure as hell can't leave her behind to tell ever man-jack in the plaza where we's headed."

Silence. Wade watched Paden, waiting for his word, put his hand on the .44's butt, wondering why everything had turned so sour, so quickly.

In the back of the stable, the dun horse kicked the stall again.

"Tie her over the saddle then," Paden said urgently. "We'll bring her with us."

Dawn broke, clear and cold, as the horses moved wearily upstream in the Río Chama. How they had ever managed to make it this far, Britton Wade figured, could only be called a miracle. The snow had stopped falling shortly after midnight, and a few hours later they could see stars. Northwest of Santa Cruz, the storm hadn't dumped so much snow, and, although the wind that morning still felt like winter, Wade knew the clear skies would mean a warm sun.

Spring, perhaps, had finally won out, and he thought of something Dickens had written: "Spring is the time of the year, when it is summer in the sun and winter in the shade."

They eased out of the river and into a fortress of juniper, sliding, almost falling, from their saddles, to loosen the cinches, and let the horses rest. Wade's shoulder felt stiff, and he was wet, weary, almost frostbitten, but he moved to the big dun horse, and knelt to untie the shadow's hands and feet.

She wasn't a shadow any more, not in the daylight, not with her red hair hanging almost to the ground. He could see the knot just above her temple, bruised and cut from Stew's vicious slap with the .22's barrel, could see her red lips crusted with something she had vomited up sometime during the night. Her face, now pale, was freckled, and, as he helped her off the dun, and watched her collapse onto the glistening snow, he realized that, even covered in filth, even after miles riding like a corpse, she was a beautiful woman, in her twenties, with delicate nose, and eyes like emeralds, only harder than diamonds. She wore a black riding skirt, black boots, a navy blouse.

Wade stood there, staring at her, as she rubbed her head. From the opposite bank, a raven *kawed,* and he looked away from the woman, studying the country, wondering why he had even tried to pull off this damned fool scheme, then heard Clint Paden's drawl.

"It ain't polite, I know, but I reckon I got to ask you your name, ma'am."

Squatting in front of the redhead, Paden handed her his canteen, and watched her drink. "Not too much," he warned. "Stew hit you pretty good."

"A fine gentleman he is," the woman said, spit some water to her side, and returned the canteen. "Fine gentlemen you all are."

"Well." The toes of Paden's boots dug nervously in the already melting snow.

"You wasn't exactly lady-like your ownself," Randy said, and pointed toward the river where Jeremiah Cole knelt, cupping his hands, slaking his thirst, and washing dried blood off his face while Stew stood guard over him with the pump rifle. "You was about to gut our prisoner like a fish."

She glared at Randy, but he wasn't even looking at her, then turned her blazing eyes on Clint Paden.

"Ma'am?" Paden said softly. "If I knew what I should call you. . . ."

"Fenella Magauran," she said. Her accent sounded like County Cavan. "And I aim to kill that man."

Slowly Paden rose, wiping his face. "What for?"

"What for?" She looked at him sharply. "What for, you say? What do you think, you dumb oaf? Do you think only the Mexicans want that scoundrel to die? Do you think a woman cannot know the power of Roman Cole?" She pointed at the German silver crucifix hanging from her neck. Paden was looking away, embarrassed, but Wade couldn't turn from the Irish girl. "Father Vasco was my priest, too! And he. . . ." She spit at Cole, still at the river. "He murdered him!"

# CHAPTER NINE

Rivulets of water carved furrows in the red earth, weaving through cheap grass and *chamisa,* moving around rocks, finally pouring into the river, wide here in the flat, open country. By midday, most of the snow had melted, and the blue Chama shimmered with reflected sunlight, so bright it hurt one's eyes.

Somehow, they had made it past the confluence of the Ojo Caliente, riding in the middle of the Río Chama when they could, on the banks when they couldn't, sometimes, when the road looked clear, on the trail itself to make better time.

If they could just get past Abiquiu, the next village—the only place of any significance between here and Tierra Amarilla—then make it to the red rock country, they might survive. *At least until we hit the deep cañon,* Britton Wade thought. Clint Paden had been right back in Santa Cruz. There was a pretty good chance Chama Cañon would kill them.

Paden took the point, with the red-headed Irish girl trotting alongside him on her big dun. Beside Paden rode Jeremiah Cole, head down, wetting his cracked lips, no longer acting like the cock-of-the-walk boy who felt the world owed him something. Randy and Stew brought up the rear on their bay horses. Wade didn't like the idea of having those two tramps behind him, and kept his right hand near the Merwin & Hulbert, kept listening for the metallic click of a revolver being cocked behind him. It wasn't good for his nerves.

They had been on the Abiquiu road for three quarters of an

hour, trotting, then slowing to a walk, and had not seen one person. *Lucky,* Wade thought. *How long will it hold?*

Paden reined the sorrel to a stop, told the girl to hold up, his saddle *creaking* as he turned, jutting his chin toward crumbling adobe walls near the river, maybe a quarter mile off the road. Dead weeds piled up against a *carreta,* one of the ox-drawn carts so common in the territory, in front of the old house. The cart looked about as ancient as the adobe.

"We could rest our horses there a spell," Paden said. "Got a good view of the road."

Wade's head bobbed. Rest the horses, rest themselves.

When they reached the abandoned home, Paden helped the girl down, dusted off the remains of a fireplace's hearth, and suggested that she sit there, out of the wind. He kept busy, loosening the cinches, barking orders, always smiling. Wade wished he still possessed that kind of youthful energy.

Paden ordered Randy to grain the animals, then lead them down to the river, two at a time, to drink. He told Stew that the cottonwood tree near the Chama would be a good place for him and his Colt Lightning rifle, told him to keep a sharp lookout for anything, anyone. He told Wade: "You wouldn't happen to have some whiskey in that grip of yours, would you, pard? Something to cut the trail dust?"

Rye sounded good.

Wade swung wearily to the ground, and untied the leather thong holding the Gladstone. "Lot of stuff was spilled out," he said to no one in particular as he headed for a rock near the Irish girl, letting Randy take his buckskin. He sat down, looked inside the grip, and sighed. The laudanum was gone. He rummaged through the books, stopped, pulled one out, stared at it, not comprehending.

"You can preach to us, too," Paden was saying, "but I'd prefer some whiskey before the sermon."

Wade opened the Bible, closed it, traced his finger along the cross cut into the leather cover, shook his head, returned the Bible into the Gladstone. *A present,* he thought, *from Father Marcelino. When was the last time I've held a Bible?*

He found the flask, took a swallow, tossed the container to Paden, and reached back inside the bag, retrieved his shaving kit, and walked to the river where Randy was watering the two bays.

"Every tale I ever heard about Britton Wade says he's savage as a meat axe," Paden said. Hat tipped back, he leaned against the adobe, near the Irish girl, legs stretched out in front of him, crossed at the ankles, smiling that big smile of his, the flask, empty by now, leaning against the rock under Fenella Magauran's legs. "Yet here he is, a man who wants to shave every day."

"I like to be clean," Wade said. He removed his hat, ran his fingers through the hair, looked up and down the trail.

"Shaving won't keep you clean, mister," Jeremiah Cole said bitterly.

Randy, having watered and grained all the mounts, laughed. "He sure won't get clean with what he's got for shavin' soap." He cackled even harder. "You should have seen it, Clint. He ain't got no shavin' mug, just a worn old piece of soap he put in his palm, and it's just a thin wheel. That's all that's left. Middle of it's all gone, used up." He slapped his thigh with his hat. "I mean to tell you, Clint, most folks I know, they'd toss that morsel away, buy a new one."

"Wade's always been a miser." Paden re-crossed his legs.

"How long y'all knowed one another?" Randy asked.

"Oh, we was acquaintances ten years ago or so, when I was just a green pea." Looking at Wade now. "I heard about what you did in Chloride, pard, after I went up to Santa Fe for two years."

"So did I," Wade said.

Paden yawned, stretched, slowly climbed to his feet. "You and me are a lot alike," he told Wade.

"Not really," Wade said.

"Sure we are. Even our last names are similar, Paden and Wade. You could hang 'em names on a shingle if we was lawyers or a troupe of Thespians, and bring in customers by the score." Paden faced Fenella. "Ma'am, it's like this. Brit Wade, he got to wear a badge. Clint Paden, he's . . . that would be me, ma'am . . . he's had badges chasing him most of his life. But we're both clay-eaters, just poor white trash from the South. My mama always told me that I was born on the wrong side of the tracks to amount to nothing. Now, Britton Wade, he was born on the same side of the tracks as me, or so I suspect, only he amounted to something. Got his name in the newspapers, got wrote up in three or four half-dime novels. Got to be a big man."

"Not so big."

Paden grinned harder. "Not now, I guess. Even old Goliath met his better."

"We should go," Wade said.

The girl was looking at him. "You," she said. "You are a lawman?"

"Sometime back," he said.

She didn't look away, just stared at him with those green eyes, as if trying to understand him.

*Hell,* Wade thought, *what's the point? I don't even understand myself.*

"Why do you do this?" she asked.

"I'm bringing him in." Wade pointed at Jeremiah Cole. "It's as simple as that."

She laughed, without humor, shook her head, and rose from her seat on the stones. "I do not believe you. I believe you are taking this fiend to Senator Cole. For money!" She spit out the last words with a vindictiveness that almost matched her hatred for Roman Cole.

He heard Cole's fingers snap, saw him pointing at the girl. "I know you. Now I remember. You used to clerk in Jimmy Gage's mercantile in Chama."

"That is right. And I remember you, Jeremiah Cole."

"Well, I never hurt you. Don't think I ever spoke to you much. You ain't got no call to come trying to cut out my heart."

"Don't I?" She spun quickly, facing Wade again. "How much is Senator Cole paying you?"

"Ma'am," Clint Paden answered, "was we working for Mister Cole, don't you figure we'd be having an easier go at things? Don't you reckon the rich senator would be hurrying his boy south to Mexico, maybe to some hide-out in Texas? Don't it stand to reason that we wouldn't be bringing the boy to that rope awaiting him at T.A.? We're men seeking justice, ain't that right, Brit?"

"You are not just men," she said, still bitter, "no matter how many badges he has worn."

*I cannot deny that,* Wade thought.

"And you're a just woman?" Randy said, mocking her. "You tryin' to stab him to death?" He shook his head. "Clint, I wish we had rode on to Las Vegas to join the fight in Cuba. Everybody in the territory has gone plumb loco."

"Let's ride," Wade repeated.

"Two hundred dollars!" the woman shouted, and everyone inside the adobe walls stared at her. "Two hundred dollars," she said again. "That is the reward Father Amado and Father Virgilio will pay."

"How's that?" Stew had rejoined them, holding the rifle

against his right leg.

"I told you to keep a look-out!" Paden barked.

"Yeah." Stew stared at the woman, but only briefly, then looked at his boots. "You did. What about that reward?"

"Two hundred dollars," Fenella repeated. "If you are not riding for Senator Cole, if you truly want justice, the money can be yours. Perhaps you knew of this already. The priests in the valley took up a collection. I gave them three dollars and seventeen cents myself. Two hundred dollars, to be paid when that man"—she spit at Jeremiah—"when he is delivered to the devil."

Jeremiah Cole's laugh broke the brief silence. "My pa would pay two thousand. Or more." Then his eyes became slivers, and he stood in Wade's face. "You," he said, remembering. "You so all high and mighty, saying you're working for the law, justice, all that bullshit. You told me you were working for those two *padres*. You're bringing me in for money!"

Clint Paden was laughing now, walking to the picketed sorrel. "I do declare, Brit, you was holding out on me. Two hundred dollars. A reward. And you told us that you was doing this job for nothing. Let's ride boys. Into the river for a few miles. We can camp tonight in the rocks. And figure out how we're gonna split up that reward those good *padres* have offered us."

Chalk-colored boulders lined the cañon floor, its walls stretching into the darkening sky, as they made camp that evening. The ground remained wet, the wind cooling as the sun dipped lower in the horizon. No coffee. No fire. Another cold camp. But they had made it this far. There was that.

"That was mighty sly of you, pard," Clint Paden said, dropping his saddle beside Wade, who was lying on the ground as Randy and Stew picketed the horses, and Jeremiah Cole and Fenella sat across from each other, leaning on their saddles, as well. "Not telling me about that two hundred dollars."

"It's only a hundred and fifty," Wade said. He wished they could have a fire that night, heat up some of his coffee. The cañon would likely prevent anyone seeing a small fire, but someone might smell it. Better to play it safe.

"How's that?"

Wade cleared his throat, then coughed into a handkerchief. "Father Amado advanced me fifty." Had to. I was dead broke. He shook his head at the memory, opened up the cotton rag, and shook his head again at the flecks of blood.

"I guess if I didn't like you so much, Brit, I'd say that was your tough luck, that you'd already collected your part of the reward, and me and the boys would divvy up the rest. But I like you, pard. We'll split the rest of the money four ways. Might be harder to cipher that way, but that's what we'll do. It's only fair. After all, it was you who got the Cole kid out of the jail."

"I appreciate that." Paden didn't catch his sarcasm.

" 'Course," Paden said, staring across their camp. "There is the other thing. What the boy said. That his pa would pay two thousand dollars to see his son alive."

"Yeah." Waiting for Paden to make his play.

Instead, Clint Paden shook his head, still looking at the Irish girl. "On the other hand, a woman like that, well, she could almost make you want to do right by her."

Wade sighed. "You ever tried to do right by yourself, Clint?"

Paden's head turned, and he looked at Wade for a long time, puzzled, wondering, maybe thinking. He started to answer, stopped, and found Fenella again. "She's a fair sight, don't you think?"

"More than fair."

"Strong, too. Like to have cut Cole's throat." He chuckled slightly. "That would have been something. Having a girl stop us cold." Sighing heavily, he stretched out his long legs.

"Randy's right. The whole territory has turned crazy. You ever seen anything like it?"

Wade's head shook.

"I reckon we lost 'em boys in Santa Cruz."

"Maybe. But there will be others. Dan Augustine. Riders for Roman Cole's brand. Who knows how many more."

Paden wasn't listening. He was scrambling to his feet, sweeping off his hat, hopelessly love-struck, as Fenella Magauran approached them.

"Do you really believe this piece of filth will hang?" She hooked a long thumb at Cole. Before Paden could reply, she asked again: "Do you really believe you cannot be stopped by Senator Cole?"

"Well, ma'am," Paden said, "we ain't been stopped yet."

"Then you may let me go. I will not harm you any more."

Paden scratched the palm of his hand against his pistol's hammer. "Well," he drawled.

"Surely, Mister Paden. . . ."

"Call me, Clint, ma'am."

Those Irish eyes danced. "Clint. Surely, Clint, you have heard the saying that a woman has the right to change her mind." She tossed back her head, red hair bouncing, and laughed. "I do not have to kill him. He is not worth it. He is cursed, anyway. The entire Cole clan is cursed."

"Shut up!" Cole said.

"Cursed to hang," she said, eyes still dancing, turning to mock the doomed Jeremiah Cole.

"Shut up!"

"Like his brother. Like his. . . ."

Roaring in anger, Jeremiah Cole sprang to his feet, charging. Wade was pushing himself up, drawing the .44, and the girl was screaming, ducking, eyes no longer so bright. From the picket line, Randy yelled something, but Wade couldn't hear it.

Paden dived, tackling Cole, pinning him easily on the ground, and, when she saw he no longer remained a threat, the Magauran girl chuckled again. "Cursed to hang," she said. "To die from the rope. As they all must die. As many have already. . . ."

"Shut up." This time, Britton Wade spoke the sharp words, holstering his revolver, staring into her hardened eyes, staring until she looked away.

On his feet, catching his breath, Clint Paden hurried to the girl. "Well, Miss Fenella, I reckon I'd enjoy your company. So if it's all the same to you, ma'am, you can just ride along with us. Dangersome country, ma'am. Not fit for a woman to be riding through alone."

Trying to speak easily, Wade figured, but Paden's voice was as strained as his smile. Knowing what the girl had been doing, riling Cole, hoping Paden or Wade would kill him. Getting no response from the woman, Paden put his hat back on, and walked to the horses, shrieking orders at Randy and Stew.

Fenella Magauran's eyes glared again at Britton Wade before she went back to her saddle and sat, while Jeremiah Cole scrambled into the rocks, away from the girl, closer to Wade.

"Damn her to hell," he said. "Damn that curse! Damn. . . ." His voice cracked. "Damn my family."

Back at the church, during one of his long-winded history lessons, Father Marcelino had mentioned the *bruja*'s curse of the Cole family. Wade hadn't given it much thought, more folklore and superstition as common across New Mexico as coyotes, and he considered asking the prisoner more about it now, but decided against it. Superstition or not, it had riled Jeremiah Cole. Or something had. Maybe it had just been the Irish girl.

"Five thousand dollars," Cole said urgently. "Even ten."

Wade looked at him.

"Ten thousand. That's more than those bean-eaters around

Chama could ever raise in twenty lifetimes. Ten thousand dollars. Just get me to my pa."

With a slight laugh, Wade opened the Gladstone. He had a little light left, just enough for. . . . He found the Bible, put it back, withdrew Dumas.

"You don't know what it's like, Wade." Cole's voice kept faltering, still upset by the girl's comments, combined with his approaching execution date. "I been rotting in that dungeon in Santa Fe for months while my lawyers were appealing my case. You don't know what it's like, Wade, to have a death sentence hanging over you."

"Son," Wade said, "I've had a death sentence hanging over me for nigh sixteen years." He opened *The Man in the Iron Mask.*

# Chapter Ten

"So, throughout life, our worst weaknesses and meanness are usually committed for the sake of the people who we most despise."

Roman Cole reread the sentence, dog-eared the page, and slowly closed Great Expectations, having already forgotten what he had read. Too noisy. One reason he preferred the solitude of his ranch headquarters, where he could see the Brazos Cliffs from the window of his library, where he could enjoy the quiet, the loneliness. One reason he hated Chama.

He tossed the book on the dresser of his hotel room, on the second floor of the High Mountains Hotel, just above the saloon. A poor location for peace and quiet, but it was the biggest room in the hotel, the biggest room in Chama. The floor seemed to shudder from the shouts and laughter below, the *clinking* of glass, the *thudding* of balls on the billiard table, the cacophony of forty-rod whiskey and thirty-a-month cowhands. *Might as well join them,* Roman Cole decided, grabbed his Stetson, and left his room.

Only he didn't make it to the saloon.

He saw her leap from the davenport by the window overlooking Front Street, dark hair pinned in a bun, a pencil tucked above her ear, making a beeline for him. How long had she been waiting in the lobby? Probably since the news had spread throughout the gossipy little town that Senator Roman Cole had checked in. That woman galled him something fierce.

"A word with you, Senator?" Rachel Morgan said, removing the pencil and producing a notebook.

Ignoring her, he strode across the parlor and into the saloon, found an empty corner along the long mahogany bar, and barked an order for a beer to the nearest bartender, then searched his coat pocket for a cigar.

"I won't be denied an interview, Senator."

She, a damned woman, had followed him into the saloon. The woman had sand, but no pride. He bit off the end of his cigar and spit, not caring that he missed the spittoon. *Women in saloons. Women editing newspapers. Women demanding suffrage. The world had gone to hell.*

"Make it bourbon," he told the bartender. He looked around the saloon, found a few friendly faces, spotted another man near the taps, the little solicitor who had argued long and hard, and won, for a change of venue for Jeremiah's trial, said a fair trial could never happen in Río Arriba County. For both sides, he had argued, due to the reputation of the defendant's father and due to the most heinous crime on record for which the defendant is accused. He had gotten the trial moved to San Miguel County, to Las Vegas, started the whole damned ball rolling downhill. Cole struck a match, looking over his cigar, the smoke, glaring straight at the firebrand of a lawyer, until the cad gulped down whatever he was drinking, and, pulling down his bowler tight, headed outside.

"Your son is scheduled to be executed one week from today," the newspaper editor said.

"I read that in your newspaper." The barkeep gave him a glass. Cole killed it, motioned for another.

"Is Britton Wade working for you?"

*Insolent bitch.* He sent a blue stream of smoke in her face, hoping she would cough, turn green, but she didn't even blink, damn her. Hearing the whiskey refilling his tumbler, he reached for it, stopped, decided to answer her question. "Britton Wade has never drawn time from me. I don't know the man. Only by reputation. And that reputation smells like a rotting coyote."

"Some say the same of your reputation, Senator."

"Some. . . ." He held his tongue. Had been about to remind her how people had been killed for words like those, that he had killed men himself, and if not for the fact that she wore a skirt. . . .

"Do you believe your son will hang?"

"I believe my son to be innocent." Two men nearest him nodded. Pandering to him, the mealy-mouthed, gutless bastards. His eyes blazed until the two looked away, one of them moving to a table in the saloon's darkest recess.

"There's a story, among many of the original families to the Tierra Amarilla Land Grant, that, if Jeremiah Cole hangs, it will continue to fulfill a prophecy. That all of the Coles are cursed to die from the rope."

He lifted the glass.

"One of your sons hanged by his own hand. They say the other put the noose around his neck when he killed Father Vasco."

He drank. The bartender had left the bottle. He refilled his glass.

"Is it true that your late wife also hanged herself?"

Another man, standing to his left, turned on his heels. "Miss Morgan," he said. "No offense, ma'am, I don't mean to be eavesdropping, but it's bad manners to mention a woman in a saloon. Missus Cole deserves some respect." He tipped his hat, lifted his wine glass.

To Cole's surprise, that seemed to fluster the shameless hussy. She shuffled her feet nervously, looked at her notes, wet her lips.

Cole sipped the bourbon.

"You done?" he asked.

He should have kept quiet. Her resolve returned. Again she looked straight into his eyes, unwavering. "Sheriff Murphey purchased the timbers for the gallows from the Cole Lumber Company."

The saloon had turned silent. Some drunk looked up from a table, slammed his empty glass on the felt cloth, asked what in hell was going on, stood up, wobbled toward the player piano, said something about needing music. A tall railroad worker stopped him, told him to sit down and shut up.

"I have many businesses," Cole told her. He looked at the man who had come to his late wife's defense. "Isn't that right, Jimmy?"

James Gage's head barely moved, and he finished his wine.

"You mean to profit from your own son's death?"

He took another sip, placed the tumbler in her hand, and smiled through his cigar. "Jeremiah isn't dead, yet."

Tossing the cigar into the spittoon, he left, pushing angrily through the batwing doors, across the lobby, and out the front door onto the boardwalk, looking across the muddy street, and down the hill at the railroad depot and tracks, over to the water tank, back to the telegraph office next to Gage's Mercantile. That's why he had come to town. Be closer to the news. He saw the telegrapher, busy jotting something down. For him? Maybe not. He looked southward. The Jicarilla Saloon sat a few doors down, but he'd have to cross that bog to reach it. He didn't want to look over his shoulder, troubled that he might find that newspaper editor waiting to ambush him again. He wished somebody in Chama had the sense to lay some planks down across the thick soup. Wished they had purchased those planks from the Cole Lumber Company.

Hell, yes, he had sold the county lumber for the gallows. Same as he had provided timbers for the gallows in '96 when

Perfecto Padilla and Robert Torres had been executed. Hell, yes, it had been about profit, but he had never figured those gallows would have been used for Jeremiah. Wouldn't be worried about that now, if not for Britton Wade.

He turned, decided to find some escape in the Jicarilla, had just sunk his right boot into four inches of bog, when someone called out his name. It was the baldheaded, rail-thin telegrapher, waving a slip of paper in his bony left hand, slogging through the street, reaching the boardwalk, leaving a trail of mud on the pine planks.

Roman Cole pulled his muddy boot back onto the wood.

"This come for you, Senator." The relic handed him the paper, his head bobbed once, and he was hurrying back across the street.

Cole swallowed, unfolded the paper, steeled himself for the worst.

*STONE ON TRAIL STOP*
*SHOULD HAVE J SAFE STOP*
*WILL BRING HEAD YOU DESIRE STOP*
*NEAR ABIQUIU STOP*

It had been signed Archie Preston. He let out a long breath, hadn't realized he had even been too scared to breathe, but now Roman Cole smiled as he folded the paper, and tucked it inside his coat pocket. Turning slightly, he spotted the newspaper editor in the hotel lobby, talking to mercantile owner James Gage, furiously taking notes.

Good old Archie. He didn't know how his foreman had managed it. Probably ordered a string of riders to the nearest telegraph office to send the wire. Archie Preston deserved a bonus, would get one, once Jeremiah was safe.

Cole started down the boardwalk, away from the Jicarilla, away from the High Mountains Hotel, toward the livery, where his stallion was boarded. No longer would he wait for news, good or bad, wait to be ambushed by that pesky newspaper woman, forced to drink in watering holes alongside pettifogging lawyers, poor businessmen, and a bunch of Judas Iscariots. And damned Mexican fables.

"Louise died of cholera," he said bitterly to the lady ink-slinger's back. "And William was no son of mine."

North of Abiquiu, in a box cañon a half mile from the river, Wade held a firm hand over the buckskin's mouth, listening as a dozen riders loped on the road above. Stew knelt nearby, having ignored Wade's demands to keep the horses quiet. Instead, the gunman aimed the Lightning rifle at the road. Paden kept one hand on his sorrel, the other held the Bulldog revolver under Jeremiah Cole's throat.

The sound of hoofs died away, and Britton Wade filled his lungs with air, quickly swung into the saddle.

"Close." Paden holstered the revolver, and mounted the sorrel.

"We should have turned him over to those riders," Stew said after he angrily shoved the rifle into the scabbard. "Cole men, likely. Could have collected the senator's reward, and not that change offered by them starvin' poor priests."

"Stew, Stew, Stew." Paden shook his head. "Those gents would have just taken Jeremiah from us. So as they could get a bonus from the boy's daddy. No, the only way we could collect anything from Senator Cole would be to turn young Jeremiah over to the senator, in person, face to face, *mano a mano.*" Grinning, he turned to Wade and Fenella. "That is to say, if that was our intentions, which it ain't. We're deputies, working for Deputy United States Marshal Britton Wade, and we've given our word to bring Jeremiah Cole to jail, or the closest church to Chama."

Wade kicked the buckskin into a walk, easing out of the cañon, then nudged the horse into a trot, making for the river, away from the road.

It had been going like that most of the day. Yesterday, they had seen no one, but today they had spent more time hiding from riders than riding for Chama Cañon. Skirting a wide loop around Abiquiu, picking up the river again, looking over their shoulders at the flat-topped mountain known as El Pedernal looking down on them.

"River's rising," Paden said, reining up at the Chama's banks.

"Yeah." Still, Wade kicked the buckskin, splashing into the water, cold, deep, swift, heard the others follow him.

The buckskin shook, urinated, and moved on, into the woods. Wade led the group another mile, near the river, although they were deep enough in the trees now that they couldn't see the road. The problem was the forest didn't go on forever, and soon they'd have no more cover.

He reined in, letting the horses rest, letting his own nerves settle down, and he let out a small laugh. There it was again. That fear. "It's funny," he said, not meaning to speak his thoughts aloud.

A voice sounded to his left.

*"Buenas tardes."*

His hand started for the revolver, stopped. Behind him, Stew cursed, drew his own pistol, but Wade barked: "Hold it!"

A little man in duck trousers and a muslin shirt stood just a few rods away, axe over his shoulder, sweat-stained sombrero in one hand at his waist, worn boots on his feet. The woodcutter had appeared out of nowhere, but he didn't seem a threat. Not yet.

Wade nodded a greeting at the Mexican, listening as Paden told Stew: "Gunshot would bring that posse back, Stew. Let's see what the fella wants."

After a gracious bow at Fenella, the Mexican leaned the axe against a tree, and pulled his big hat back over his sweaty black hair. Behind him, in a small clearing, waited a patient donkey loaded with firewood.

"I am Carlito Martinez."

"You speak English," Randy said stupidly.

The woodcutter kept his eyes on Britton Wade. *"Un poco."*

"We're. . . ." Wade laughed again, stopped his lie before he could think of one. The man knew who they were. "I'm Britton Wade."

*"Sí.* A pleasure, *señor."*

Wade introduced the others, stopping at Jeremiah Cole. "You know this man."

"I have never seen him before this moment, but, sí, I know who he is. Everyone knows who he is." Carlito Martinez spoke English more than just a little. "Everyone knows who you are, *Señor* Wade."

"And you don't want to kill Cole?" Paden shook his head. "That's a first. Every Mexican in the territory wants this boy dead."

"Not all." The donkey brayed. The woodcutter ignored him. "Not all are cursed by the madness afflicting our people. Afflicting your people, too. Two nights ago, men camped at the place my grandmother once called El Muro de Muchas Voces. Today, they come to Abiquiu. They ride up and down the trails, across the mesas, through the desert. To kill you."

Wade pushed back his hat, waiting for more, but the woodcutter had finished, except for an *adiós.*

Carlito Martinez picked up the axe, returned to the donkey, grabbed the rope, and, clucking his tongue, eased the pack animal through the trees, heading southeast toward Abiquiu.

Again, Stew began easing the rifle from its scabbard.

"Let him go," Paden said. "He's harmless."

"He's seen us."

Paden kicked the sorrel, took the point. "First man we met in a 'coon's age who don't want to kill us on sight, and Stew here wants to shoot him in the back. Let's ride, boys."

# Chapter Eleven

"Do you know where that there . . . what is it that woodcutter called the place?" Paden asked.

Riding alongside Britton Wade, Paden looked comfortable in the saddle, whereas Wade kept shifting his weight, trying to find a position, any position, that didn't hurt so damned much.

"El Muro de Muchas Voces," Wade answered, his voice tired.

"What's that mean?"

"The Wall of Many Voices."

Paden's head bobbed in approval. "Mexicans sure have a way with words. That's right pretty."

"I think so, too."

"So where is it?"

Wade's left hand shot out quickly, pointing northeast, toward the main road. Almost as quickly the hand pulled back, fumbling inside the Mackinaw's pocket, jerking forth a handkerchief, and then Wade bent over in the saddle, coughing savagely, although never stopping the horse, barely even slowing down. When he straightened, he shoved the handkerchief out of sight, turned sideways, and spit out phlegm.

"Glad I ain't ridin' downwind of you." Paden glanced over his shoulder, and laughed. "I warrant that cough of yours scares Randy and Stew more than your gun."

Wade rubbed his shoulder—stiff, almost as sore as his thighs and backside. He tried to fill his lungs with cool air.

Shaking his head, Paden looked back at Wade, then focused

on the trail they were cutting, looking ahead, but addressing Wade as he spoke.

"You got bad lungs, pard. You lost a right smart of blood from that bullet back in Santa Cruz. You ought to go see a doctor in some big city."

"I've seen a doctor. I've seen a big city."

Paden's head shook again, and he sighed. "Be a whole lot easier on you. You're an old man, just wastin' away."

With a slight laugh, Wade informed him that he was only forty-one.

"Like I said . . . an old man."

"How old are you, Paden?"

"Be twenty-nine in August. You're game, pard. I will grant you that."

They rode in silence for a while, frightening a few ducks off the river.

"That means you were nineteen when I arrested you," Wade said.

"Eighteen."

"That's right. Eighteen. Reason the judge gave you only two years. On account of your youth."

The sorrel stopped, and the saddle leather *creaked* as Clint Paden turned, his face no longer jovial, staring hard at Wade. "Age had nothin' to do with it, pard. First off, that fellow didn't die."

"I wouldn't call him living," Wade said, equally bitter. "His brother had to spoon him his breakfast, dinner, and supper, clean up his mess. He wasn't alive, Clint. Not hardly."

"He called my mama a *puta*. You speak that language. A lot better than me. Just now we was talking about how pretty that Mex lingo is, but there ain't nothing pretty about the way *puta* sounds, especially the ugly way that big miner in Winston said it, first to my back, then to my face."

"It's not a pretty word in English, either."

Paden didn't hear Wade's comment. "Called her a *puta,* and then he laughed. Laughed at me in that damned bucket-of-blood, and it chockfull of folks. Called her a *puta,* and me a *hijo de la puta.* I ain't sorry for what I done to him. Not hardly. He was fifteen years older than me, an Army veteran, twenty pounds heavier, and neither one of us was wearing a gun. It was a fair fight."

"Judge and jury saw things different."

"So did you. I don't begrudge you for what you did, Brit. Tracking me down all the way to Silver City. Buffaloing me with that pistol barrel of yours. Hauling me back to the calaboose in Winston. Don't begrudge you at all. Just like I don't begrudge that judge or even all those former soldier boys they picked to serve on that jury. Jury of my peers. Like hell it was. They was peers of former Sergeant Norman Wilson, not me, and Winston was his town, their town. But I don't blame 'em none for finding me guilty. Had Sergeant Norman Wilson whupped the devil out of me, left me with vacant eyes and messing in my britches every day, they would have found him not guilty. I know that. But if that had happened in Memphis, Tennessee, then I would have gotten off, or, if the sergeant had won the fight, the true and righteous citizens of Shelby County would have sent him off to prison. Maybe. Just the turning of the cards. That's all. Sometimes you get the card you need. Oftentimes, you don't. But you tell me this, pard. You tell me the difference between what I done ten years ago and what you done seven years later in Chloride. Tell me that."

Wade wet his lips, and kicked the buckskin back into a walk. "No difference."

"Not a damned bit of difference." The sorrel followed. "And you killed your two men." Paden chuckled. "Maybe if Sergeant Norman Wilson had died, I would have got set free. Maybe that was the difference."

"Maybe you should have gone free, Clint," Wade said. "What I did was worse, far worse. The only reason I didn't get sent to prison was because I was respected."

The mirthless laugh came again. "You wasn't respected, Brit. You was feared."

For another two hundred yards they rode in silence before Paden spoke again. "The damnedest thing is this, pard. My mama was a *puta.* I called her that to her face . . . not *puta,* but whore . . . when I lit shuck of her. I was fourteen at the time, tired of getting whipped every night by that rum-soaked procurer she worked for. Tired of living in that crib she had the gall to call a home. Maybe that's why I swung that singletree so hard on Sergeant Norman Wilson. He reminded me too damned much of that plug-ugly back in Memphis. Anyhow, she didn't say nothing when I called her that, either, because it was truer than gospel. The point is . . . I can call my mama a whore. But nobody else can."

A stillness returned as they rode, the only noise the whistling of wind and the plodding of horses. Behind them still loomed El Pedernal, and ahead of them rose the towering cliffs of red and vermillion, but mostly that golden yellow clay. Here marked the true beginnings of the Tierra Amarilla country, the Yellow Earth that was everywhere, in the old adobe buildings, in the pottery and body paint of the Indians, the yellow dirt now caked on their clothes and horses.

They entered the Chama again and rode upstream, but the current was strong now, getting stronger, the water cold and rising, so, after three hundred yards, they forded the river, and let the horses rest while the riders drank water from canteens, and looked all around them. It had been hours since they had seen or heard anyone, which might have given them some measure of relief if not for the Chama. As they approached the rugged cañon country, the river began to look more menacing.

Wade slid from the saddle to tighten the cinch, then wearily pulled himself back up, and nudged the buckskin forward, pushing himself, pushing hard.

"I forgot what I had been wanting to bring up, pard," Paden said cheerily, again easing the sorrel closer. "You've worn yourself to a frazzle, pard, you being an old man."

"Forty-one isn't that far around the bend for you, young man," Wade said.

"So here's my proposition," Paden continued, ignoring Wade's comment. "You ride back to Abiquiu, find a nice little *señorita* to take care of you, and you wait for me and the boys . . . and Miss Fenella . . . and we'll deliver young Mister Cole to the law in T.A. And I promise, personally, to bring you your share of the reward we collect from 'em priests."

Stew's sniggers seemed to annoy Paden almost as much as they pricked Wade.

"I appreciate the offer," Wade said. "But I'm feeling fine as silk."

"And I'm feeling finer than frog's hair cut eight ways. But this country ain't getting no easier." Paden pointed ahead. "I'd hate to have to bury you in that cañon."

"I'd hate for you to try."

"Hate to see you swept down some rapids we're bound to come across."

"I'm a pretty good swimmer."

"Hate to see a rock fall on your head."

"My head's mighty hard."

Paden's head shook. "This is no foolish thing, pard," he said, surprisingly urgent, almost as if he cared about Britton Wade. "Even money that nary a one of us makes it to the far side. Game or not, you're one sick man. And even if we do somehow get to the Chama valley, what then?" Paden's thumb hooked toward Jeremiah Cole riding behind them. "That boy's daddy ain't gonna see his only surviving son hang. On the other hand, all those Mexicans living up yonder will be bound and determined to kill the kid before his daddy kills us. And 'em odds might be better than even money."

"Could be," Wade said, smiling despite his nerves, despite that cough he had been trying to hold back for the past mile. "So here's my proposition. You and the boys ride back to Abiquiu, and take Miss Fenella with you. I'll deliver young Mister Cole to the law. And I promise, personally, to bring you your share of any reward I happen to collect."

Clucking his tongue, shaking his head, Clint Paden let out a defeated sigh. "You're a stubborn, stubborn man, Brit."

"I'm holding on like grim death."

With that, Clint Paden swung the sorrel away, and circled back quickly, pulling up alongside Fenella Magauran, and starting a conversation with her, although Paden did much of the talking as he dominated any conversation.

Wade gave up on holding back the explosion in his lungs, spit when he was finished, and heard that sinister, barely audible laugh of the man called Stew.

He felt those nerves again, pushed back the coattail, and let his hand rest on the .44.

An hour later, his courting done, Clint Paden rejoined Wade at the point, immediately picking up where he had left off, pointing out the ominous country that lay ahead, saying how Wade should retire from this forlorn hope.

"Forlorn hope," Wade said thoughtfully.

"How's that?" Paden asked.

Wade shook his head. "Nothing."

Paden started talking again, his drawl reassuring, folksy, friendly, while Wade looked over his shoulder, beyond Randy and Cole, Stew and the redhead. He wet his chapped lips again with his tongue, looked ahead, behind, to his side. What day was it? He had lost track of time back at the Holy Cross Church. How long would it take them to claw their way through Chama Cañon? How much more would the river rise? That late snowstorm, which had saved their lives in Santa Cruz, might wind up killing them, after all. Flooding from the snow melt. . . .

He tried to shake off the next thought, but it kept echoing in his tired head: *how many more mistakes can you survive?*

When they dropped into an arroyo, Wade reined in his horse, twisted in his saddle, gripping the saddle horn, and looked back down the trail.

The others stopped as well, Randy dismounting to adjust his saddle, and the girl kicking free of the stirrups to stretch her long legs. Stew stared hungrily at those legs, even though they were covered by her black denim skirt and black leather boots.

"Pard," he heard Paden saying again, "I know I keep on saying the same old thing, but if you're gonna turn back, well, you best do it now because what's waiting for you up yonder. . . ."

"Is a lot easier than what's back there!" Wade snapped, angry now, mad at his so-called partners, mad at his own stupidity, his carelessness, mad at the consumption killing him, mad, as he had been for years, at God for saddling him with this wretched luck.

Paden and the others jerked their heads around, staring off back toward El Pedernal and the tree-covered mountains below the peak.

"If you boys had spent more time looking and less time jawing," Wade said, "you would have known that we're being followed, and have been followed for the last two hours or more."

"By who?" the one named Randy blurted.

"Who do you think?" Wade barked back.

# Chapter Twelve

From *Sixty-Two Years In The Southwestern Territories*
by Colonel Zechariah X. Stone

Thus, it was sometime in the spring of 1898 that I found myself recruited out of my self-imposed exile to Jawbone Mountain.

Having wintered in that warm log home, and, indeed, having spent the past three springs seeing hardly any human, Ol' Griz, that hearty German shepherd of mine now entering her fourteenth year of loyal companionship, and I were not prepared for company. As I savored the taste of a bear-grease biscuit, Ol' Griz, curled up by the fireplace, lifted her head, and commenced a low growl.

That high up in the Tusas, that far from civilization, and that early in the spring—if my memory is right, we had just received a fresh snowfall of twelve-fourteen inches two days earlier—I suspicioned the motives of any visitor, figuring whoever it was that had woke Ol' Griz either had to be "sent for supplies"—as some sheepherder would call it—or after blood. My blood.

A passel of enemies I had made by my sixtieth year, so I swallowed a biscuit, and fetched the Tranter .38 which Major General James H. Carleton had presented me during the war to preserve our Union, and, as always, my .54-caliber Hawken that had hardly ever been out of my hands, and never my sight. Donning bearskin cap and coat, I left the cabin's comforts for the freezing out-of-doors, followed by Ol' Griz, and picked a path into the pines, locating a good spot behind a snowdrift. We waited to see who had come a-visiting. We waited, quiet as a mouse in a church. Waited, and watched.

Fifteen minutes later, horse and rider came plowing through the snow, reining up a few rods from the cabin. The horse was a zebra dun, carrying a rider in blue greatcoat, heavy gloves, and scarf wrapped over his gray hat and bearded chin. It was hard to tell who looked more miserable, mare or man.

"Hallo, the camp!" the man called out, which seemed a good sign that the gent meant me no harm, nor was touched in his head, but I let him wait in the cold for another five minutes, looking around to make sure he indeed had come up alone, and looking at Ol' Griz to make sure she didn't smell out any other varmint.

"Colonel Stone!" the voice yelled again. "It's me, Archie Preston! Foreman of the Triangle C!"

Ol' Griz's tail started wagging, and I rose, startling both horse and rider I was so close to them, and said: "Archie Preston, as I live and breathe. Light down, old hand! I got biscuits, bear grease, and bitter coffee on the hearth."

It took Archie about thirty-five minutes to thaw out from the hard ride, standing in front of the fire, sipping scalding coffee. Archie Preston was a man in his fifties, I suspect, proud of his chin whiskers—he wore no mustache—with blue eyes, and hardly any meat on his bones. I had met him about twenty years earlier, when I was helping his boss, Senator Roman Cole, and the Army round up some Jicarilla Apaches who had fled the agency at Parkview.

As I said, having lived in the mountains and shunned towns like the plague, I was unaware of any of the news Archie Preston related to me once he had thawed the marrow of his bones. He told me about the goings-on in Cuba, the gold strike in Canada's Yukon, and the troubles involving Senator Cole's son, who was being transported by gunman Britton Wade to Tierra Amarilla to hang by the neck till he was dead, dead, dead.

"Sheriff Luke Murphey will deputize you," Archie told me, "just as he deputized Dan Augustine."

I had never met the gunman Dan Augustine. Never wanted to. Cavorting with a man of such a bad reputation was not a thing I desired.

"The county will pay you twelve bits a day plus one-half cent for each five miles you travel. And, on top of that, Senator Cole will pay you." He sipped his coffee. "Handsomely."

"To fetch his boy home?" I said. "So he don't catch hemp fever?"

Archie nodded.

Truth is, money had never interested me in the slightest. Certainly Dan Augustine did not interest me, and, upon hearing why Jeremiah Cole, the senator's son, had been convicted and sentenced to die, I had practically made up my mind to thank Archie for the visit, but to decline the invite. I had a warm cabin and Ol' Griz. What more did a man like me need? I had solitude, and, in most cases, the Tusas Mountains all to myself, with nothing to do but hunt bears and elk, and watch the eagles fly across summer's bluest skies.

The law had convicted Jeremiah Cole, had ordered him to pay for his crime with his life, and I had never ridden against the law. Something gnawed in my craw, though, and that was the fact that I reckon I owed Roman Cole, as I have mentioned in previous chapters of this narrative. Owed him my life. He had saved my hide once from the Utes.

It was at that moment that Archie Preston told me how much money his boss was willing to pay, and, faster than greased lightning, I heard myself taking that job, saw myself shaking Archie's hand. Saw myself for the greedy rascal that I was. Oh, I told myself, later, that I had agreed just for the adventure, for the challenge, but most importantly to repay a debt to my friend, the senator. Never had I come across Britton Wade's trail, and I figured him for a low-down skunk. I told myself that I did it because Roman Cole had kept a Ute buck from sending me off to glory. Yet, dear reader, I will admit the truth in these pages, in black ink, of my own volition, in my own hand: I took the job for money, plain and simple.

A great deal of money it was. Out of respect, I will not share the true amount, and now, more than a decade later, I often wonder how I let money lure me to do something so dastardly. I had never needed money. Odd, I think, how we humans work.

Tierra Amarilla was, and so remains, a town of yellow adobe and Mexican farmers, and not much else. Back when it had been founded, in 1860 or '61, it had been named Las Nutrias, after the beavers that had lured me up that way from Taos. When it became the seat of Río Arriba County, in the year 1880, the name had been changed to Tierra Amarilla.

We came down from the mountains, Archie Preston, Ol' Griz, and me, and met Senator Cole in front of the county courthouse, one of those pitched-roof structures so common in this part of the country. A couple of Mexican kids were up in the attic, tossing down corn, and it struck me funny as the way things worked in northern New Mexico Territory. People were practical, I believe, using the attic of a courthouse to store food.

Briefly I talked to the senator, who looked much older than I remembered, but a few years had passed, and I supposed I had aged myself. And unfortunately Roman Cole had lost a wife and a son since our trails had previously crossed, and was on the verge of losing the only remaining blood kin he had left.

When we had first met, Roman Cole had not been a senator. It was after the late war, and he had arrived as a sergeant-major with the troops that built Fort Lowell—originally designated as

Camp Plummer—along the Río Chama southwest of Tierra Amarilla, or, as I have already mentioned, Las Nutrias as it was known back then. Clinging to General Carleton's recommendation and letter of introduction, I found myself hired at that fort as a scout, and often led soldiers on missions to stop the Utes, who were committing all sorts of depredations in those wild and woolly times. In an earlier chapter of this narrative, during which I recall my accounts in the Ute wars, I have described the campaign during which my life was spared, thanks to Roman Cole.

The fort did not last long, as the reader should remember how we ended the Ute troubles rather quickly, and by the early 1870s the fort was no longer an active post but instead the agency headquarters for the Utes and Jicarilla Apaches. Roman Cole served as Indian agent there until 1875, before being first elected senator. By the time the agency was consolidated with the agency up in Pueblo, Colorado, around 1880 or 1881, Roman Cole was considered among the most powerful men in the territory.

As we talked outside the courthouse, the senator told me he would wait to hear from me, or Archie Preston or Dan Augustine, at the High Mountains Hotel in Chama. Then he brought out the county sheriff, an Irishman of no account or honor, and I was duly deputized. After a dinner of mutton stew, Archie Preston and I rode south for Abiquiu to meet up with Dan Augustine. Roman Cole had given me a wad of greenbacks and simple instructions: fetch his son home alive, and bring him the head of Britton Wade.

By the time we arrived in Abiquiu, however, we received word that Jeremiah Cole and Britton Wade were trapped in a church in Santa Cruz, a small community a couple of miles due east of Española. Archie Preston and I hurried our horses, catching up with Dan Augustine and his party of rogues, but a great snowstorm slowed us, and we reached the church too late. Our prey had vanished in the blizzard, much to the anger of Dan Augustine.

I was glad, for now I felt that I might earn my pay from the senator. What was the challenge of a siege? What was the honor in starving out a gunman and gambler racked with consumption—none other than Britton Wade—who had pleaded for sanctuary, and gotten it from a Mexican priest? He had also gotten some help. Four men had joined Britton Wade's posse, or so I thought at the time. Within a few days, however, having picked up the trail, I realized that one of those men was actually a woman. I've often been asked as to how I could guess a person's gender when on the trail, but all I can say is—it's never a guess. I know it as a fact! Signs never lie, if you know how to read them.

Ours was an odd party, filled with a few gunmen Dan Augustine had recruited, and cowboys who took wages from Senator Cole. I think, however, that I would have preferred to have ridden with Britton Wade. A smart man. A brave man. Just a mite careless.

He used the rivers to his advantage, first the Santa Cruz, then the Chama, but I realized what he was doing fairly quickly, and, when I discovered a pewter flask at some abandoned homestead not far from Abiquiu, I knew it would only be a matter of time before I had my prey. The flask was empty, forgotten I suspect, with Britton Wade's name etched underneath an eagle's outline, and some words in Latin, or so I was informed by a rather educated gunman, his name lost after these last hard years, hired by Dan Augustine.

Dan Augustine was not educated. Nor was he patient, whereas I have always been a cautious man. I wanted to see what exactly Britton Wade had planned. Would he risk taking the road north of Abiquiu, or would he try something even more strenuous, and head up the Chama River and through its tortuous cañon?

Late in the day after we had passed through Abiquiu—where Archie Preston sent a telegram off to his boss—using my spyglass, I could view Britton Wade and his gang, and by that time I had a difficult time reining in Dan Augustine and his Hessians.

"You can't chase them across open country," I warned the notorious shootist.

"And you'll never catch 'em just watchin' 'em run, you old fool," he said.

Twenty or thirty years earlier, such words would have provoked a round of fisticuffs, but I was wiser at sixty years, and saw no need to muddy my buckskins. Letting his comment pass, I informed him that, if we went charging up to those men (and woman), they would likely shoot Jeremiah Cole dead. The territory's Mexicans and sky pilots did not care how the senator's son died, by rope or lead, just as long as he died. "And the senator," I said, "isn't paying us to bring him Jeremiah's corpse."

That shut up the man-killer, but my victory lasted scarcely a moment, for one of the Triangle C cowboys suddenly shouted: "Look!"

Off in the distance, the chestnut horse exploded out of the arroyo, splashing through the mud and grass, heading for the Abiquiu-Chama pike.

"That's Jeremiah!" another cowboy cried. "He's getting away!"

White smoke drifted above the arroyo, then a pistol's report, and an instant later, the buckskin was charging after the chestnut. Britton Wade, riding hard, chasing Jeremiah, still hatless, riding harder. A bay horse climbed out of the arroyo, and its rider cut loose three or four rounds from a rifle, then stopped. Jeremiah crouched in the saddle, but I didn't think any bullet had found its mark.

Still, I cursed, furious, for Dan Augustine and two of his men were already loping across the country, swearing oaths, whipping their mounts furiously. The rider on the sorrel saw them, then he was shouting something, and a moment later he led the rest of his party toward the cañon of the Chama River.

I swung around, crying out: "Archie, you try to head off those making for the cañon!"

More gunfire erupted.

"The hell with that!" shouted a Triangle C rider. "I ain't lettin' that lunger kill Jeremiah!" He cut dust after Dan Augustine.

"You do as I say!" My rebuke proved hopeless, but, when another Triangle C waddie tried to join the race, I cut him off as quickly and as cleanly as he could sort out one of Roman Cole's shorthorns. This rider had the misfortune to stare down my Hawken rifle. When another man reached for his six-shooter, Ol' Griz practically tore off his arm, knocking him from the saddle and into the rocks.

"Griz!"

I called off my shepherd, leaving that gunman with a bloody arm, sitting up, his face pale as pale can be, and just a-whimpering as he looked at his mangled flesh.

"You go after them riders!" I barked out, madder than I had been in twenty-one years. "Keep them out of that cañon. I'll light out after those other two, just in case I'm wrong!"

I spurred my blue roan.

The horse of one of Dan Augustine's men had stepped in a hole, spilling its rider and breaking its leg. I loped past both man and steed, lying on the rocky ground. The killer was lucky to have come away from such a wreck with just a busted collar bone. I've often wondered if he knew how much he owed that horse, for saving his life.

The riders hit the road, turned north for a few miles, loped around the bend, then spurred off the road, and I felt that Britton Wade had hornswoggled us again. By the time I caught up, I found a bunch of winded horses, pawing the earth, longing for water: a chestnut, a buckskin, and the lathered mounts of Dan Augustine, a gunman named Andy O'Neill, and a young cowboy called Buttons.

I couldn't see the men, for they had disappeared in the thick of trees, mostly piñon and juniper, but also Douglas fir and mountain mahogany. Off to my left, El Pedernal remained in view, but, closer, more ominous, rising above the trees and cactus stretched a cliff wall, painted red, white, and yellow, the top a brown limestone dotted with more piñon and juniper. In the middle of the wall, God had carved out an opening, not quite a cave, but a natural amphitheater, one that, for my money, rivaled anything the Greeks built at Epidaurus.

"Jeremiah!" came the cry of Buttons. "Where are you, pal?" His second shout was almost drowned out by an echo, and a gunshot followed, bouncing across El Muro de Muchas Voces, The Wall of Many Voices.

Another shot. I turned one way, then another, circled around, listening, realizing, at last, that the voices came from the right, the echoes rolling off to my left. Ol' Griz growled, and started through the trees, down the rocks, but I called her back. I wasn't about to lose her. Not for the likes of that priest-killing boy. Not against a man like Britton Wade.

"Hornswoggled," I said again with a snigger, and heard the shouts, the shots, the chorus of echoes.

Spirits of the dead, the residents from Abiquiu to Chama often said, haunted The Wall of Many Voices.

"Wade!" It was Dan Augustine's voice. The name reverberated across the rocks and trees.

Wade. . . .

"It's me, damn you."

Damn you . . . damn you. . . .

"Shut up, Dan!"

That had been O'Neill. He was smarter than his boss.

A gun roared. The whine of a ricochet, and the sound sang repeatedly off the cliff, through the forests, from hell to heaven and back again. Voices weren't so bad, too faint, but the echoes of gunshots and ricochets bounced all asunder. Even though I knew where I would likely find my prey, I was sweating like it was July in the Mojave.

Honestly I hated to go into that place, but I had taken Roman Cole's money, had given him my word, and owed him my life.

"Stay here," I told Ol' Griz. "Watch the horses, girl. I'll be back."

At least, I hoped so.

The first one I found was Buttons, leaning against a boulder near a dry wash, tears rolling down his cheeks, a mixture of blood and saliva seeping from his lips, clutching his belly, trying to keep that lifeblood from pumping out of his body.

I knelt by him, heard another shot, and its echoes.

"I'm sorry, boy," I said. There was nothing I could do for him.

"It . . . it was . . . A-A-Augustine . . . who . . . sh-shot me." He coughed, shuddered, his face masked in agony, his voice frail, young, and pathetic. "Didn't even . . . s-say . . . he was . . . s-s-s-sorry."

He was dead before I climbed up the sandy hill. I wonder if he knew he had died for nothing. A loyal rider for the brand, who had gone off trying to save his boss's son—or maybe he had been chasing that reward—but I had known it back near the river, or had at least suspected it. Jeremiah Cole hadn't been riding that chestnut horse. They had switched mounts, swapped some duds, and lured us into an ambush.

One savvy man, Britton Wade.

Another cannonade ripped through the thicket. My ears rang without mercy, trying to pinpoint the direction of the gunfire, trying to hear above the echoes. Trying to get out of this place alive.

What likely saved my life was my own cursed luck. One minute I was picking my way down the rocks, clutching the .38 revolver in one hand, using the Hawken to balance, and an instant later one of those rocks give way. Too many bear-grease biscuits, I concede, and down I fell. Hard. Started a little rock slide, and above all that noise the crack of bone jarred me as the pain raced through my leg. I'd heard that sound before, felt that agony before. There I lay, half covered with rock and dirt, the Hawken out of my reach, the revolver somewhere under yellow earth. Pinned like a jack rabbit in a hawk's talons. My right leg busted just below the kneecap.

But I had the best seat in the balcony, as they say, for what was about to transpire.

Yonder stood Dan Augustine, shucking spent cases from his Colt, his back pressed against a giant Douglas fir, blood dripping from a cut above his right eye. He pulled bullets from his shell belt, reloaded the short-barreled .45, crouched, and peered around the pine's trunk.

A pistol cracked again, echoing. Augustine moved, stopped, turned, addled, sweating, and then, just as the echoes of the report faded, someone called out the sidewinder's name. Closer, though, and Augustine was spinning, dropping while thumbing back the Colt's hammer.

Next came the deafening roar of a nearby gun, so close my ears rang, and I'm sure I could smell the sharp odor of gunsmoke. Augustine fell against the tree, a splotch of red on his shirt front blossoming, but, game as ever, the savage man still gripped his Colt, tried to bring it up as he himself slid down the pine. The other gun spoke. Augustine shuddered as he was hit again, and he pulled the trigger, but the bullet dug into the earth at his feet, and he fell over to his side.

Just a few yards ahead of me, a man appeared from behind a mound of reddish-yellow rocks, lean, not as tall as I had expected, wearing a Mackinaw and a used-up Stetson, the smoking pistol in his right hand still aimed at the fallen form of Dan Augustine. He moved cautiously forward, kicked the Colt away from Augustine's hand, kept the barrel trained on the gunman's head, which lifted for just a moment, then fell back onto the ground.

Another sense, the acute awareness of an experienced gunman, turned the man in the Mackinaw, none other than Britton Wade, toward me. Looking right into my eyes, he brought up the big pistol, and I bet I was about to cash in my chips. The man who had just killed Dan Augustine, a pale man, clean-shaven except for a mustache and long under-lip beard, with the merciless eyes of a killer, walked toward me.

He said nothing, still cautious, almost frail-looking, stopping about ten paces in front of me.

"Who are you?" he asked softly.

As I answered him, Andy O'Neill, the other black-hearted henchman hired by Augustine, came into my view near the back of the amphitheater, some twenty yards behind Britton Wade.

"Name's Stone," I said, never giving away the fact that I was eyeing a man intent on putting a bullet in Wade's spine.

O'Neill brought up his rifle.

"I'd be obliged if you'd dig me out of this mess," I said.

"Hey!"

At first, I thought O'Neill was being a man, refusing to shoot

Wade in the back, but the warning had been voiced by another fellow, and he was calling out O'Neill. Wade dived to his left, turning in the air, fast, smooth, smart, but, before he knew how close he had been to death, somebody else practically blew Andy O'Neill's face apart with a rifle blast, and the gunman tumbled down the incline.

I thought the echoes of that final gunshot would never end.

A tall man, wearing the prison shirt that had been on Jeremiah Cole, walked over to O'Neill, made sure he was dead, then rushed over to me and Britton Wade, who picked himself off the ground, and shoved his big pistol in a holster.

"I guess I'm beholden to you," Wade told his companion.

"You are." His friend was taller, heavier than Jeremiah Cole, for now that I could see him up close, I realized how short the sleeves were, how poorly the striped shirt fit. Oh, he had sandy hair like Roman Cole's son, but he looked nothing like the kid I had viewed from my spyglass.

Like I said, hornswoggled.

"But," the sandy-haired gent told Wade, "it would have soured my stomach to let that fellow do you like that, pard." He pointed the rifle barrel loosely at me. "Who's your pal?"

"Zechariah Stone," Wade said, and I was honored that he knew me.

"No foolin'?" The sandy-haired one looked at me with respect. His trousers were torn above his right boot, and I could see blood, but he didn't seem to be hurting. "The senator hire you to track us down?"

"No," I said, irritated. "He hired me to fall and break my leg."

"He's half buried, Brit. Want me to finish the job?"

Wade shook his head, and looked at me. "You leave a man guarding those horses?"

"Nope."

"There were three of you lopin' after us," Wade's hatless companion reminded me.

"You'll find the third one about a hundred yards back yonder. Augustine shot him in the belly. Accidental, I think. He's dead. I sent the rest after your pards. No man's back that way. Not alive."

I'm not sure they believed me, but, when they started to go, I called out, not for help, but a bit of a warning. "Listen," I said, when both gunmen were looking back at me, "I said no man, but . . . I got a dog."

My first thought had been to let Ol' Griz chew them up, but the more I studied on it, the more I worried for my great shepherd.

"She's old, but she's ornery. You go over there, without me, and she'll rip your throat apart. The lucky one amongst you would have to kill her."

They said nothing.

"My dog ain't dying with Dan Augustine. And not for some priest-killer, no matter what I owe his pa."

They looked at each other.

"You dig me out, help me back to the horses, I'll call her off."

Much has been written about Britton Wade, about his drinking, his brutality, but I will say this of the man: on that spring day, he done me a world of right.

They pulled me out of those rocks, carried me back to the horses, and left me a canteen and my pipe and pouch of tobacco. The taller one, the man who had killed Andy O'Neill, even squatted and scratched Ol' Griz's ears, but only after I let that great canine know that everything was all right. And it was. All right, I mean. Then they mounted and rode away, most likely cutting through the rocky hills north of The Wall of Many Voices, and down into the cañon.

A half hour later, Archie Preston and the riders returned, finding me smoking my pipe to take my mind off the pain in my leg. One of them explained that they had heard the gunfire, and came loping back to assist Dan Augustine and me, although I had them pegged by now, and knew they returned to reap the senator's reward.

"The only thing Augustine needs," I informed them, "is burying."

"He's dead?" Archie Preston looked like he had been struck by lightning.

"And O'Neill. And your cowboy. And almost me."

"How about Jeremiah?" another asked. "He ain't dead, is he?"

"You fools!" I was riled. "He was never here. That's why I sent you after that other bunch. Only y'all let him get into the cañon!"

After hearing what had happened, Archie Preston swung back into the saddle, said he was riding back after Jeremiah.

"No need for that," said I. "They got to come out of that cañon, if they live, so I figure to get some splints on my leg and wait for them up north."

Archie looked tired and old. " 'If they live.' " He sighed heavily. "Like you say, Roman Cole isn't paying me to fetch home Jeremiah's corpse. Reckon I'll follow them into the cañon. Chama Cañon's not the Río Grande Gorge."

"Nor is it a stroll across the Santa Fe plaza," I warned him, and pointed at my busted leg. "I can't go through that cañon with you, though. Wish I could."

"I know, Colonel. I wish you could, too."

Archie told two of his riders, Tom Oliver and Matt Denton, to get me to a doctor in Abiquiu, then see to it that we got back to Chama, to tell the senator what had happened. Tom Oliver, however, allowed that he would ride into the cañon with Archie, so another cowboy—whose name I disremember—took Oliver's place as one of my nursemaids.

Now I must draw to quick conclusion this ignominious episode of my life. My dear reader might have heard or read other accounts, most based on the imagination (or lack thereof) belonging to some no-account writer churning out blood-and-thunders who never laid eyes on the Southern Rockies.

Yes, there is more to this story, as I have always been bound to my word, and my word had been given to Roman Cole. We retrieved my Hawken and revolver, and buried Dan Augustine, the cowboy called Buttons, and Andy O'Neill. Some men, gutless wonders that they were, quit us for the comforts of the Abiquiu saloons, and I was relieved to see them go.

Often, though, I wish I had quit, too, for the events I later witnessed haunt me still, especially when I recall the despicable act a man I had trusted and called a friend did ask, nay, ORDER, me to do.

That is all I will say on this subject.

# Chapter Thirteen

It took them a day to reach the Chama.

They galloped north along the road before turning off into a narrow cañon cut by a long-dry river, following it as far as they could, then beginning the tortuous climb, forging a path through junipers and boulders, eventually camping that evening atop a mesa, Clint Paden staying near the horses, and Britton Wade heading into the rocks with his books, both men sleeping hard, heavily, exhausted from what they had done that day, and knowing what faced them over the coming week.

Rest revitalized Clint Paden, for he was chatting at first light, jovial as they continued up, down, and around the mesas, jumping narrow chasms, winding through a forest of boulders, moving through the high-walled country.

"You sure you know where you're going?" Paden asked.

Rubbing his shoulder, Wade didn't answer.

"I thought you said you'd never been in Chama Cañon before."

"That's what I said."

"So how come you know so much about it?"

"You knew a lot about it. You knew about Dead Man's Peak and Mesa de las Viejas."

"Yeah, but I'd just heard about 'em places. You knew where to tell Stew and Randy to meet up with us." He leaned to massage his right leg, wrapped tight with a bandanna just above his boot top. "I think you're holdin' back on me, pard."

Wade reined in the buckskin, stood in the stirrups, staring ahead at a vast emptiness, beautiful but daunting, humbling.

"I don't even see no river," Paden said. "Maybe what you're holdin' back is the fact that you're lost, that you don't know nary a thing about this country. I think. . . ." A gust of wind silenced him.

Wade had to hold his hat to keep it from being swept into a patch of cholla. When the breeze died down, Wade spoke. "You wish you had stayed behind with the others?" He didn't wait for an answer. Leaning back in the saddle, Wade gave the buckskin plenty of rein, letting the horse pick its own path down the rocky ground. Loose stones tumbled, but the horse kept its footing. So did the chestnut Paden rode.

"I'll tell you this, Brit." Paden combed his tangled hair with his fingers. "I'd like to be in my own shirt, wearing my hat. I never should have let you talk me into that harebrained scheme."

"It worked."

"Yeah, it worked, but Cole's shirt itches like it's chockfull of graybacks." He reached inside his shirt, scratching furiously. "And I feel naked without my hat. This sun'll bake you blind. If the wind don't blow your eyes out first."

"Now you know how Jeremiah Cole feels. He hasn't worn a hat since we left Santa Fe."

Paden quit scratching. "And I don't like him wearing mine, even if your idea got us out of that jam. That hat's new. Cost me two whole dollars. The lady at the mercantile in Magdalena said it's called The Governor, and I thought that would be just fine, maybe folks would call me governor. Governor Clint Paden. It's got a nice sound to it, don't you think?"

Wade found a piece of jerky, took a bite, handed the rest to Paden. The dried beef didn't shut him up.

"A man should better himself, pard." Paden kept talking, Wade thought, to keep his mind off that hole in his leg. "That's why I joined up with you. Oh, not at first, I mean, 'cause when we lit out after you from Española with 'em other fellows, that was just something to do, something fun, something different. But that reward, whoo-wee, I could make my pile at last. Start fresh. I'd have more to me than a hat with a big name to it. I'd be able to put this life I been livin' behind me."

Wade washed down the jerky with a sip of water. "You know how many men I arrested who sang that same tune?" He put the stopper back in the canteen, and hung it from the saddle horn.

"At least one." Paden grinned. "Me!"

"You think your share of one hundred and fifty dollars will buy you a new life?"

Paden rested his hand on his Bulldog. Wade let his right hand fall on the .44's butt.

"Well, I been thinking," Paden said, deliberately thickening his drawl, "there might be some other rewards."

"I wish you wouldn't think that, Clint. I'd hate to kill you."

"It would be a plum shame, I admit. Your killing me. And it would break my heart, a little bit, if I had to kill you. But it is a temptation . . . Roman Cole's money."

"Like I said, the senator would pay you off in lead."

"Maybe. Maybe not."

"Then why didn't you let that gunman shoot me in the back?"

Chuckling, Paden put both hands on the reins. "That bothers you, don't it? You a gambler and all, you want to be able to read the fellow sitting across from you at the poker table. Only you just can't peg Clint Paden, can you? I told you yesterday, it would have made me sick, letting you get done in that way." He pushed wet bangs off his forehead. "Damn, I miss my hat."

"We'll get you back to your hat."

"Well, it ain't the hat that truly worries me."

"Can you walk?" Wade pointed at Paden's wounded leg.

"Bullet went clean through. Didn't hit no bone. Think it was a confounded ricochet, curse my luck." He rubbed the leg, before swinging from the saddle, gripping the horn, and leaning against the chestnut for support. "Yeah, I can walk. Long as it ain't too far."

Wade eased off his mount, and they led their horses through a slot cañon, its red and yellow walls high, barely enough room for them to move through the path of eroded Zs and Ss.

"We'll catch up," Wade said.

"I ain't rightly sure I can trust Stew and Randy. Leaving our prisoner alone with 'em was risky."

"You picked them as partners."

"Well, it was more like they picked me. Randy ain't too bright, but Stew, he can be devilish. Devious. And greedy."

"They're both killers," Wade said, adding, before Paden could say the same thing: "I'd know."

"Yeah."

They made it to the other side, staring at more rocks, more cholla, snakeweed, and sagebrush, and another hill to climb.

"Randy and Stew can't turn back." Wade spoke with a false confidence. "Someone in Stone's posse's sure to follow us into the cañon. There's nowhere to go but north."

Paden nodded. He checked the cinch, then mounted, grimacing as pain raced up his leg. "Sure, but there's the girl to think of. I don't like her being left alone with Stew. Or Randy."

Wade swallowed. He hadn't thought of her. Swearing softly, he mounted the horse, kicked it into a trot up the hill.

"Figured I'd be in the Army by now, on my way to help the Cubans," Paden said when they reached the top. "Whip the tar out of 'em Spaniards."

"It's not exactly where I thought I'd be, either." Wade shook his head. "This might strike you as funny, but this isn't the life I had chosen for myself when I was a kid."

With a laugh, Paden pulled up alongside the buckskin. "No? What was you gonna be? A doctor? A schoolmarm?"

Wade didn't answer. He looked around, trying to find an easy way down.

"It might strike you as funny," he heard Paden saying, "but this ain't exactly what I had planned for myself, either."

"What did you want to be?"

Paden shrugged. "It ain't what I wanted to be. More like it's what I didn't want to become. Memphis wasn't nothing short of hell."

"Never been there." Wade wondered why he had become so talkative, almost as windy as Paden. "But I always figured it would be a charming city on the river and all."

"Charming?" Paden sniggered. "You never lived through a yellow fever outbreak. Seemed like we had one every year when I was a kid. Wasn't even a city, lost its charter when I was ten or so. I hear it's gotten better of late, but it was rough back then."

"Baltimore wasn't much better," Wade admitted.

"That where you come from?"

He nodded.

"Huh. I had you pegged as hailing from some place farther south. Anyway, like I was saying, I just wanted to get out of Memphis, so as I wouldn't become one of 'em riverboat swine that come calling on my mama, or those sons-of-bitches she worked for." The smile hardened into a bitter frown. "That's why I had to shoot that fellow before he killed you. Had I let him gun you down like that, Brit, well, hell, then I would have become one of the vermin I swore I'd never turn into."

The words sank in. The wind blew harder, and Wade stared at Clint Paden, not speaking. What could he say to that?

Paden spoke softly, pointing: "How about that way?"

"Good as any." Wade dismounted. "But let's walk them down, if your leg won't vex you." He swung his arm out. "See the light green down below?"

"Uhn-huh. Cottonwoods. They think it's spring, even if the wind don't."

"Right. That's the river."

They led the horses down the hill, hoofs and boots kicking up dust, starting a small rock slide, then landed on a ledge. Thirty minutes later, they could see the winding river, and the vast, forested land, more valley here than actual cañon. Yellow walls rose in the distance, covered with dense vegetation, and behind those popped the curved peaks of mountain tops.

"Which one's Dead Man's Peak?" Wade asked as he mounted his horse.

"I think we're standing on it," Paden joked.

Wade had to laugh at that, before kicking the buckskin, now hesitant, down the rocky slope.

"Some road you chose for us," Paden said.

Fifty feet below ran the muddy Chama, the roar of the rapids almost drowning out the cold wind. The opposite bank looked practically impenetrable with brush.

"People have been using this river as a road for ten thousand years," Wade said.

"So you say."

"We're not riding in the river. We're riding with it."

"All the way to Chama?" Paden's head shook doubtfully.

"No." Wade studied the wide valley, trying to spot a landmark. Nothing he could recognize. He withdrew the telescope he had stolen from Zech Stone, looked upstream, then down, decided to take a guess, and turned the buckskin downstream, closing the telescope and returning it to the Gladstone. "We can't follow the river to Chama."

"I thought that was your plan."

"It was. If no one found us. Stone found us."

"Reckon he'll follow us?"

"Stone can't. Not with his leg busted. But someone will, sure as hell. And Senator Cole will be waiting for us at the far side. Or riding down to meet us."

"So what's your plan now, pard?"

"We follow the river upstream, then find a way out of the cañon, pick another way to the jail in T.A. or Chama. But first, we rendezvous with the rest of our partners, and our prisoner."

They rode another mile before Wade stopped, dismounted, opened the Gladstone, and withdrew *The Man in the Iron Mask.*

"Let's rest our horses. They've had a rough go of things lately. So have you. Want me to look at that leg?"

Paden shook his head. "You and your books." He stared at the river below, and dropped from the saddle. "That's a lot of river."

"You won't go thirsty."

"I don't know about that. I've felt mighty thirsty since we polished off your rye." Sighing, wrapping the reins around his left hand, he sank onto the ground, letting his boots drop over the ledge, watching the Río Chama rumble around the bend.

The river twisted, turned, forming islands and oxbows, red cliffs jutting into the graying skies between the riders along the ledge, and the Chama.

"This river's a lot like you, Brit," Paden said brightly, pointing to calm brown water. "Peaceful one minute, then roaring like Beelzebub himself the next."

Wade hadn't been listening. He figured he had guessed wrong, that Stew, Randy, Cole, and the girl were somewhere upstream, and was about to turn around, head back up the river, deeper into the cañon, when Paden urgently reined the gelding to a stop, and leaned forward in the saddle, listening, right hand on the rifle, pulling the Marlin from the scabbard.

"You hear that?" Paden asked in a fierce whisper.

The chestnut snorted. Wind. River. Chirping birds. Then, the soft *pop* of a rifle.

"Damn," Wade said, and kicked the buckskin into a lope.

# CHAPTER FOURTEEN

What she wanted most was a bath.

They rode close to the Chama River, already running hard and high, but those calm pockets here and there looked so inviting, even in the cold wind, beckoning her to wash off that trail dirt, to baptize her again. Only, Fenella Magauran knew she could never be truly clean, and the Chama wasn't exactly holy water. She knew that from washing her clothes in the town of Chama, where the clay and silt from the river left white clothes dyed a reddish brown. Nor was she about to take a bath in her present company.

She hated the men she rode with. Maybe she hated them more than she despised Jeremiah Cole. The greasy one named Stew with his leering eyes, and the other one, Randy, clutching that shotgun while hardly speaking a word. She hoped they would hook up with Paden and Wade soon, hoped they hadn't gotten themselves killed trying to lead the posse away. Hoped she wouldn't have to spend another freezing night alone with Randy and Stew.

Under different circumstances, she might have felt bemused by Clint Paden's boyish good looks, his childish banter. She might have felt that motherly instinct to help nurse Britton Wade back to health. Instead, she felt herself damned to this purgatory, her insides gutted by a hatred to kill a boy not even twenty-five, her heart blackened by revenge. She didn't even know why she felt that way. Hadn't the law sentenced Jeremiah

Cole to death? Even if his father somehow managed to free him from the hangman, the boy could never show his face in New Mexico again. Her Irish temper had gotten the best of her again, and now she rode with men with less morality than the one she had sworn to kill.

Thick brush clawed at her, ripping her sleeves, scratching her flesh until Stew, riding point, had the sense to lead the horses into the river for a few rods. They came out on the flattening bank, following a series of Ss the Río Chama cut through shale and sandstone.

Ahead of her, Jeremiah Cole sat slumped in the saddle, wearing Paden's blue shirt and Sears, Roebuck and Co. hat—both a size or two too big for him—riding Paden's sorrel, or, rather, the horse that Santa Cruz priest had procured for him. Behind her came Randy, his breathing heavy. She could hear it when they were near the calm sections of the river, but not along the rapids.

With a heavy sigh, Fenella cursed her stupidity. What had she been thinking? Quitting her job. Leaving her church. Taking a ten-inch Wilson's butcher knife from Gage's Mercantile, and riding her dun all the way to Chamita, where she planned to wait for Jeremiah Cole to step off the Chile Line train, and kill him. Instead, she had heard that the murderer of Father Vasco was holed up in the Holy Cross Church in Santa Cruz, so she had made her way through a blizzard, sneaked into the churchyard unseen, found the horses in the stable, and waited.

It had almost worked.

Maybe, deep down, she was glad it hadn't. Only now, instead of taking her confessions to a priest, she was praying for her life, riding with ruthless men in a lonely wilderness.

It was late afternoon. The wind had turned colder, harder, and the sky looked gray farther down the valley.

As the river cut sharply, she looked to the hills to her right, a multitude of colors with little life to them except for the piñons and junipers in the distance. No sign of Wade or Paden, and now, the way her luck had been, she presumed they were dead. Presumed she'd soon join them.

Here the current flowed fast, deep, and ahead she could see the shallow rapids around the next curve. She was looking at those rapids, not paying attention, only thankful that the current drowned out Randy's hoarse breath, when a shot sang out.

Ahead of her, Stew's bay dropped as if it had been pole-axed, pinning the long-haired killer underneath. Horse rearing, Jeremiah Cole dived off the sorrel into the muddy bank, rolling, moving quickly into dead brush. The sorrel dashed toward the hills, and her dun, snorting furiously, wanted to follow. She pulled the reins hard as the dun fought the bit. Looking up, she heard Randy ear back the hammers of his shotgun, heard the leather creak, heard the wind, heard the river, then heard a man's voice.

"Don't be a fool, sonny. Pitch that shotgun into the river."

The gun roared again. Not at Randy, but at Stew, who was clawing for his revolver.

"I've never shot a man before. That's the only reason you're still alive, but my next bullet kills one of you fool bastards. Which one'll it be?"

She spotted them now, two men, standing on the opposite bank, atop a cliff that rose steadily, layered with granite and red boulders, sprinkled with some trees at the top, maybe forty feet above the river. The two men book-ended a dead piñon, its branches stretching into the sky like a spider web, both of the men holding rifles. The older one, tall, lean, wore a graying beard with no mustache, tails of his canvas range coat flapping in the wind, shapeless hat pulled low. Near him, now kneeling, was a younger cowboy, in shotgun chaps and a bib-front shirt, rifle stock pressed tightly against his shoulder, aiming straight at

Randy. His thick brown mustache drooped over his tight lips like a dead snake.

Cursing, Stew moved his hand away from the revolver, and fell back on the bank. Something splashed behind her. Fenella knew it was Randy's shotgun.

"Now the six-shooter," the older man said.

Another splash. Randy's big revolver.

"And you," the man said, keeping his rifle pointed at Stew, "you lift yourself back up, and you just ease that pistol, toss it over your dead horse. Just forget about that rifle. It won't do you no good. That's right. Easy. Nice lad."

Stew started to push out from underneath the dead horse.

"No. I like you where you are."

"It hurts like hell!"

"So does a bullet in your gut."

Stew dropped back down, silent, fuming.

"Archie!" Jeremiah Cole's voice startled Fenella as he shot to his feet, smiling, raising his bound hands, putting Paden's hat back on his head. "Tom! By grab, it's great to see y'all!"

"It's good to see you, kid. Where are the other two men who took you? Where's Britton Wade?"

Cole shook his head. "Haven't seen them since they cut out. I'd hoped y'all had killed them."

"Didn't work out that way. So let's light a shuck before they show up. Ma'am, are you all right?"

It took a moment to realize the bearded man was talking to her. He had stepped away from the tree, worked his way to the edge of the cliff.

She could only bob her head slightly.

"If you'd ride back around the bend, ma'am, you can ford the river there. We'll take you back to Abiquiu."

"The hell with her!" Cole shouted. "She's with them. She wants me dead."

"Shut up, Jeremiah. I ain't leaving no woman behind. Not in this country. Pick up that pistol by that dead horse."

Cole lifted his hands, revealing the rawhide binds.

"You." The one named Archie swung his rifle back toward Randy. "I see that knife. You cut him loose, but you be real gentle, you hear?"

Laughing, Jeremiah Cole started back toward Randy, shaking his head, talking as much as Clint Paden would, but Fenella wasn't listening. She kicked her dun, let it take a few steps away from Randy, all the while watching the two Triangle C men on the bluff, watching, but not really understanding, wondering why the younger one had quickly swung his rifle around, not really believing as the Winchester roared, knowing she would never forget the look on Archie's face as the bullet slammed through his body, blood erupting from his chest like a volcano, the rifle clanging on the rocks at his feet as he pitched over, and dropped into the roiling river.

Her horse danced, confused, then she knew what was happening as the young cowhand with the big mustache levered the rifle, hurried a few steps, aimed quickly, and fired.

Fired at Jeremiah Cole!

Screaming, Cole dived behind a boulder. A bullet *spanged* off the rock. Her ears rang. Another splash. It was Randy, diving into the river. His horse, squealing, took off downstream, and again the dun wanted to follow. The Winchester above her roared. She tightened her grip on the reins. Urged the horse back, knew the cowboy named Tom didn't care about her, wouldn't hurt her. She posed no threat.

Stew moved quickly, pushed against the saddle, dragged his leg from underneath the bay. A bullet dug into the sand near him, and he forgot about the pump rifle in the scabbard, crawled behind the horse, and cowered there. Randy was out of the river, hugging the bank, wondering what was happening.

The rifle boomed. Three times. Maybe four.

"Damn it, Tom!" Jeremiah Cole's voice. "This ain't right!"

Another shot, which ricocheted off the boulder. Tom moved downstream, working the lever. He fired again.

"Tom! Jesus, Tom! You got no. . . ."

Tom didn't speak, so focused he was on killing Jeremiah Cole. But why? She'd never seen him before, not at church, and, if he had come into Gage's Mercantile, she couldn't remember him.

The Winchester *clicked.* Empty.

Silently he thumbed five or six cartridges out of his shell belt, and fed his rifle.

"Tom!"

Tom jacked another round into the Winchester, brought it up, sighted down the barrel.

"Tom!"

She could see Jeremiah Cole pressing himself into the boulder, his face ashen. A bullet clipped the top of the boulder, showered Cole's hair with dirt and pebbles.

"Tom! For the love of God, man!"

Another shot. Jeremiah Cole tried to sink lower.

"I'd never sell you down the river!"

The rifle roared. She smelled the sulphur of hell. Her horse pawed, still wanting to run. She kept the reins tight. Randy and Stew lay still, watching, shocked.

"Tom!"

He cocked the rifle again, took another step, trying to find a likely spot, started to walk, then ran back upstream. Stopped. Smiled.

Too late, Jeremiah Cole realized what was happening, and pushed himself up, saw Tom, the rifle aimed at him. He pushed himself away from the boulder, fell onto his rear, tried to back away. Crying now. Begging for his life.

"Tom! Don't do it, Tom! Please. We're. . . ."

Another shot, but this one came somewhere from the yellow hills behind her. Tom spun around as the bullet clipped a tree behind him. He looked. Aimed. His Winchester drowned out the shot that killed him. He staggered back, swallowed, dropped the rifle into the dirt, and sank slowly to his knees.

"Hell."

It was the only word she ever heard the man named Tom speak.

Then, he toppled onto his side, his right arm dangling over the cliff. His hat rolled down the slope, held there for a moment, then a gust of wind lifted it over the edge, and it dropped into the river, swept downstream.

Hoofs sounded, and the buckskin loped toward them. Fenella let out a breath, swung off the dun, confused, looked into the hills again, and found Clint Paden mounting the chestnut, shoving his big rifle into the scabbard, hurrying to catch up with Britton Wade. Movement brought her out of her trance. Stew was up, grabbing his rifle, and Randy was fishing for his pistol and shotgun. Jeremiah Cole started to run, stopped, knew he'd never make it, and slowly walked to the edge of the river. He looked up at Tom's body.

"Damn your soul to hell, Tom Oliver," he said. "I didn't testify at the trial that you were with me that day. And I wasn't going to speak your name, or none of the others, on the gallows. If I ever got there. You didn't have to do this, damn you. You. . . ." His voice cracked, and he quickly turned away, hurried down the bank, desperately searching the river.

She found him first, the older man, dead. The current had swept him into a nest of boulders at the river's bend, pressed him there, kept him there, pinned. Jeremiah Cole looked back as Britton Wade stopped the buckskin, and dropped from the saddle.

"We can't leave him like this. Please don't leave Archie like that." Staring at the old man's body again, Jeremiah Cole sank to his knees, shaking his head, bawling like a newborn. "We can't. . . ."

Fenella loathed herself for it. Fingering her crucifix, she bowed her head, wondering why, how she could ever feel sympathy for a rambunctious, cocksure, evil kid like Jeremiah Cole.

# Chapter Fifteen

Wade reached them first, his shouts stopping Jeremiah Cole's tears.

"Everyone all right?"

Uncertain, Fenella nodded before Stew roared: "That sumbitch killed my horse!"

Wade turned in the saddle, saw that Paden had caught up the sorrel Cole had been riding. Letting out a breath, he looked downstream.

"My horse run off," Randy said, pointing past the farthest bend.

"I'll see if I can't fetch her." Wade kicked the buckskin, yelling back as he loped down the bank, "Find their horses! Likely up on that bluff!"

Muttering an oath, Randy waded through the calmest part of the river, the deepest part reaching just over his waist, and shouted back at Stew: "Come on, man, lend a hand!"

By then, Paden had ridden up, handing Fenella the reins to the sorrel without thinking, then plunging the chestnut into the river, shaking a loop into his lariat, somehow managing to rope Archie's boots and drag the body to the shore.

"Thank you," Jeremiah Cole said softly, sniffed, and knelt to close the dead man's eyes. "I'm sorry, Archie, sorry that you had to die for my pa."

They had no shovel to dig a grave, so Paden, Fenella, and Jeremiah began piling stones over the body. A sudden, loud splash caused all three to look up. On the cliff top, Stew, laughing, bent out of sight to pick up Tom Oliver's Winchester while the current took Oliver's body past the rocks in the bend, and on downstream, eventually pulling him under the surface.

"That's despicable," Fenella said.

"So was Tom killing Archie like he done." Jeremiah Cole went back to searching for stones. They were still at it when Stew and Randy returned, coming down the rise and crossing the river, now riding Triangle C mounts—Stew on a zebra dun, Randy on a roan.

Pounding hoofs announced Wade's return, but he pulled no horse behind him. "Couldn't find the bay," he said. "We need to. . . ." The words died as he watched the burial, and slowly he dismounted, removing the battered hat from his head.

"That sumbitch"—Stew pointed at the corpse's face—"shot my horse dead."

"They had us cold," Randy interrupted. "Nothin' we could do. Must have ridden past our camp last night, got ahead of us, and waited for us to ride into their trap."

"Then the other one blew his pard's heart out," Stew said, "started poppin' away at Cole here."

Still mounted, wiping his wet Greener with his bandanna, Randy sniggered: "Reckon he wanted that reward for hisself."

"That wasn't it." Cole covered the wet, bearded face of Archie Preston with a bandanna, and placed a rock gently over it.

"No?" Stew asked. "He wanted you dead, certain sure."

Another rock covered the body, and Cole climbed off his knees. He had done most of the work, bound hands never stopping him. First he glared at Stew, but quickly turned to Fenella, staring hard.

"You wanted me dead. Everyone wants me dead. Because of Vasco. Everyone thinks that would be fair. Fair. Hell, I wasn't alone at that church, and everybody in the valley knows that.

There were five men, including me. Even that damned witness said as much at the trial. Five men. But I'm the only one who was put on trial. I'm the only one who's looking at a rope around my neck. Is that justice? Nobody's even tried to find the others. Well, one of them's floating down the river now."

"Was he with you?" Fenella pointed at the grave.

"No. Archie had no part in that priest's death. Archie's only fault was he picked the wrong brand to ride for. Let's get the hell out of here."

Fenella stared at the grave while the others mounted. She bowed her head, crossed herself, and swung into her saddle. The last to mount was Britton Wade, who looked at the grave for what seemed an eternity, not blinking, just staring, hat by his side.

"Brit." Paden's voice. "We don't know how many others might be coming up that river. Best light out."

Nothing.

"Brit."

He nodded. Putting on his hat, he turned to the buckskin, grabbing the horn, then looked back at the final resting place of Archie Preston. He seemed to start to make the Sign of the Cross, but stopped, and was on the horse, kicking the buckskin into a trot, leading them into the widening cañon.

They made camp in a clearing on an island a few miles up the Chama, surrounded by juniper and brush, exhausted, the clouding skies matching their own moods.

Now they sat hunched around a small fire, coffee brewing, on a sandy island, weary, wondering, hiding like rats in a land whose vastness spoke of loneliness, as the wind blew furiously and the temperature dropped swiftly.

"I'll take my hat back, kid." Clint Paden snatched it off Jeremiah Cole's head. "You shouldn't keep things that you borrowed. And my shirt. Would've taken it back yonder, but it didn't seem the polite thing to do, what with us burying your pal, and all." He unbuttoned the scratchy prison woolen, which he tossed in a ball at Cole's feet. "This thing stinks like a slaughterhouse. You ought to take a bath in the morn. No sense in letting all this water go to waste."

He was trying to be funny, but failing.

"Hey." Paden snapped his fingers. "Now I got two folks here who owe me their lives. I saved Brit's hide at The Wall of Many Voices. And I stopped that waddie from sending Jeremiah Cole's soul to hell before its time."

Paden grabbed his shirt, pulled it over his head, jammed on his hat, and tried to think of some other joke, but couldn't. Walking away, favoring his right leg, he sat near a dead tree, and sighed, shoulders suddenly slouched, the smile replaced by a worn look.

Suddenly Britton Wade doubled over, coughing into his cupped hands and shivering. Fenella made her way to the stricken gunman.

"I'm all right," he said weakly.

She knelt, placed the back of her hand on his forehead. "You're feverish."

"I'll be fine."

Yet he didn't resist when she helped him up, pulled off his Mackinaw, unbuttoned his shirt, and examined his shoulder.

"When's the last time you changed this bandage?"

He tried to smile.

Shaking her head, she walked away, into the trees, every eye in camp following her. A few minutes later she returned, holding strips of some undergarment, and she knelt back over Britton Wade.

"Fetch me some hot water," she barked in that Irish brogue,

and, like a child willing to please, Clint Paden limped over to the fire.

He woke to the blaze of lightning, tried to sit up, realized the woman slept next to him. His stirring caused her to sit up, rubbing her eyes. The dark skies lit up with another flash, and he waited for thunder, only it never came.

"I didn't mean to wake you," Wade said.

"I couldn't sleep," she lied. "How do you feel?" Her hand was on his forehead before he could answer. "Fever's gone."

Clint Paden was awake, too, over by the fire, stoking it, adding more pieces of driftwood, his back to them.

"What is it," the woman asked, "that happened to you in Chloride?"

Wade remembered the conversation with Paden on the trail. She had been listening.

"You don't have to tell me. . . ."

"I know I don't." He frowned. Hadn't meant to speak sharply. Lightning lit up the sky again. He could smell the coming rain. She stared at him.

"I killed two men," he said.

She turned away, looked at Paden's silhouette by the fire. "And Paden?" he heard her ask. "Is it true that he beat that man senseless? In Winston?"

"I would have killed him."

"Because you have mercy." She was looking at him again.

Now he heard it. Thunder, faint. The wind seemed to have stopped.

"I have no mercy," he told her.

"Nor did he." She hooked a thumb toward the fire. "To let a man live. In that condition."

Wade's head shook. "He was just a kid. Didn't know what he was doing."

"That is what Jeremiah Cole's lawyer said during the trial in Las Vegas. I read of it in the newspaper."

"That's different. And you know it. People die in this country for the wrong choice of words."

"Or their religion," she said. "Or the color of their skin."

He ignored that. "You insult a man, or his kin, you can pay for that with your life. That's what happened to Clint. Me, too."

She said: "Father Amado, the priest at Parkview, he preached often that the rebellion in Cuba is what should be going on in New Mexico, that the oppressed should rise up against the tyrants."

They were having two conversations.

"I shouldn't have gone after Clint," Wade said.

"Father Vasco said similar things," Fenella said. "Perhaps that is why he was murdered by Cole."

Wade shook his head. "Shouldn't have arrested him."

"That is why the people, so peaceful, so God-fearing, in the valley have become so angry."

"But it was my job. Or I thought it was."

Her eyes bore through him. "Was it your job to kill those men in Chloride?"

The rain started, softly at first, large, cold drops that hurt like tiny hailstones. He wanted to answer her, although he wasn't sure he could find the words to explain what had happened to him in Chloride. He felt her trembling, and wanted to put his arm around her, pull her close, warm her, comfort her, kiss her, but she was standing now, walking into the trees, seeking shelter he knew he could never provide.

He heard the *hissing* of the fire, heard Paden's soft grumbles as he pulled his Governor's model hat down tight, and limped toward the picket line to check on the horses.

The rain fell harder, slanting, pounding, and soon became mixed with hail.

Chloride.

He couldn't even remember what had brought him to the town. Most likely, it had been the need of a drink, or lure of a card game. In the autumn of '95, he still had that commission as a deputy marshal, even wore a badge, but unlike the time he had gone after Clint Paden, few people would have called him a lawman.

With the discovery of silver ore, the town sprang up and boomed in the Black Range, south of the Plains of San Agustin. There were probably three thousand people there, when he had first seen Chloride in the mid-1880s, but he doubted if there were more than three hundred when he had ridden up to The Bank Saloon on that October afternoon. The price of silver had dropped, kept dropping. Gold, the United States had declared, would be the monetary standard, and the silver market crashed. Barely worth digging up. Only the most stubborn remained, or the hardest.

Or the unluckiest.

He could remember leaning against the bar, talking to John Beeson, the saloon owner, dipping their cigars in their brandy snifters like they were wealthy, refined men.

"Who you trailing this time, Marshal?" Beeson had asked.

Lifting the bottle, Wade had smiled as he read the label. "Castarede Armagnac." He had set the brandy down, adding while Beeson chuckled: "Mount Vernon Rye. Old Forester. Irish. Claret. Beer. The whole damned gang." He had started to join Beeson, but a cough halted his laugh. Shaking his head, he recovered, wiped his hands on his trousers legs, and finished the brandy.

"John," came a voice down the bar, "quit servin' that lunger son-of-a-bitch, and give Mickey and me another whiskey."

"Yeah," echoed the partner.

John Beeson's laughter stopped, and he stepped away from the bar.

Wade straightened, looked down the dusty wood, pushed back his coat to reveal the five-point star on his vest.

"You're badge don't scare me." He was a stout man, with a heavy red beard, dusty, rugged, wearing duck trousers and a muslin shirt, a relic of a Colt stuck in his waistband.

The second man, pointed to the sign over the bar.

*NO SCUM ALLOWED*
*Management*

Taller than the red-bearded one, with beard stubble, a pockmarked face, and a nose that had been broken more than once. He wore a flap holster on his left hip, the butt forward. He cracked his knuckles.

Wade looked at the sign, and laughed. He was reaching for the bottle, shaking his head, when the second man spit on the floor, saying: "Damned lunger. Belongs in a sanitarium, not a saloon."

"Or a church," the first man said, "for his own funeral."

The laugh died in Wade's throat, but he poured the snifter, set the bottle in front of John Beeson's trembling hands, and downed the Castarede Armagnac in a gulp. Then he was walking past the two miners, stopping in front of them, speaking evenly.

"I'll be waiting for both of you in the street. I'll give you two minutes."

"We ain't fighting you with no pistol," the second one said.

They had been looking for a fistfight, but Wade wouldn't oblige them.

"You're wearing guns. Two minutes, or I'll come in here, and come killing. I don't give a damn."

"Listen. . . ." The second man wanted to apologize, withdraw the insults, but Wade wouldn't let him.

"Two minutes." He opened the tarnished silver Illinois watch, its *ticking* eerily loud in the deathly quiet saloon. "Starting now."

Neither waited long. He had been leaning against the hitching rail across the dusty street, holding the watch in his left hand, when both men stepped outside, the taller one firing immediately with a Remington, running down the boardwalk, cocking, pulling the trigger, then slamming against The Bank's façade, a bullet in his temple.

A scratch shot, Wade knew, although the reporter at the Black Range newspaper and the writer of that five-penny dreadful attributed it to Wade's "coolness, coldness, and alchemy with a revolver."

"Look, mister!" Red Beard had started to toss away the Navy Colt he had begun to pull, wetting his lips, trying to lift his hands. "I don't want. . . ."

Wade had killed him, too.

Now, as the hail stopped, the rain slackened, he could still picture John Beeson standing in The Bank's doorway, looking at the dead men, looking up at him, his face pale. John Beeson, who minutes earlier had been pouring him brandy, clipping his cigar, laughing with him, sharing news, talking about the old days, now telling him: "You didn't have to do that, Britton."

"It was them or me." He was drunk. Hadn't realized it until then.

"I wish it had been you."

Beeson had slammed the door. A crowd was gathering, whispering, pointing, wondering.

"Me, too," Wade had said.

Raindrops rolled off the brim of his hat. He pulled the

Mackinaw tight, pushed his way back against the juniper, found a little more shelter from the shower. The Black Range had published an account of the killings, the coroner's inquest that ruled self-defense, and a scathing series of editorials against Britton Wade, killer with a badge, ruthless gunman.

He remembered words more recent, something Clint Paden had told him: *You wasn't respected, Brit. You was feared.*

He recalled something else, a passage from Romans, from another life: "Render therefore to all their dues: tribute to whom tribute is due; custom to whom custom; fear to whom fear; honour to whom honour."

# Chapter Sixteen

Dawn broke to blue, cloudless skies, with no wind, as though the night's storm had pushed out winter. Britton Wade lay still, listening to the gurgling water, savoring the aroma of coffee and wood smoke, smiling at the memory of a seasoned tracker who had given him sage advice on one of his first trips as a federal peace officer: *Never get up first in the morn. First man up's gotta get the fire goin', gotta brew the coffee. Always wait for some other dumb idiot to do them chores, then roll up your sougan and pour yourself a fresh cup of Arbuckles.*

He closed his eyes, but a scream jerked him to his feet, .44 in hand, slinging off his bedroll, climbing to his feet.

Clint Paden, britches pulled down to his ankles, stood hopping by the fire, spitting out a litany of curses, staggering, gripping his right leg, before tumbling to the ground.

"Shut up!" Fenella Magauran barked back at him, and dropped to a knee. "Be a man. Buck up!" Something in her hand reflected the sunlight. A container of some kind, and she poured its contents onto Paden's leg.

He screamed.

"You want to lose your leg?" A flip of her head sent her long red hair out of her eyes. "Cole isn't the only filthy man in this group. Yes, you're one to talk. Lie still!" She reached down again.

Paden roared.

Standing near the horses, Stew elbowed Randy in his ribs,

both of the gunmen grinning at the spectacle. Near the trees, Jeremiah Cole sat on his bedroll, scratching his hair, staring in disbelief.

Wade shoved the Merwin & Hulbert into his holster, grabbed his hat, and moved slowly to the fire. He tried to mask his amusement as he stepped over Paden's boots, squatted, filled a cup with coffee, and took a sip as he turned.

"Good morning." Wade lifted the cup again, stopping, though, with a grimace as Fenella finished drawing a whiskey-soaked silk bandanna through the bullet hole in Paden's calf, Paden yelping during the entire process.

The redhead splashed the last of the whiskey from a flask over the bleeding hole, shook her head as Paden cursed, and tied another strip of her chemise over his leg, tightening it, smiling herself as Paden groaned, his fists clenched, eyes squeezed shut. She went to the river, washed her hands, returned to pour herself some coffee.

"A fine hero he is," she said, sitting down to sip her drink.

Slowly Paden sat up, wet his lips, opened his eyes, and looked at the bandage, then climbed to his feet, pulling up his pants, almost falling over backward.

"He finds a flask of whiskey in one of those dead men's war bags," Fenella went on, "but does he try to clean his bullet wound? No. The fool drinks it. Drinks whiskey in the morn. Before breakfast. You're as bad as my own father, and almost as bad as my former husband."

"I think you had a morning bracer yourself, ma'am." Wade tested the coffee again.

"Aye. I needed something to help me through my task. Needed something to block out the brave man's wails."

Paden sat down. "Fool woman liked to have killed me."

"She probably saved your life. At least your leg." Another sip. The others, summoning their courage, quietly walked toward the fire. "You might thank her."

Paden glared, first at Wade, then at the woman. "Thank you, ma'am. And I'm sorry for the salty words I used during your doctoring."

They were all in a good mood, all except Jeremiah Cole. Even Paden, although he still scowled. Maybe it was the new day, the clear skies, the sun already warm. Maybe it was something else. He wondered how long it would last.

"You scream like a catamount," Stew said.

"I was hollering," Paden said, "over the loss of that good whiskey I found."

"Serves you right for not sharin' with us," Randy said.

Paden shook his head at his saddle pals. "Serves you right for not having the brains to look yourself. Else you could have drunk it all."

Jeremiah Cole left the fire for the riverbank, settling on his knees and leaning over to wash his face. Widening his grin, Stew set down his coffee cup, and sneaked over behind the prisoner, then kicked him hard, laughing as Cole plunged head-first into the Chama.

"Maybe he won't smell like no pig no more!" Stew roared, turning to watch his companions, not paying any attention as Cole floundered, sank, came up spitting, slipping, his face masked in panic. Wade was about to stand, realizing that the young man couldn't swim, but the water wasn't that deep, the current not so swift, and Cole had found his footing, was climbing out of the river, swinging his bound hands hard to the back of Stew's head.

Randy laughed so hard that he spit out his coffee, but Paden and Wade were moving in quickly, Paden stopping Stew from drawing his pistol, and Wade pushing Cole onto his backside.

"He's no good to us dead, Stew," Paden warned his companion.

"You keep that bastard away from me," Jeremiah said. "My pa'll kill him if he lays a hand on me again."

"Your pa." Paden shook his head in contempt as he turned from Stew. "You been riding on your pa's reputation all your life, ain't you? Don't you think it's high time you stood on your own two feet?"

"You just keep him away from me." Water ran down Cole's face. Like a dog, he shook his wet hair, moved to the fire, squeezing out the water from the tails of his prison shirt, shaking, from the water, and his rage. Suddenly he turned.

"You don't know anything about my pa!" he barked back at Paden. "Or me."

"He knows your pa'll pay us ten thousand dollars to bring you back to him alive," Randy said, scraping mud off his boots with a piece of wood.

"None of you know anything about me!"

"I know you murdered Father Vasco," Fenella said, stepping back quickly from Cole's wrath, fearing she had said too much.

He seemed to be about to lunge at her, but Britton Wade blocked his path. The killer took a deep breath, slowly exhaled, and held his hands over the fire.

"You think you're better than everybody else," Cole said. "You, a divorced Irish strumpet."

"My marriage was annulled, you. . . ."

"I had my reasons."

"For what? For murdering an innocent priest? Killing a man of God?"

Now Wade found himself blocking Jeremiah Cole from Fenella's rage.

"I know what the boy means." Randy examined his mud-covered stick, inspected the soles of his boots, then flung the stick into the river. "First man I ever wanted to kill was a preacher. Well, he was a deacon anyway. Caught me takin' some coins from the collection plate they was passin' around in the Methodist meetin' house when I was, oh, eight years old, I reckon." For once, he looked at the man he was addressing. "Is that what you was doin', Cole? Was you stealin' from that priest? That why you killed him?"

"Shut up!" It was Paden who spoke, shoving his way past Cole, pointing at the horses. "We got a hard ride today. We don't know who's coming up the trail behind us, or who's waiting for us up in the cañon. Let's mount up and ride."

Wade tossed the last of his coffee on the fire, staring down at the smoke. It hadn't taken long at all for the good mood to go up in flames.

*This country,* Wade thought, *seems to swallow up time.*

Steep cañon walls rose one thousand five hundred feet above the water as they picked their paths around the sandstone outcroppings. No one spoke as they rode, the only sound the roar of the rapids and the *clopping* of metal horseshoes against the hard rock. Gradually the walls sloped downward, and the Chama resumed its twisting path.

He had lost track of the days, wondered if he would be able to bring Cole in before his scheduled execution. What would happen if he made it—a mighty big if, he realized—after that date? He smiled suddenly at something he hadn't thought of until now.

*Jeremiah Cole was to hang on Friday the 13th.*

Stew had taken the point, riding alongside Randy. Jeremiah Cole rode behind, closely followed by Paden and the girl. Wade brought up the rear.

The day turned warmer, almost hot. Maybe not truly hot, but at this elevation, somewhere between seven thousand and eight thousand feet, the sun always felt hotter.

They rode near the river, calm now, the sheer walls well

behind them. Here the valley widened, the hills covered with juniper and sage, some cholla, with rugged buttes to the east, and over to the north and west cliffs rose behind a thick forest like a castle, the rocky walls painted red and yellow.

Wade had almost fallen asleep in the saddle, lulled by the sound of the hoofs, the sun, and his own weariness, when Stew cursed loudly, and water splashed.

His head jerked up, and he spurred the buckskin, charging between Fenella and Paden, the latter reaching for his Marlin, and loped past Stew and Randy. Ahead of him, Jeremiah Cole urged the chestnut across the river, making for an island. Cole leaned forward, desperate, as the chestnut struggled in the deep water.

A rifle ripped from the brush in the island, and Wade reined in.

"It's the senator's men!" Randy yelled.

Wade had pulled the .44, cocked it, gripping the reins in his teeth. Another bullet sang over his head. Randy must have spotted the riders, hidden on the island, and made a dash for the cover. Cole must have thought the same thing—that the men on the island were riding for his father.

"My God!" Randy yelled. "Them ain't Cole's men! They're. . . ."

A gunshot drowned out his warning.

A bullet splashed water near the chestnut, struggling now, snorting, panicking, then pitching Cole into the deep water.

Yips, shouts, and gunfire came from the island as four, no five Indians plunged out of the timbers. Wade fired, swallowed, ripped the reins from his teeth, tugged desperately, turning his horse away from the Chama.

"Help me!" Cole yelled, coughing, spitting out water.

"My God!" Randy's voice again.

A bullet tore through Wade's hat. He saw the woman, off her

horse, moving through the water, lunging, catching the collar of Jeremiah Cole's shirt, somehow stopping him before the current took him into the rapids some two hundred yards downstream. She struggled to keep his head above the surface.

One of the riders swam his horse toward Fenella and Cole, firing a double-action revolver as quickly as he could pull the trigger. Fenella screamed as a bullet singed her hair. Wade aimed at the rider, but an arrow spoiled his aim before he could shoot, caused the buckskin to buck. He yanked hard on the reins, kept his seat, heard Paden's Marlin *boom,* watched the Indian with the pistol slide off his horse into the river.

Wade fired again, jumped from the buckskin, let it run into the trees. The riders stopped in midstream, firing, some at Wade, Stew, and Randy, the others at Paden, the girl, and Cole. Wade shot again. They had to find cover.

Wade spotted a giant cottonwood, its wide limbs without leaves. He wasn't sure if the cottonwood was dead, or just slow to realize it was spring at last. A few feet below the cottonwood stretched the remains of a dead cottonwood, uprooted, reaching from the high bank to the river's shallows, its bark long gone, trunk almost bleached white.

"Over here!" he yelled. It was the best cover he could see.

He fired, stopped, let Randy rush past him. Stew galloped past, leaping off his horse behind the dead tree. Wade fired again, stepped into the Chama. He saw one rider, closing in on Paden and the girl. How many bullets were left in the .44?

He squeezed the trigger. The rider fell off the side of his paint horse into the river.

Paden leaped out of the saddle, into the chest-deep water, near Cole and Fenella, fired the Marlin once, helped Cole to his feet, shoved him. Moving for the shore. Bullets tore into the water's surface all around them. Smoke and sweat burned Wade's eyes. A bullet grazed his neck. He bit his lip.

Coughing, spitting up water, Cole reached the bank.

Wade fired again, ran to help. "To the tree!" He pushed Cole, grabbed Fenella's arm, hurried, pulling her behind him.

Paden's rifle barked as he ran. He levered the big rifle, shooting as he raced for the dead cottonwood. The Indians returned fire. Wade pulled the trigger, heard the hammer *click* on an empty chamber. Running. From the shelter of the cottonwood, Randy cut loose with Stew's pump rifle. Stew lay slumped over in the mud.

They ran, Cole staggering ahead, Paden just a few steps behind Wade and the girl.

About ten yards from their fortress, Cole grunted, stumbled, fell to his knees. He'd been hit. A rider had reached the shore, kicked a black horse, yelled while hurling a lance that *thudded* in the tree. Randy killed him with a rifle shot.

Wade pulled the woman, practically swung her into the timber, grabbed at Cole. Dived. He landed in the mud. He couldn't hear. Could hardly breathe. Wade coughed, made his lungs work, sat up. Paden was beside him, sweating, the Marlin booming like a cannon.

An arrow whistled overhead.

Wade rolled over, thumbing shells from his cartridge belt. Fenella was beside him, hands over her ears, tears streaming down her face, or maybe that was just water from the river. Cole was crouching, biting his lip, clutching his side, blood pouring between his fingers.

"Mother of Mercy!" Randy's voice sounded higher than normal. "The whole damned Apache nation must be out there!"

# Chapter Seventeen

From *Concerning the Jicarilla Apache Incident Occurring in New Mexico Territory, May 8–15, 1898; 56th Congress, 1st Session; U.S. Senate Executive Document 47, 1899*

Distinguished Gentleman of the United States Senate:

I have the honor to present to you a brief report pertaining to the so-called Jicarilla Apache outbreak of last year.

Shortly after the "Assembly for Buglers Call" on the evening of May 9th, 1898, I was instructed to report to headquarters at Fort Lewis, where I was stationed with my troop of 9th Cavalry, near the town of Durango in southwestern Colorado. I met Major Timothy B. Duncan, at that time serving as temporary post commander, and Victor Frazier, a dispatch rider from the Jicarilla Apache reservation that had been established in 1887 in the northwestern corner of New Mexico Territory, perhaps one hundred miles in distance from Fort Lewis. Major Duncan promptly handed me a hastily written note from Lamont Sanders, agent at that reservation.

I copy from that correspondence:

*Quarter till Midnight, 8 May 1898*

*To the Commanding Officer, Fort Lewis:*

*Sir:*

*Earlier this evening, approximately ten to fifteen Jicarilla*

*Apache males, most of them teen-agers but under the leadership of a plug-ugly known as Escorpión, a hard-bitten, recalcitrant leader, approximately fifty years of age, who has been known to incite riot, did leave this reservation without proper authority.*

*No one has been able to provide a reason for their departure, but, as I know Escorpión, I fear it is to inflict harm on white settlers in this region. For the past few months, Escorpión has vowed to avenge Roman Cole, the territorial senator who lives in the Chama Valley due east of here, for some long-ago incident.*

*The wards were not armed with anything more than lances, and bows and arrows, but were well mounted, and believed to have been riding in a general southeastern course toward Cañon Largo.*

*It is urgently requested that you order a battalion to pursue, apprehend, and return the Indians to this reservation, as I fear we are in a state of emergency. I have also written a letter to the commanding officer at Fort Wingate in which I also request immediate assistance.*

*(Signed) L. Sanders*

"He seems overly excited," I said. "Two to seven companies, chasing a dozen or so Apache bucks?"

"Don't make light of this, Captain," I was rebuked. "Twenty minutes before Mister Frazier arrived with his dispatch, a deputy marshal said he had just received a complaint that the trading post at Boulder Creek was plundered. They made off with sugar, coffee, and perhaps a dozen or so rifles and revolvers, plus ammunition."

Mr. Frazier interjected: "If those bucks wasn't armed well when they skedaddled, they are now."

"Yes, sir," I said, "what is it the major desires, sir?"

Major Duncan quickly outlined my orders, instructing me to form my company and with all due haste proceed into New Mexico Territory, pick up the trail of the fugitive Apaches, using the Navajo scout, Joe Bitsillie, already at the fort, and capture and return the hostiles. Major Duncan also informed me that he would send two companies of cavalry, one to the town of Chama and the second to the nearby village of Tierra Amarilla, to assuage any fears that might arise among the white settlers in those New Mexico settlements once word of the outbreak reached them. If I needed help once I had found the fleeing savages, I could send a galloper to Tierra Amarilla and request reinforcements from one of the troops.

My troop would be outfitted with sixty rounds of ammunition and rations (three-quarter pounds meat, one pound hardtack per day) for two weeks.

"I will not be responsible for another Wounded Knee, Captain," the major said. "You leave immediately."

If I may address the plight of the Jicarilla Apaches on the reservation, allow me to state that the total population at this time was perhaps three hundred to three hundred and fifty men, women, and children. They have had a difficult go of things adjusting to life on the new reservation, raising sheep, goats, and some cattle, trading with whites and Mexicans, and watching many of their children be shipped off to boarding schools so that they may learn to exist in the white man's world. Major Duncan's use of words such as "hostiles" and "savages" seemed overzealous to me, as I thought these Indians had left the reservation to go hunting, and this was not an act of war, but the result of boredom.

Still, I, too, had heard of the Jicarilla leader Escorpión, so I proceeded into New Mexico Territory with 2nd Lieutenant Dean McCrea, Sergeants W.B. Boone, A.J. Kennedy, R. Boyd, R. Claude and T.T. Madison, seven corporals, and twenty-three privates, along with the aforementioned Navajo scout Bitsillie.

Bitsillie located the Jicarillas' trail along the eastern slope of the Continental Divide, and we stopped at Taylor's Trading Post on Boulder Creek, where we learned that Apaches indeed had robbed the post.

We traveled through the forest, and into the rugged country, and I must take time to praise my men for never complaining nor shirking their duties, traits I have come to respect of these fine Negro soldiers. Although the newspapers in Denver, Albuquerque, and Santa Fe, credited B Troop with stopping the uprising, I must report that there never was an uprising, per say, and that B Troop did not locate the Apaches.

We merely ran into them.

Approximately four hours after dawn on May 11th, nine riders, two of them severely injured, the oldest not more than sixteen years of age, rode toward us, waving a flag of truce from a worthless trade rifle without a stock. Following orders I gave to them, which were translated into Spanish, a language the Apaches spoke fluently, by Bitsillie, the Apaches tossed away their weapons. We immediately started fires to heat up water and treat the injured braves, while Bitsillie and I interrogated the oldest of the Apache runaways.

They had left the reservation, we were told, and I have no reason to doubt the veracity of the statements given by three of the Jicarilla boys, to find and kill Jeremiah Cole, the son of the aforementioned senator from New Mexico Territory, who was being transported from the territorial capital to Tierra Amarilla to hang for a murder committed earlier in that year. It seems that Escorpión told his followers that killing Senator Cole's son would exact a stiff payment, as Escorpión believed that the senator had stolen the Apache lands, and deflowered a few Apache maidens.

"Where is Escorpión?" I inquired, and was immediately told that the leader of the escape lay dead in the Río Chama, along with five young warriors.

The survivors said they had found the posse bringing in

Jeremiah Cole deep in Chama Cañon, had waited on an island in the river, and attempted an ambush. As I have mentioned, the Apaches in this party were not seasoned warriors but mere boys, and the attack failed. Escorpión was killed early in the fight, they said, and quickly the posse, led by notorious gunman Britton Wade, as it has been reported in a myriad newspaper articles, repulsed subsequent attacks.

I dispatched most of my command back to Fort Lewis, under the command of Lieutenant Dean, but insisted that one of the Jicarilla boys take me to the spot of this engagement, and so I continued into Chama Cañon with Joe Bitsillie, 1st Sergeant Trevor Madison, Trooper Skip Cooper and Trooper Tony Oscar, along with a Jicarilla Apache boy of thirteen named Ben-Mundo.

By the time we reached the site of the ambush, carrion had turned the scene into a nightmarish scene of blood and bone. The gunfight must have been intense, for we found many brass casings. On the banks of the Chama and, indeed, in the river itself, we discovered the remains of four horses, two Indians, and one white man who had died of a single gunshot wound to his head. Ben-Mundo said this white man, with long black hair, no taller than five foot seven, perhaps one hundred and fifty pounds, died early in the fight.

Another young Indian's corpse was discovered by Sergeant Madison, bloated and ugly, lodged in an uprooted tree, about four miles downstream. The bodies of Escorpión and the other Apache youth were never found, but I believe they were indeed killed during the attack, and are somewhere beneath the surface of the Chama River.

On the 15th of May, I arrived back at Fort Lewis with the rest of my command, and Ben-Mundo.

The Jicarilla boys who were not seriously injured were confined in the post guardhouse for one month, while those with grievous wounds were treated at the post hospital. Post surgeon Adalric Grün was forced to amputate the left leg, below the knee, of one patient, who succumbed to infection, shock, and loss of blood, in the late evening of May 30th, and was interred in the post cemetery the following morning. The other patients recovered, and were returned, along with the prisoners in the guardhouse, to Agent Sanders on the 27th of June, 1898.

Many editorials have been written demanding further retribution, but I believe any debt these Apache boys owe has been paid with interest. Escorpión and six of his followers are dead, buried in the post cemetery, on the banks of the Chama River, or sunk deep in the water in the cañon. Using hides, ponies, and other trade goods, the Apache leaders also paid Jim Taylor for his losses sustained during the raid at his trading post on Boulder Creek.

Punishment is neither desired nor warranted, as it would only add to the degradation these Apaches have already suffered. The incident of May 8–15, 1898, was truly an insignificant affair, with tragic results.

Respectfully Submitted on this 19th day of March in the Year of Our Lord 1899,

Your obt. servant,
Robert A. Campbell IV, Capt.
B Troop, Commanding
9th U.S. Cavalry
Fort Lewis, Colorado

## Chapter Eighteen

"My God."

Wade stepped back, the revolvers suddenly heavy in his hands, and leaned against the dead cottonwood, coughing, not from the tuberculosis slowly killing him, but from the acrid smell of gunsmoke and the stench of death.

It had grown quiet, eerily still, the only sound coming from the river gurgling. He shoved the Merwin & Hulbert into the holster, dropped the Colt he had taken from Stew's gun belt. He forced himself to walk to the nearest Apache, put his boot underneath the body, kick it over. A man's shadow fell across the dead Indian's face, and Wade knew it was Paden.

"Hell, he's just a kid," Paden said.

Wade just looked at unseeing black eyes staring back up at him.

Paden stepped over the dead boy, went to the river, and dragged another body to the shore. "Hell, he's a boy, too," Paden said with disgust. "Ain't a one of 'em a man."

"Like hell!" Randy called out. "I shot one of 'em dead, and his hair was gray as Robert E. Lee's coat. And they was all tryin' to kill us, sure enough."

Spitting out a savage oath, Paden hurled his Marlin repeater into the sand next to the corpse, ran his fingers through his hair. "What's this world coming to? I'm killing boys!"

"Apache nits!" Randy shouted. "I druther 'em be kilt, than me!"

"Kids." Paden pointed at Wade. "I side with you, pard, but if I knew it would come to this. . . ."

"Murderin' savage red niggers!" Randy yelled. "Look what they done to Stew! They killed him, damn it. I don't care if they was suckin' their mama's teats. They was damned Apaches. There ain't nothin' weighin' heavy on my soul for sendin' those red devils to hell's hottest fires!"

Still not speaking, Wade ducked underneath the ancient trunk into what had been their fort. Fenella sat beside Jeremiah Cole, packing a mud poultice against his bloody side. Tears had carved lines down her dirty face. She knew he was staring at her, but refused to look at him.

"I thought you wanted him dead." Randy stepped over Cole's legs. "Women are so notional."

"Like Paden said . . . 'He's no good to us dead.' " Her voice cracked. "I'm just saving him for the gallows." She wiped her eyes, sniffed, her whole body trembling.

Chuckling, Randy dropped beside Stew. A purple hole in the gunman's temple had only now begun to leak blood, and Randy went through his dead partner's clothes, shoving coins and greenbacks into his trousers pocket, unbuckled the gun rig, then dragged the dead man out of the fort, up to the higher ground, and rolled his body into a shallow ravine. "So long, Stew," he said. "You was a good pard these past two, three years." He came back, smiling, the only one, it seemed, to have put the gun battle behind him, the only one no longer scared.

"You think 'em others might come back?" Paden asked. "Looked to be ten or so, though some of 'em was wounded."

Wade shook his head. He asked the woman: "How's Cole?"

"He'll live. Bullet carved a furrow in his side is all. He'll bleed a mite, but. . . ." Then she was crying, backing away from Cole, and Paden had dropped beside her, pulled her close, let her sob on his shoulder, holding her tight, running his fingers through that long red hair.

"Hey," Paden said softly, his face revealing his surprise and awkwardness, "it's all right, ma'am. It's all over."

Wade watched a moment, glanced at Cole, and turned back toward the river. A bay horse lay dead in the water, in the shallows near the island. The woman sobbed. He felt Randy standing beside him, breaking open the breech of the shotgun to eject the shells and replace them with fresh loads.

"I gotta say one thing to you, Mister Wade," Randy said. "What you done . . . that, was, well, that . . . well I just ain't got the words, but they should write all about how you saved our hides in some book or newspaper, maybe in that there *Frank Leslie's Illustrated* I've seen some. I'd write it up myself, but I don't know how. You was something else."

"Something else." Wade coughed.

He remembered little about it. Tried to piece it all together. He had pulled the Colt from Stew's holster, heard Paden duck behind the cottonwood, his rifle empty, and cry out: "Here they come!" Then Paden was diving to Fenella, covering her body with his own, knowing they would all die.

Closing his eyes, Wade could picture it now, clearly, as if he were looking down on himself, viewing what had happened on the banks of the Chama through one of those peep-show, penny-operated Mutoscopes he had seen in El Paso.

Cocking both pistols, standing, leaping over the dead tree, yelling: "Come on, you sons-of-bitches, let's start the ball!" Firing, walking, feeling bullets and arrows buzz past him, waiting for one to kill him.

Just like he had waited at Chloride in 1895. Just like he had waited countless times before.

Waiting for someone to kill him.

But the Lord Jehovah, that jokester, would never let that happen. God wanted Britton Wade to die little by little.

Firing, knocking one Apache from the saddle into the river, killing a piebald gelding when it reached the banks, watching it send its rider into the sand. Clubbing the Apache with Stew's Colt, now empty, crushing the skull, lifting the Merwin & Hulbert, squeezing the trigger. Yelling: "Come on, you sons-of-bitches, let's shout at the devil today!"

He could hear God laughing at another fine joke.

Watching them retreat, gathering some wounded, but shaming themselves, leaving most of their dead on the banks, in the river, riding away, running.

Yelling: "Come back here, you damned cowards! Come back!"

"I never seen the likes," Randy said.

"How's the woman?" Wade asked.

He sat on a boulder away from the cave, closing *A Tale of Two Cities* as Clint Paden walked up to him.

They had made camp, no fire this time, farther from the river, in a small cave in the rocky ground, later that afternoon, after gathering their horses, not bothering to bury the bodies.

"She's all right. Kind of rough on her, all that killing today. It's one thing to think you want to kill somebody, but different when you see what killing is really like. Rough on all of us. But I reckon you don't owe me no more. For savin' your life, I mean. You saved all our hides today. I appreciate it. Is that a good book?"

Wade tapped the cover, started to return it to the Gladstone, then sighed and opened the worn, leather-bound edition, pulling a piece of folded parchment from inside the book and passing it to Paden.

"What's this?" Paden opened the paper, leaned against the sandstone. He studied Wade. "A map?"

"Father Amado drew it for me," Wade said. "Back in Parkview. That's how I knew where to go in this cañon."

"You had it all planned out, eh?" He handed the map back.

Wade's head shook. "Not everything."

"So that's why you was always reading your books."

He shrugged, but spoke the truth. "No, I've grown fond of Dumas and Dickens. I grew up reading Voltaire, Apuleius, Vergil, Homer, Socrates, Shakespeare, Milton, the Bible. But I've found a lot of truth in Dickens, a lot of adventure in Dumas." He tapped his chest. "To take me far away from this."

"I'm more interested in the map," Paden said, "than books."

"Figured you would be."

"You think it's worth the two hundred bucks 'em priests agreed to pay?"

"Let's say it's a job I need to finish."

With a mirthless laugh, Paden shook his head again. "I can't figure out why you're pushing this, Brit. It ain't like the Britton Wade I knew ten years ago. Well, the shootist today, killing, not fearing death, that was the Britton Wade I recollect. But. . . ."

"I've changed."

"No, men like you, men like me, we don't change. We can't change."

"We have to change. Sometimes."

"You got an obsession, pard."

"They're my obsessions."

"Yeah, but they are affecting a lot of people. And I don't mean me. Nor Stew, God rest his soul. But there's Fenella."

"I didn't want her in this. I didn't want you, Clint. This was something I wanted to do alone. And I'll do it alone, if I have to."

Paden exhaled. "Well, that's the Britton Wade I knew. Stubborn. Don't care beans about nobody. Forgetting that if you was doing this alone, you'd be dead in that churchyard in Santa Cruz, or dead back yonder at The Wall of Many Voices, dead somewhere."

Wade opened the Dickens novel, shut it, pulled out the map, pointed.

"A half day's ride from here, we'll leave the river, climb out of the cañon, move into the timber country."

"To take young Cole to Tierra Amarilla?"

"No."

"Then Chama. It don't make a damned bit of difference. Even if you get the boy behind bars, his daddy'll just break him out or buy him out. You'd be doing all this for nothing. I'd hate to think that poor Stew got killed, for nothing."

"You never liked Stew."

Paden ignored that. "Map or no map, it strikes me that we'd be better off just taking the kid on through the cañon, turn him over to his daddy."

"And his daddy would kill you as quickly as those Apache boys wanted to."

"I think we could negotiate some sort of truce. After all, Jeremiah himself said his pa would pay us a right smart reward if we was to bring him home."

"No."

Paden straightened. "You understand how this is gonna turn out, don't you, pard? You and me? I been holding back like all wrath, Brit. Stew wanted to put a bullet in you for a long, long time. I'd rather our partnership not go up the flume."

Wade rose, hooked his thumbs on his gun belt, waited.

Paden was looking away, into the cave, shaking his head. "That girl, Fenella, I could buy her some fancy dresses, some pearls, buy her a nice home in some city."

"She wouldn't have a thing to do with you," Wade said, "or Roman Cole's money."

Paden looked back, harder, talking a half step for Wade. "No, you ain't changed. I see the same contrary lawman who'd track me across the Black Range, bend a pistol barrel over my head, haul me back to a town where he knew I wouldn't stand a chance in a court of law, let 'em convict me, and ship me to the territorial prison."

Fenella had stepped out of the cave, watching, silent.

"You're bound and determined to bring in yet another kid." Paden hadn't noticed Fenella's presence. "Take him all the way to T.A., only this one's to hang. You got no soul, Brit."

"He killed a man," Wade said.

"So he killed a man. So have I. So have you."

"He was a priest!" Wade coughed, angry at himself, hating himself, coughing savagely, until he dropped to his knees, feeling Fenella come to him, feeling her hands on his shoulders, but he pushed her away, climbed to his feet, one hand on the butt of the .44, the other coming to his mouth, wiping saliva, blood.

"A priest," Wade repeated, and shook his head. "You want to know why I'm doing this, Clint?"

Paden stood before him, a blur. Wade tried to clear his vision. He sat down on the boulder, picked up the book and map, shoved them into the Gladstone. "I have to do it!"

He stood again, spitting out words, hating himself for revealing everything, not hearing what he said, but remembering Clint Paden's words: *You got no soul.*

"A priest. I was going to be a priest, Clint. That's right. You're looking at an altar boy, grew up in Baltimore, grew up in a Catholic family, the pride and joy. Father Britton Wade. That was my destiny. I could speak Latin, knew the Bible, the saints, knew everyone in our parish, knew the Blessed Virgin as if I had been on Calvary myself at the Crucifixion. But then I get this damned cough, and it won't go away, so I visit some pill-roller, and he gives me the news. Tells me I'm a dead man. Consumption. Says I should get out of the cities, maybe head West, says that might buy me a few more years. Says I'll certainly be dead in five years if I didn't get to that desert climate. Says I'll probably be dead in ten no matter what I do.

"And what did Father Britton Wade, good Catholic, loving child of God, do? Hell, I rejected God, told him to go to hell. Cursed him, hated him, for giving me these lungs. I spit on everything I'd grown up believing, broke my mother's heart, damned near killed my father . . . probably did kill him. I wouldn't know. Haven't written my family since I came out West, came out hating everything.

"But I fooled that sawbones in Baltimore. Oh, at first I tried to help myself, went to some sanitarium, where they'd have me bent over a metal rod like I was a blanket hanging over a clothesline. Draining my lungs. Hell, the things some people believe. Like believing that a man named Jesus could rise from the dead. Like believing that someone turned water into wine. Like believing those stories about Moses, Babel, Ruth, Solomon, David, and Paul's change of heart.

"Well, I am a miracle. Sixteen years later, I'm still kicking. That's God's mercy for you. That's God's joke. A joke on me, and it's been a damned fine one." He was looking at the sky, laughing. "I kept waiting for someone to kill me. A bullet's quicker than this." He tapped his chest. "Those two men in Chloride couldn't do it. Those Apaches couldn't. I'm blessed. I'm cursed.

"But it all struck me in Chama. In jail. I watched that sheriff, Roman Cole's man, beat up a priest, and I saw me beating up my priest from Baltimore. I saw me for the godless bastard I'd been for sixteen years. And I know I don't have much longer, know I haven't been a man. Yeah, I've changed. I had to change. I had to make Britton Wade stand for something. I'd been running from myself, but my past caught up. You can't run from God. That's why I'm here, Clint. It has nothing to do with money. It has nothing to do with justice. It's about salvation.

My salvation.

"But you wouldn't know or care about that, would you, Clint? All right. That's my story. So, if you want to make your play, you want to take Jeremiah Cole in to his father, well, let's fill our hands. You'd best remember this, Clint. I'm the Lord's avenging angel. You can't kill me. But, as God is my witness, I surely will kill you."

# Chapter Nineteen

"You shouldn't get your dander up, pard." Paden's words came out more as a whistle. The gunman bit his lower lip, exhaled heavily, and turned away.

Tense, wound so tight he thought he might explode, Wade sat, practically collapsed, staring, waiting, watching as Fenella walked slowly away from him, back toward Paden. His chest heaved as he struggled for breath, his heart pounded against his ribs, almost hurting.

The wind blew, and, somewhere in the distance, coyotes sang their song. He was alone. He'd always been alone. Slowly his heartbeat lessened, and he could breathe again. *I'd kill for a shot of whiskey,* he thought, but opened his Gladstone again, looked at the books, reached for *The Man in the Iron Mask,* but his hand wouldn't co-operate, and he felt himself withdrawing Father Marcelino Eusebio de Quesada y Azcárranga's Bible, instead. He opened the book, looked down, let his eyes fall on some random passage.

"And not many days after the younger son gathered all together, and took his journey into a far country, and there wasted his substance with riotous living."

He kept reading, and read until it was dark.

They rode in silence.

Wade hadn't even shaved that morning, although he had made a futile attempt until the remnants of his shaving soap crumbled in his hand. *Crumbled,* he thought, *like my life,* and he pitched soap, razor, and brush into the river.

The walls of Mesa de las Viejas loomed over them until they reached the confluence of Río Cebolla, more creek than river, where Britton Wade led the group away from the Chama, out of the cañon, turning east, eventually climbing from the banks of the small stream, and into the timber. There, Wade stopped, letting the horses rest, while he fished out Father Amado's map from the grip fastened behind the cantle.

He was studying the piece of parchment when Clint Paden nudged the sorrel up alongside him.

"You speaking to me, pard?" Paden asked. "Or you still riled?"

"What do you want?" He kept all emotion from his voice, neither mad nor hospitable, and tried to focus on the map while keeping his right hand near his revolver.

"Where's that map taking us?"

"A church." Folding the map with one hand, Wade looked into the dense forest of pine. The air felt crisp, clean.

"A church?"

Wade looked over his shoulder at the man who had spoken. Jeremiah Cole nervously wet his lips. He hadn't noticed how sunburned the boy was, riding hatless all these days, his hair matted, dirty, his nose so red it had to hurt like hell. Yet Cole never once complained, never asked for a hat or help. He'd give the kid credit for that.

"We should call this the Trail of Many Churches." Paden laughed at his own joke. That was Clint Paden for you. Always trying out some gag. Couldn't help himself, and Wade wanted to like the young man, wanted to be able to trust him, but knew he couldn't, not completely. "Would this be Father Amado's church? The *padre* who drawed you this map?"

Wade kept studying Cole. "No," he said. "Amado's parish is in Parkview. But that's where we're headed." He had decided to confess, to take a chance on Paden. Hell, hadn't he blabbed his whole damned life story last evening? Might as well tell everything. "It'll take us another day or two to get there. They'll expect us to bring him"—he jutted out his jaw toward Cole—"to the jail in T.A. or Chama. But that would be the same as cutting the boy loose. That's why Father Amado suggested that we hold him at the Parkview church. Keep him there for the night. Or as long as needed."

"Sort of like asking for sanctuary again," Paden said.

"Something like that. Nobody would expect to find Cole there. Anyway, that's what Father Amado thought. Keep him there, then haul him in the back of a wagon of hay up the road to T.A. on the day of the execution. Take him right to the gallows awaiting him. The gallows they thought they'd never use."

"And hang him," Paden said.

"And hang him," Wade repeated.

"For a hundred and fifty dollars?" Randy said with contempt.

"Shut up, Randy. Brit and I are talking here."

The wind blew harder. Wade looked up. He remembered the pine forests outside of Baltimore, how when the wind blew like this, the swaying treetops sounded like gently falling rain. He kept remembering a lot of things lately.

"A church. . . ." This time, the words came from Fenella Magauran, who looked equally disturbed. Wade traced a finger along the map, found the church Father Amado had marked on a woods trail, just a triangle with a cross on top, marked Los Pinos, and a warning describing the area surrounding the church.

*Bosque. COLE! ¡Tenga Cuidado!*

He hadn't studied this part of the map much, had been examining, visualizing the trail as he traveled it. The truth of the matter was he never really thought he'd make it this far.

Another symbol had been drawn due north of the church. A

star. No. Too many points. He knew then. Sawmill.

Senator Roman Cole owned two sawmills in the valley, the Cole Lumber Company farther north, over toward the Brazos Peaks, and the smaller one, El Aserradero Pequeño de Los Pinos.

"Let's ride." Wade nudged the buckskin forward. "But we might have to muzzle our horses. This is Roman Cole's country. Keep it quiet. We'll rest at the church down this road."

Randy cursed, told Jeremiah Cole to get moving or he'd blow his head off with the Greener. They rode into the timbers, and Wade let the darkness, and the scent of pine, envelope him.

There wasn't much to the settlement in the clearing below the hill they had crested: a makeshift, circular corral used to thresh grain, a few small log buildings, and a similar number of *jacales,* three or four privies, a lean-to, root cellar, two wells, the beehive-shaped oven called a *horno,* and a rugged building of adobe, rectangular, with a cross atop a crumbling steeple and bell tower. A cottonwood tree stood in the center of the settlement, the only thing living Wade could see.

Before Wade, on the hilltop, stood a large black cross, crudely but somehow beautifully decorated with bent nails. More crosses leaned in front of the adobe church. He knew where he was, knew what he was seeing, knew the hill on which they rested must be El Calvario.

"This is about as dead a place as I reckon I've ever seen," Paden said. "You see anyone?"

Wade's head shook.

"What is this place?"

Wade pointed to the church. "They call that a *morada.* A meeting house."

"Who'd meet there? Ghosts?"

"Los Hermanos de Nuestro *Padre* Jesus Nazareno."

"Reckon I'll have to take your word for it."

"Brothers of Light," Wade said. *"Penitentes."*

Paden thought a moment, his head finally jerking up and down. "Ain't 'em the fellas that whip 'emselves for punishment? To please God?"

"Something like that."

"Some dude down in Eddy told me they sacrificed virgins, too. He called 'em devil worshipers."

"I wouldn't believe anything a man in Eddy told me."

Paden grinned. "I reckon that's the gospel truth, pard. But I'm betting that Parkview priest didn't collect no money for that reward he's offering us from these folks. This place looks as poor as a prison." He clucked his tongue. *"Penitentes,"* he said, testing the word.

Fenella spoke up. "There are no *Penitentes* here." She looked back at Cole, whose sunburned face had turned ashen. "There is no one here. Not any more."

He knew then, and Wade silently cursed Father Amado for bringing him here, with Jeremiah Cole, with the Irish woman—although Amado could not have foreseen that Fenella would be with them, probably didn't know who Fenella was—drawing him a map that would take him to the place where Jeremiah Cole had murdered Father Vasco. He looked at the cottonwood, tried to picture the Mexican priest kicking himself to death, hanging from the big limbs, then, even quicker, tried not to imagine such a scene. He turned back toward the redhead.

"My understanding of the *Penitentes,*" he said, "is that they served where there were no priests. Laymen of the church, working in the country far from the churches."

Her long hair blew in the wind, and she nodded. "Yes, but this has not been a *morada* for some time. Father Vasco came to assist those who had to work at Roman Cole's lumber mill, the mill he stole from the poor Mexicans, as he stole from everyone.

Father Vasco fixed up this church. He. . . ." She looked down the hill. "He is buried in the *campo santo* cemetery."

They were moving down the hill, easily but with caution.

"How far to the sawmill?" Wade asked.

"Three miles," Fenella replied. "Maybe four. But do not worry. No one comes here since. . . ."

"What brought you here?" Paden asked. "Didn't I hear the kid here say that you worked in Chama?"

"I moved here for a man," she said. "My husband, but he proved to be a swine. Father Vasco got me out of that rotten deal."

"That why you thought so much of that bastard Vasco?" Jeremiah Cole's voice, cracking nervously, but trying to sound brazen.

"Shut up, boy," Paden snapped.

They were off the hill.

"That why you were willing to put a knife in my heart? You ain't fit. . . ."

"Boy," Paden said, "I'm going to put a hurt on you that'll take a month of. . . ."

"Quiet!" Wade barked. "All of you."

Wade swung from the saddle, wrapped the reins around one of the weathered *campo santo* crosses, and moved to the church, hand on his .44, pushing the heavy door open.

The Merwin & Hulbert came out of the holster, cocked, as he stepped inside.

The *morada* was divided into three rooms, and he had stepped into the chapel, barren, dark, a large crucifix hanging on a wall lined with carved, wooden *santos.* There were no windows, but sunlight streaked from the doorway and the widening cracks, where the cottonwood *vigas* had been set, revealed thick dust swirling in the wind. Light also flickered from the wrought iron candelabras secured to the side walls. Wade's boots *thumped* heavily as he hurried toward the dining room beyond the chapel.

"I thought you said this place was deserted." Paden's voice resonated in the Spartan quarters.

"I did," Fenella said.

"Who lit 'em candles?" The Marlin sounded treacherous as Paden worked the lever.

The wind blew the door shut, whistled through the cracks and the holes in the thick adobe.

Wade lifted a tortilla, so stale it broke in his hand, off a rough-hewn table. Beside the bread rested a wooden cup, empty, but damp. Wade moved into the storeroom, then walked back to the others.

"Nobody's here," he said.

"Somebody was." Paden spoke with an urgency, and a nervousness. "And not that long ago, pard."

Wade stared at Fenella.

"I don't know who. . . ."

Something rattled, kept on rattling, and she almost screamed, turning, blood draining from her face, as Paden brought the rifle to his shoulder, as Wade swung around the .44.

"Christ A'mighty!" Paden thundered. "You like to have just caught a forty-caliber chunk of lead in your gizzard, Randy." He butted the Marlin on the sod floor, jerked off his hat, and slapped it against his thigh.

Blankly, then bemused, Randy looked at his companions, shaking the wooden *matraca* he had picked up off a wooden table underneath the crucifix in his left hand, his right gripping the Greener's twin barrels. "Y'all is way too jumpy," he said. He dropped the rattle on the table, grabbed a *santo* to study it for a moment, then pitched it beside the *matraca*. "There anything to eat in this place, Wade? I'm plumb starvin'."

After holstering the .44, Wade wiped his hands on his trousers, let his heartbeat slow again. He had hoped to rest here, ride on toward Parkview in the morning, but now? Now he was, like Randy had just said, way too jumpy, and whoever had lighted the candles on the wall would return.

"We'd best head out," he said, not bothering to answer Randy's fool question.

No one, not even Randy, seemed to dally.

They made a beeline for the door, Jeremiah Cole in the front, Randy bringing up the rear, watching in horror as the door jerked open to reveal a tall man's silhouette.

# Chapter Twenty

"What is the meaning of this? Have you no decency? How dare you enter this sacred place with those instruments of Satan." A long, crooked finger pointed at the Merwin & Hulbert in Britton Wade's hand.

Expecting the man in the doorway to be one of Senator Cole's riders, they had reacted quickly, Wade grabbing Jeremiah Cole's prison shirt, jerking him back, jamming the .44's barrel underneath the kid's chin. Paden had stepped in front of Fenella, aiming the Marlin, and Randy had dived to the floor, bringing up the shotgun.

Yet no one fired. The man in the doorway raised his voice. "I command you to leave here at once!"

He spoke with a French accent. A silver cross hung from his neck. That cross had probably saved his life, kept the others from pulling the triggers.

"We meant no offense, Father." Wade lowered the hammer, and holstered the revolver.

"You do not offend me. You offend Him!"

A tall, sloop-shouldered man with a long face, maybe forty, with piercing hazel eyes, and a nose that had been broken more than once. More pugilist than priest, he looked like he would fight the men before letting them out of the crumbling *morada*, but he stepped aside as Wade led the group into sunlight.

"We'll water our horses before taking our leave," Wade said. It wasn't a request.

The priest said nothing until Randy began hauling water from the well.

"You are the riders of judgment." He had walked from the church toward them.

Paden looked up. "How's that?"

"It is what the people of Los Pinos say." The priest waved toward Cole. "You bring him to Tierra Amarilla, to stand before the Almighty. He is Jeremiah Cole." Staring at the cottonwood.

"Judgment riders?" Paden took off his Governor's hat to scratch his head. "I mean riders of judgment. You'll have to spell that out to me. We ain't exactly been reading newspapers of late. Been a mite busy."

Turning away from the tree, the priest slowly exhaled. "At first, my flock did not know what all of this meant, but the news has traveled across New Mexico. How you have taken him"—he gestured at Cole—"from the so-called law to bring him to the gallows." He swallowed. "At first, many said you rode for Senator Cole, that you would have this lad cheat death, cheat the law, but now it is believed that you ride for the Mexican people." His eyes fastened on Britton Wade. "But I know better."

Wade stared him down. "Believe what you want." He pulled so hard on the saddle's cinch that the buckskin snorted.

"As may you," the priest continued, nonplussed. "You may believe this, too, or no. Yesterday, a great scout came to El Aserradero Pequeño de Los Pinos, and visited here, with many, many riders, including Senator Cole." He had Jeremiah's interest. Had all of them, like trouts on hooks. "The great scout was forced to ride in a buckboard, with crutches, one of his legs being broken. He said you would be coming this way. He said he would find you."

Wade glanced at Paden.

"I told you we should have buried Zech Stone while we had our chance back at The Wall of Many Voices," Paden said.

Wade looked back at the priest.

"That is when my flock began to have hope that you would do what is right. That is when they began to call you the riders of judgment."

"But you think different," Paden said as he shoved the Marlin into its scabbard.

"I believe in the wrath of God, as well as his love, but I see too often the wrath of man. Does this boy deserve to die?"

"Father!" Fenella stepped away from her dun, her face bewildered. "You?" She pointed to the cottonwood. "This was my church, for a while. Father Vasco was my priest. He. . . ."

"Was an evil man." The priest crossed himself, bowing his head.

No one spoke. The sorrel stamped its hoof.

The priest lifted his head, tears welling in those once hard hazel eyes, looked right at Jeremiah Cole, and said something in French. He blinked away the tears. "Tell them, my son."

"I ain't telling nothing!"

"You cannot expect God's forgiveness if you do not confess all," the priest said. "Jesus in heaven knows why you did what you did." He had turned to the others, pleading. "Hear me, I do not say the boy should not answer for his crime. It was wrong for him to take Juan Vasco's life. Perhaps, he should hang . . . I do not know. How can we know? We are not God. We are humble, foolish men in a brutal wilderness. I have not been at Los Pinos for very long, but I know the truth. This boy knows the truth. If you would hear. . . ."

"Shut up!" Cole had broken away, slammed his clasped hands into the priest's temple, staggering the tall man, but not knocking him down. Randy jumped to Cole, planting the shotgun against the kid's backbone, but Cole acted like he didn't feel the barrels, like he didn't care. He turned away.

"Jesus, Mary, and Joseph, none of you know a damned thing.

Y'all don't know nothing." He pointed at the cottonwood. "That's the tree. I can show you the damned branch we used. Me and Tom Oliver. Matt Denton. Manuel Sanchez. Big Boy Davenport. We dragged that dirty rotten son-of-a-bitch out of that privy yonder. He had been hiding from us. Fool should have lit out for Colorado, but I would have chased that. . . ." He choked out the words. "I would have followed him to hell, just to kill him."

Silence.

Randy cleared his throat. "To prove somethin' to your daddy?"

"My daddy?" Cole laughed a savage, hoarse cry. "Oh, that's why them others rode with me. They weren't riding for me, for damned sure. They thought it was something Pa wanted, and maybe he did." He whirled toward Paden. "What was it you told me, Paden? Stand on my own two feet? Hell, that's what I was trying to do. At least I thought I was. That son-of-a-bitch Vasco wouldn't bury my brother. Wouldn't bury my mother. Said they didn't belong in consecrated ground."

"Because they killed 'emselves?" Paden asked, uncertain.

Cole laughed.

"That is no reason to kill a priest!" Fenella yelled.

"That ain't why I killed him!" He shook his head again, pulled at his tangled hair. Tears streamed down his face. "You ask my father, you ask anyone around here who ain't Mexican, who wasn't riled over Pa taking the Tierra Amarilla Land Grant from them, and they'll tell you . . . they'll swear on a stack of Bibles . . . that my mother died of cholera. That's what Senator Roman Cole says. Said it so much that he even believes it, but it ain't true. Not one word of it.

"Pa come here, greedy as anything ever sired. Wanted this land. The mill just north of here belonged to my mother's grandfather. That's right. I'm half Mexican, but, God forbid, don't you ever tell Roman Cole that. He'd shove those words down your throat, break your neck. He said. . . ." He sobbed harder. Stumbled to his knees, head bent down, hands on the dirt, trembling, holding himself up. "Pa thought it would be good to have a Mexican wife for what he was doing. Stealing the land. My grandparents' land. Apache land. The whole damned land grant. And when my mother found out why he had married her, what all he had done, when Father Vasco yelled her name in Mass, threw her out of this church. . . ." He pushed himself back onto his feet, staggering backward, blindly.

"Excommunicated her," the priest said.

"Branded her is what he done!" Cole stared at the cottonwood. "Shamed her. Ruined her. He drove her to the barn. He put that rope around her neck. He pushed her from the loft. He. . . ."

He seemed to be in control now, no longer crying, wetting his lips, almost smiling. "Vasco wasn't there, mind you. He was here. But he killed my mother. But, God forbid, a Catholic can't kill herself! But a priest can, can. . . . Never mind. And then Vasco wouldn't even let her be buried in her parish cemetery, alongside her parents, her people."

"So you killed him?" Fenella seemed staggered.

"I didn't kill him for that." Cole let out a chuckle. "That was years ago. I was just a kid. Me and Billy . . . that's my big brother . . . we just waited for my father to kill Vasco. To avenge our ma. But he didn't. Ma didn't mean a damn to him by then. He'd gotten all he needed from some Mexican girl. Gotten two sons. Gotten land. Gotten rich. Oh, but Roman Cole had a reputation to protect. Not my mother's, but his own. He said he buried her at the home, buried her where he could talk to her when he was of a mind, buried her so his children wouldn't have to ride all the way to Los Pinos to pay their respects. And he let it be known that she had died of cholera."

"Father Vasco was a man of God," Fenella said, unbelieving. "He wouldn't. . . ." She was looking at the French priest, praying for his help.

"You are a beautiful woman," the priest said. "He would be kind to you . . . at first."

She shook her head. "He. . . ."

"He got your marriage annulled." Cole kicked up dirt with his feet. "Hell, how much did that cost you? How long were you at Los Pinos, woman? Two months? Three? You thought you owed that lousy bastard? A man of God!" He spit out his contempt.

The priest cleared his throat. "Juan Vasco was a user."

Fenella's head shook harder.

"He used people. Women." He looked down. "Boys. He let his soul become corrupted. By power and lust. By hatred. He reminds me of those who said they were men of God during the Inquisition. Those who enslaved the Indians for their own profit. The Church brings in all kinds. Some good. Most good. Most wonderful, wonderful. . . ." His head shook slightly. "But. . . ." He crossed himself again. "It is impolite to speak ill of the dead, to soil the reputation of a man, especially a priest. There is no need to speak of this more."

"You started it, *padre!*" Cole yelled. "You all started this. Vasco drove my big brother to that same barn. And what he done to my brother was. . . . Hell, never you mind that. But he put a rope around my brother's neck. He killed Billy, just the same as he had killed our mother. But this time I was smarter. I knew Roman Cole wouldn't lift his hand. My father wouldn't even admit . . . after Billy hanged himself . . . wouldn't even admit that Billy was his own flesh and blood. Just let me and some hired hands bury him. God as my witness, Pa found Billy hanging there that morning, and just saddled his horse, left the barn, left my brother in the barn. Told Archie Preston to cut him down, to bury him. So I decided. I'm the rider of judgment. I lynched that damned Vasco. I led Pa's men here. I killed that bastard. Maybe I did it to please Pa, show him I was as big a man as he is, as hard a rock as he is. But I didn't please him, by grab. Some woman saw me here, saw what I did, hurried over to Parkview, told Father Amado, and he tells Father Virgilio, and it's like lightning has struck in the forest in the driest of summers. I'd figured to ride over to Las Vegas, join up, go off to free the Cubans, get away from this awful place. But it don't go that way. I get arrested by a deputy marshal, and this whole country chooses sides again. They wait for me to die. It's as close as they can come to killing Roman Cole."

He moved to the horse, climbed into the saddle, and laughed again. "And you know what my father said to me? When he came to jail? To see me? He says . . . 'Boy, you can't do nothing right.' Roman Cole don't care a damn about me. So let's ride, boys. Come on, you sons-of-bitches, you lousy whore, you riders of judgment. Let's ride over to T.A. Let's get this damned thing over with. Let's fulfill that witch's curse on the Cole family."

It sounded like thunder. Off to the west. Wade looked up, spotted the clouds, but figured the noise must have been his imagination.

"Come." The priest motioned for Cole. "Come with me, my son. Inside." He pointed to the church.

"Y'all coming?" Cole kicked the horse into a trot, rode toward the trees, reined up, waiting.

Randy had already mounted, spurring his horse, holding the shotgun, catching up with their prisoner.

The priest spoke in French, pleading, but Cole turned away.

"Come on!" Randy waved the Greener over his head. "Didn't y'all hear? Senator Cole and his men are hereabouts. Let's get out of here, get to Parkview. Collect our reward!"

Wade grabbed the reins, heard Paden telling the redhead: "You stay here." Heard Fenella whisper: "No, I've come this far. I'll see this through." He saw her look at the cottonwood, saw her dab her eyes with the torn hem of her blouse, saw her mount the dun.

Paden swung into the saddle. "You comin'?"

Wade nodded. "I'll catch up," he said, and watched Clint Paden lead the riders of judgment and their prisoner into the forest. He walked the horse toward the priest.

"I'm Britton Wade." He held out his hand.

"I know." The priest drew a deep breath. "I am Father Alain Girard."

"You're a long way from Paris."

The priest forced a tight smile. "Denver," he said, "by way of Colorado City." He shrugged. "We go where we are called."

"I understand." Wade looked over the saddle at the forest trail, started to mount, but swallowed, and turned back to Father Girard. "I was wondering," he began, uncertain. Scared.

He laughed.

Scared. Again.

He looked at the church, longed to go inside, but didn't want Paden and the others to cover too much ground. He rubbed his hands on his trousers, decided he'd face this as he had done countless fights. *Mano a mano,* or however one wanted to put it. Out in the open. On some dusty street. His head dropped, and he heard his own quaking voice: "Bless me, Father, for I have sinned. It has been sixteen years since my last confession."

# Chapter Twenty-One

Father Juan Vasco leered at her.

Every time she closed her eyes, she saw his face. Fenella woke with a start, trying to forget those images, trying to forget her nightmares. In the early morning light, she sat up, sighing, her heart racing, throat dry.

Out of the forest, they had camped beside an abandoned log cabin, its roof caved in, on the old trail along the Río Brazos to Parkview. She knew this meadow well, had seen the decrepit cabin more times than she could count. They easily could have made it from Los Pinos to Parkview yesterday, but no one seemed in any hurry to get there. Except maybe Randy.

And Jeremiah Cole.

Apparently she was the last to wake. Hard to figure, for she doubted if she had slept more than an hour during the night, succumbing to weariness only to jump awake from another nightmare after what felt like only seconds of sleep. The men were up and about, Jeremiah sitting by the campfire, waiting for the coffee to boil, Randy over by the cabin, working to pry a cactus spine out of his middle finger, and Clint Paden staring at the Brazos. There stood Wade Britton, on the banks of the river. Waiting.

Everyone was waiting.

Fenella Magauran had never had any luck with men. Her father had spent more time in taverns than at home, finally disappearing in Durango when she wasn't yet thirteen. A couple of men she had known hadn't been much better, and then along came Kurt Borgos, that Norwegian lumberman who had stepped off the train in Chama, hired by Roman Cole to run the sawmill at Los Pinos. A fine man he turned out to be. She wondered where he was now. Not that she really cared.

She tried to close her eyes, only to see Juan Vasco once more.

*Accept it. Vasco lied to you, like all the others. That French priest was right.*

This morning, she could see Vasco for what he was. Not a priest. No, far from a man of God. She could also picture the people of Los Pinos, especially the mothers. How could she not have noticed their faces before? She had thought they had feared God. Simple people. Peasants. No, she now realized, it hadn't been God that they feared, but Juan Vasco.

Looking at the men she had ridden with, Fenella waited.

Randy and Paden no longer believed Senator Roman Cole would pay for his son's freedom. Jeremiah had convinced them of that much yesterday. The kid's father didn't care about anything, except his own reputation. Yet Father Amado and Father Virgilio were still offering $150, and wages like that meant the world to men like Randy, and Clint Paden.

The wages of fear.

The wages of sin.

Death.

She liked Clint Paden. What woman wouldn't? So she watched, knowing it had to come to this, that Paden and Britton Wade would face off, fight for Jeremiah Cole. How did that saying go? To the winner go the spoils. She didn't want Paden to die, but she knew that he could never take a man like Britton Wade.

He was walking away from the Brazos, and Paden rose, wetting his lips. Fenella shot a glance at Randy, but the dumb oaf, tongue sticking out, still seemed only interested in his cactus injury.

Wade walked straight to Jeremiah Cole, pulled out a folding knife, opened it, and sliced through the rawhide bonds that secured his wrists. Without a word, Wade jammed the knife's blade into the stump, walked back toward the Brazos, not stopping till Paden, standing near the picketed horses, called out his name.

Slowly Wade turned around, let Paden approach him, took a few steps toward him. They stopped maybe a dozen paces from one another.

"You ain't turning him loose, Brit. Not after all the trouble we went through to get him here."

"It's over," Wade said. "For me. For all of us. I thought I could do something right, for just once in my life. Only. . . ."

"You don't believe all 'em stories that kid was tellin'. About that priest he killed. Those were the biggest falsehoods I ever heard."

"It was the truth."

Paden shook his head. "It don't make a lick of sense. If that priest was such an evil man, if he did half the things Cole here said he done, then why does everyone in the territory want to see the kid swing?"

"Retribution. For his father. That's part of it."

"Yeah? What's the other part?"

"Amado, the priest in Parkview, he's been preaching rebellion most of his life, from what I hear. That priest at the Holy Cross Church said the Mexicans in northern New Mexico don't cotton to outsiders, and that's true. They didn't ask to become part of the United States. More like they got stuck with us. And they sure didn't want a bunch of *norteamericanos* to take their land from them. Same with the Jicarilla Apaches. So that's part of it. Father Virgilio, well, I think he's a God-fearing man, a kind man, who sees good in everyone, who thinks he's doing right, who thinks he's protecting his sheep. But we didn't find anyone in Los Pinos waiting to kill us, wanting to lynch the kid. And those men in Española and Santa Cruz, well, I warrant they were too far from the Chama valley to understand what really had been happening up this way. All they knew was what they'd heard, what they'd read in the newspapers, that Jeremiah Cole killed. . . ."

"That's what you keep forgetting, Brit. You, a lawman." He pointed at Cole. "He killed a man, pard."

Wade threw those words back in Paden's face. "You've killed men. I've killed men. So what?"

"So what?"

"Best thing for the boy to do is get out of this country," Wade said. "Join the Army. Like you planned to."

"Well, he sure as hell can't join the Army in Las Vegas. Everybody in town would remember that face. That's where he was tried for murder. Convicted. Sentenced to swing. Remember?"

"There are other places to enlist."

"The law says he's to hang. You never once turned your back on the law."

"I turned my back on everything. And the law sent you to prison for two years, Clint. Remember? Was that right?"

Paden looked flustered. He swept off his hat with one hand, dropped the other near his revolver. Wade let his right arm brush the Mackinaw away from his own holstered weapon.

The river rolled. A raven *kawed.*

"You know his father won't pay you a penny for turning Jeremiah over to him," Wade said.

Paden's head bobbed slightly. "But those priests. . . ."

"Is a hundred and fifty dollars worth a man's life?" Wade asked.

"You took fifty from those Catholics already." Paden sounded desperate. "What about that? You've already struck a bargain."

"I'll pay them back."

"How? Work like a beaver? Swamp saloons?"

"That's for me to figure out."

Silence.

Wade said: "It doesn't have to be this way, Clint."

Paden let the hat drop to the ground. "You always figured it would, though." He smiled, sad, but sweet. "Reckon I did, too . . . pard."

Then, Paden was screaming, his eyes wild.

"No!"

The shotgun blast was deafening. As if it had been fired over Fenella's head. Only then did she turn to find Randy, who everyone had forgotten, ignored, who hadn't appeared interested in the least. He stood to her side, just a few feet away, behind Wade. No one had seen him move. Everyone had focused on Wade and Paden. The Greener shotgun Randy held was smoking. The gunman was grinning, and Wade was on his knees. Paden stepped toward him, then drew his pistol.

Randy swung the shotgun toward his partner.

Paden dived.

The shotgun roared.

Paden rolled. He had dropped his pistol. Ran for the snorting sorrel. Randy pitched the empty shotgun to the grass, clawed for the revolver in his waistband. Paden desperately pulled at the Marlin in the scabbard, but the sorrel was stomping, frightened, rearing.

Randy's pistol roared. Again. Again.

The sorrel was down, pinning Paden.

Britton Wade fell, face down.

Fenella moved then, grabbed at the knife Britton Wade had sunk into the stump, went for Randy, who kept grinning, thumbing back the hammer of his revolver as he walked toward Paden, to finish the job. To kill him. Take the money for himself.

He clubbed her with the long barrel, and she fell on her back, dazed, head bleeding. Knife still in her hand.

"I'll be back for you later," he said, and laughed.

Randy walked on.

Fenella heard Paden's curses. Slowly she sat up, but the world began spinning. She had to do something. Had to stop. . . . A gun *popped.* She blinked. Pitched forward. Vomited. Started to cry. The gun *popped* again, and again, and she forced herself to sit up, pulled the knife closer, held it tightly, found her resolve.

Another shot. Another.

The world came into view, and Randy had dropped the pistol, staggering back, twisting with each *pop.* She had forgotten about Jeremiah Cole. So had Randy, the numbskull. Cole worked the pump action of Stew's rifle. Pulled the trigger. Randy fell to his knees with a grunt. The rifle spoke again, and Randy was on the ground, face down. Cole walked over, placed the barrel against Randy's head, squeezed the trigger again. Once more. Then he straightened.

"Put it down!" Paden's voice. He had dragged himself from underneath the dead horse. He didn't have the Marlin, couldn't get to it, but Cole didn't notice, or care, that Paden was unarmed. He let the Lightning slip from his hands, and Paden stumbled across the meadow.

He dropped by Britton Wade, gently rolled him over. Jeremiah Cole took a step toward them, but Paden held Wade's revolver now, which he pointed at Cole. "You stay right there. You don't move. You take one more step, and I'll kill you, damn it. Damn it!" He looked back at Wade. Grimaced. "Damn it all to hell!"

Fenella made herself stand, dropped the knife, walked the few rods to the two men, pressing one hand against the deep cut in her forehead. Cole just swayed in the gentle breeze, above the bloody body of Randy.

Wade coughed once. He had taken most of the charge from Randy's shotgun in the small of his back. The blood was so dark that the wet grass looked black, and blood seeped from both corners of Wade's mouth.

"I didn't . . ." Paden choked out a sob. "Want. . . ." He couldn't finish. He looked up at Fenella. "Not this way."

I know. Fenella could only mouth the words. She was clutching her crucifix, sinking to her knees, grabbing Britton Wade's hand, squeezing, letting her forehead bleed freely, wanting it to run into her eyes, blind her, but she could see clearly. She couldn't even cry.

The gunman coughed again, tried to swallow. His eyes turned to Paden. "Finish. . . ."

*Finish what?* Fenella shuddered. *Finish him? Finish the job?* She shook her head, kept squeezing Wade's hand, then she was looking at Paden.

"Clint." Wade's voice. Surprisingly strong. "Can you hear the angels singing? What beautiful voices they have."

Fenella stared at Wade, as did Paden. She heard the rustling of grass, and glanced up. Jeremiah Cole stood above them, looking down, watching Wade. Her eyes locked once more on Britton Wade. She wanted to feel strength in the hand she gripped so fiercely.

They looked into the eyes of Britton Wade.

Maybe five minutes had passed before they finally accepted the fact that those granite eyes they were looking into were no longer staring back.

# Chapter Twenty-Two

Using dead limbs, knives, the stock of the Colt Lightning rifle, but mostly their fingers, their hands, the three of them clawed out a shallow grave for Britton Wade. The ground was soft, and gently they laid the gunman in the pit. No blessing, no prayers. Paden, Fenella, and Jeremiah Cole looked at the body, peaceful, eyes closed, his hands folded across his chest, clutching the crucifix that had belonged to Fenella Magauran.

Finally it was Jeremiah Cole who spoke.

"What about his books? Should they go in there with him?"

Paden shook his head. "Brit wouldn't want 'em books." He stopped, swallowed. "Wouldn't want 'em books buried. He'd want 'em read. I'll take 'em." He tilted his head toward the horses. "Y'all go. I'll handle this," he said, his voice barely audible.

Fenella and Cole walked away, letting Paden cover the grave.

She gathered brush to cover the dead sorrel, while Cole dragged Randy's blood-soaked corpse into the ruins of the cabin. Using strips of rawhide, a cross had been fastened from rotting timbers, and Paden carved Britton Wade's name on the cross with the gunman's folding knife, misspelling his first name, giving it only one T, but it didn't matter. Paden stuck two folded papers between the rawhide and the dry, black wood: a battered commission as a deputy United States marshal, and a poem or something titled "Lungers Club".

Afterward, Fenella and Jeremiah Cole mounted their horses,

and waited as Paden walked to them, blue shirt and hands filthy with the dark clay along the Brazos drainage. At first, Fenella thought he had escaped the fight with Randy with nothing more than bruises, but she noticed where a few of the buckshot had hit his shoulder, and one had carved a crease along the side of his neck. Blood mingled with mud and sweat. Suddenly Clint Paden looked older. Serious. Determined.

His own horse dead, Paden mounted Wade's buckskin.

They rode an hour before he reined up.

"Listen." Paden stared ahead at the mountains. "I don't know much about the law. I don't know if you should hang or not. What I do know is that I'd be dead back yonder if it hadn't been for you, Cole, and I ain't one who forgets a debt like that."

"I don't. . . ."

"Let me finish!" Paden took a deep breath, and slowly let it out. Suddenly he smiled, hooking a leg over the saddle horn as he relaxed, remembering. "Brit asked me something a while back. I didn't think much of it. Maybe I didn't even hear his words, till just a few hours ago. 'You ever tried to do right by yourself?' That's what he asked me. Well, that's what I'm tryin' to do now. I owe it to you, Cole. And to my pard back yonder."

He settled back into the saddle, and nudged the buckskin into a walk.

They rode away from Parkview. Toward the mountains.

"Somebody in Santa Fe told me he figured they'd be training those volunteers to whip the Spanish down in Texas," Paden said. "San Antonio. I ain't never been there. That's where I'm bound. If you still want to enlist, want to say *adiós* to this country, get away from this place, you might as well ride along with me, kid. War might even be over by the time we get to San Antone, but I figure I'm done with New Mexico. Well?"

"I'll ride with you," Jeremiah Cole said, adding, softly, testing the name, "Clint." A few seconds passed, and he murmured, mostly to himself: "I'm done with New Mexico, too."

"Ma'am?" Paden looked at Fenella.

"I'm with you," she said.

They rode.

"Let them come. Let them come. A little farther. That's right, come along, you damned fools. Easy. Easy. All right, boys." Roman Cole gripped the saddle horn. "Bust 'em!"

He smiled as the first rifle *boomed,* watching the ambush commence. The buckskin dropped, but the rider landed on his feet, pistol in his hand, while the dun began bucking and pitched the red-headed woman over its head. Jeremiah kicked free of his stirrups, slid off the horse, and ran to help the girl.

The other one fired once, wildly, running for the holding pens Roman Cole had put along the road eleven years ago. A Winchester slug tore up the grass in front of his feet.

"I want him alive!" the senator shouted above the cannonade.

The man had reached the pens. A bullet splintered the rotting wood inches from his hand. Another clipped the nearest post. He started to duck beneath the weathered rails, but gunfire roared. Cole's riders had galloped out of the woods, firing, yelling. Matt Denton and that Mexican rider whose name Cole could never recall loped over to Jeremiah and the girl, while the rest surrounded the man by the holding pens, sending bullets all around him. Slowly the man straightened, dropping his pistol into the wet grass, raising his hands.

"Well done," Cole told Zechariah Stone, who sat on the buckboard's seat, smoking his pipe. Cole kicked his bay into a walk, and eased across the battlefield, not casting even a glance at his son. Cole's eyes locked on the man by the bullet-scarred lumber, and he slowly dismounted, handing one of his riders the reins. Behind him, Colonel Zechariah Stone urged the buckboard out of the woods.

"You're not Britton Wade," Cole said. He stood directly in front of the man. Big Boy Davenport and a newly hired cowhand called Cooper positioned themselves on either side of the stranger, each pointing a revolver at the gent's head.

The man said nothing.

"Who are you?"

Nothing.

Cole slapped him savagely, dropping him to his knees.

"I'll ask you again," Cole said after Davenport had jerked the man to his feet. "Who are you?"

Game. This fellow sure beat the Dutch. He'd say that much about the man when he kept his tongue from wagging. He reminded Cole of the good, strong, silent riders that used to follow his orders. Too bad. After a nod, Cole watched Davenport jam the barrel of the Colt into the silent man's groin. He wasn't silent, not by a damned sight, after that, but Cole figured he'd never tell him anything. Not even his name.

"Stop it!" the redhead shouted, running over to her injured friend. She dropped to her knees, and lifted the groaning man's head, cradled it in her lap. He had seen the Irish woman, just couldn't place her, couldn't recall the name.

"Pa!" Jeremiah hurried over, too. He smelled like a skunk, looked like some saddle bum. Sunburned. Hair needed more than a tonsorial artist's touch. More like a currycomb and brush. Still in that striped prison suit, to boot. Big Boy Davenport was about to kick the man's side, but Jeremiah shoved the cowhand away. "Stop it!" he yelled.

"Pa!" Jeremiah had turned. "Pa, this guy was helping me. He and the girl. He. . . ."

"What happened to Archie?" Cole asked his son.

The boy's head dropped.

"Archie Preston," Roman Cole said. "You might remember him. And Tom. . . . Hell." He had never been good with names.

"They're dead, Pa."

He had been expecting that. Just didn't want to hear it. Poor Archie. About as true a man as he'd ever hope to find. Cole looked at the man trying to sit up, his face pale, the woman's hands on his shoulders. Cole kicked him. Wanted to break the man's jaw, at least his nose, rake him with the rowels of his spurs, but the toe of his boot just glanced off the side of the silent man's head.

The woman cursed, and Jeremiah tried to grab his father. That was a mistake.

Cole's backhand sent his son to the ground with a split lip.

"You got Archie killed, boy. Archie Preston. And Tom Oliver. . . ." The last name had finally come to him. "Tom Oliver was your pard, boy. And you got both of them killed."

"It wasn't like that, Pa. Tom. . . ."

He kicked his son in the chest, knocking him flat. Turned around, had to grip the fence rails for support, only to have a jagged piece of timber slice through his palm. He cursed. Then fell silent while wrapping a handkerchief around the wound, watching Matt Denton ride over with some kind of grip, pitching the bag to the ground.

"This was on the back of the horse," Denton said. He seemed uncomfortable, but most riders these days looked off their feed when they had to address Roman Cole.

Cole nodded an order to the man named Cooper, watching as the cowhand opened the bag, brought out a stack of books, handed them to Cole. He tossed the Bible over the pen's rails, then stared curiously at the other titles. He studied the silent man on the ground a little closer.

"Never bothered to read Dumas," Cole said as he threw away *The Man in the Iron Mask,* "but I have heard about that book. But this." He held up *A Tale of Two Cities,* smiling, nodding in approval. "I've always been partial to Dickens." He handed the book to Cooper, who looked like he had never held anything in his hand other than a lariat, branding iron, or pistol. Probably hadn't.

"Pa." Jeremiah was pleading again. Begging. Like a coward.

"Shut up!" Cole thundered. "You damned near set this whole territory ablaze. Look what you've done. Soiled my good name, for one. Got Dan Augustine killed. Got Archie killed. And a lot of other good men. You got me having to dodge newspaper writers wanting to know how me, a senator, a rancher, how a great man like me could have sired a boy who killed a priest."

"Pa," his son tried again, "you got to listen. . . ."

"No. You listen. You!" He pointed at the Mexican. "You get him back to the ranch. Cooper, you go with them. And, boy, when you get there, you stay put. You don't go outside for nothing. You stay in the room till I get back. I got to get you out of the territory, ship you up to Montana. A man I know outside of Miles City owes me a favor or two, and that's where you're going. If you think it gets cold in these mountains, wait till winter up there, boy. You see what you've done? See what kind of fix you've got me in? Got yourself into? Hell!"

"What about them?" Jeremiah asked.

He looked at the woman, the silent man. "I'll deal with them."

"Pa, they were helping. Britton Wade's dead. And I'd be dead if it hadn't been. . . ."

"Get back to the ranch!" He looked at his bleeding palm, saw Cooper returning the book to him, then just stared at the Dickens book and his hand while Cooper and the Mexican shoved Jeremiah toward the horses. "Make sure he stays put!" he bellowed, without looking up. He didn't lift his head until the sound of the hoofs had faded.

"Well, Senator?" Zech Stone was sitting in that buckboard, bracing himself with his old rifle while tapping his pipe against the wooden bench.

Cole shot an angry glance at the scout, then looked at the riders, at the woman, at the man, and finally up and down the road before staring at Zech Stone. "You owe me, Zech."

Just like his name, the old scout's face turned to stone.

"You men ride for my brand," Cole said, his gaze locking on the eyes of each hired hand. "You ride my horses, eat my grub, sleep in my bunkhouse and line shacks. You work my cattle. You live off my land. You're my men. Anybody care to argue with me? That's good."

He lifted the book, laughed, and tossed it at the silent man's feet. "So you like Dickens." He looked down upon the silent man. "That's a good thing. Maybe you'll recollect these words . . . 'It is a far, far better thing that I do, than I have ever done.' I think that's right. 'It is a far better rest that I go to, than I have ever known.' " He laughed again. "You know, when I first read that, I thought Sydney Carton was the biggest fool who ever lived." He shook his head, laughing harder. "Imagine. A man willing to trade places with a guy about to get his head chopped off. But that's kind of what you're going to do, Silent Man. And I'll borrow a little twist from your pal Mister Dumas." He whirled to face Stone.

"Zech, you deliver him to Luke Murphey. You tell Luke to keep him in the T.A. jail. No visitors. No priest. Nothing! But then you get the word out that you've brung in Jeremiah. And tomorrow . . ."—his grin widened—"tomorrow, my son hangs. Just like he was supposed to do. Maybe that'll pacify them lazy-ass Mexicans."

"You're mad!" Fiery, the redhead was. Looked like she was about to rip out Cole's heart, and undoubtedly would have tried if Davenport hadn't held her back.

Mad? Maybe he was. Yet it seemed a good plan. A tad melodramatic, but the editors loved those kinds of stories these days. Newspapers all across the country would print this article.

Hooded because of all his shame, Jeremiah Cole went to the gallows. He dropped through the trap door while his father, the powerful territorial senator, watched from the streets. Roman Cole was a man of justice, the papers would write. He witnessed his own son's execution for the worst crime in history. That's how much Senator Roman Cole supported the law. Yeah, that might land him a few extra votes in the next election. That might make those damned Mexicans think a little better of him. That might, at last, end all of those headaches regarding the Tierra Amarilla Land Grant.

And Jeremiah? Well, he'd have to spend the rest of his life in Montana. Roman Cole could never see his son again. He sighed. He could live with that. The boy wasn't much of a son, anyway.

Of course, there would be rumors. The hood would lead to stories, suspicions that someone had hanged in Jeremiah's place. But Roman Cole would produce the coroner's report, the county sheriff's report, and he'd point to the tombstone behind his house. Too bad, he thought, that this silent man was so stubborn. Roman Cole would always wonder who was really buried in that grave.

"What about her?"

Matt Denton pointed at the redhead.

Cole took a deep breath. Everything now depended on his riders. "Matt," he said. He eyed Davenport. "Big Boy. The law never has to know that you were at Los Pinos with Jeremiah. I've protected you all this time, and I'll keep on protecting you. And the others."

He let those words sink in. Denton and Davenport understood.

"You take her into the woods. Do what you want, but you cut her throat. And you bury her, deep. On my land."

A horse snorted. The only sound.

"You do that, boys," he said, looking up at Stone, making

sure. "You do that, and you never have to worry about having your neck stretched. You do this, and you'll find a nice bonus for every man jack one of you come Christmas. And for every Christmas to come as long as you're riding Triangle C horses, and nursing Triangle C beef."

Slowly he walked to his horse, and mounted the bay. "But cross me," he warned. "Get greedy. And you'll be wishing you was buried with her. And him."

# Chapter Twenty-Three

From the *Northwest New Mexican,*
*Chama, New Mexico Territory,*
*Friday, May 13, 1898*

Word was received in this office Thursday evening, just as we prepared our Potter Press to print today's edition, that the condemned priest-slayer, Jeremiah Cole, lone surviving son of Senator Roman Cole of this valley, had been turned over into the hands of Sheriff L. Murphey, and, thusly, the long-awaited execution is to be held this morning, Friday the 13th, outside the courthouse in Tierra Amarilla, our somnolent, neighboring burg that somehow serves as county seat.

Your diligent editor quickly dispatched her trustworthy correspondent, R. Fox, to T.A. in an attempt to interview the sheriff, and the prisoner, and indeed confirm those reports. Yet long before the mare rented from our local livery man, Tom Richards, carried Mr. Fox to T.A. and back, the news had been confirmed, loudly.

Church bells are ringing in Chama this night, and in Parkview as well. Church bells are ringing in our county seat, in Cribbenville, and across the Chama Valley. Church bells, as far as we can ascertain, are ringing on the streets of glory.

The execution will be the first—and let us pray the last—in our fair county since Perfecto Padilla and Robert Torres were sent to face their Redeemer almost three years ago. It might be recalled that the former villain was so petrified, the deputy sheriffs had to hold him up after he was placed over the trap door. Perhaps a similar fate will befall the newly condemned prisoner before he is dropped into Eternity.

Earlier this week, the editor had the chance to visit the scaffold, built of the sturdiest pine and oak from the Cole Lumber Company of this county, owned by the senator whose son committed the most heinous crime in memory.

The trap door is about three-by-four feet, braced into position by a piece of timber that is hinged in the center. A wire runs from the brace around a pulley and up to the platform, connected to the release mechanism, which is within easy reach from near the condemned man's platform. When the lever is pulled, the brace falls, opening the door, and the killer becomes the killed.

Sheriff Murphey, who says he will spring the trap himself on the killer Cole, kindly demonstrated the action of the gallows scaffold earlier this week for this editor, using a hundred-pound potato sack supplied by the nearest mercantile in Tierra Amarilla. A few hours later, a Chama businessman snickered at the editor's report of how well the scaffold will operate, saying: "That sack's the only thing that'll ever drop from that bit of lumber. Waste of taxpayers' money."

Yet, providing some unforeseen happenstance, the Chama doubter will no doubt become a believer today between the hours of 8:00 and noon.

Regarding the rope, Sheriff Murphey assured the editor that it is pure manila, incredibly strong, having been imported from St. Louis, Missouri, where murder and hangings are common. The "peculiar tie" of coiled rope will be tightened over Jeremiah Cole's head, with the large knot positioned upon the doomed murderer's jaw. Thus, the sheriff says, when the murderer drops through the trap door, he is thrust to one side in a twist that snaps the spinal vertebrae. Death is instantaneous, and while it is painless, we can assure the condemned slayer of Father Juan Vasco at Los Pinos that the fires of Hades are anything but painless.

It should be noted that although the gallows platform has been finished, the compound that was to enclose the execution site, per the presiding judge's and eventually the Supreme Court's decision, remains unfinished. Only two of the four walls have been erected, which had led many citizens to believe that no one would ever test the rope. Asked for an explanation, Sheriff Murphey blamed the weather, it being a wet and cold spring, the lack of carpenters in the area willing to work for what the county pays, and the fact that: "It would be a shame if not everyone had a chance to see the show."

While still eagerly awaiting the return of Mr. Fox from Tierra Amarilla, we learned more news last night, as a bulletin, in the human form of one of our faithful gossipers, shot through the office doors of the *Northwest New Mexican* to inform us that our senator, face grim, had checked into the High Mountains Hotel, so the editor told our tramp printer to wait until she returned from an attempt to obtain an interview and ascertain the truth of the reports.

Within twenty minutes, the editor had returned, having found a tired Senator Cole alone at a table in the hotel restaurant, fingering his cup of coffee, and looking completely devoid of hope. A polite request for a moment of his time was waved off, and he sighed heavily, saying: "Can't you leave a man alone on the eve of his son's execution? I tried to raise the boy right. He was just wrong, and wrong-headed."

"There were reports," the editor said, "that you did everything in your power to keep him from the law of the land."

"He's in jail, isn't he?" the senator replied. "He wasn't brought in to Luke Murphey by any lawman, or any hired killer.

He was brought in by Colonel Zechariah Stone, a man of my employ, a man whose reputation is not stained with shame. Could you say that of a man like Britton Wade?"

Wade, of course, is the shootist of some renown who was said to have kidnapped Cole from the tombs of the jail in the territory's capital, and was attempting to bring him to Río Arriba County. The senator's declaration that Colonel Stone had done the deed instead surprised all of those—this journalist included—in the dining hall at that time. Waiters stopped pouring drinks, and hungry diners silently held forks and knives as if frozen in time, for a chance to catch another important bit of news.

Another question was formed, but the senator said: "That's all I have to say. Leave me alone." The editor was then quickly escorted out of the restaurant by the restaurant manager, where she promptly returned to the *Northwest New Mexican* offices.

An hour later, when we were about to give up hope of putting the finishing touches and most important facts on this article, hoofs sounded in our street, and, moments later, Mr. Fox dashed through the doors, waving his notebook, yelling: "It's all true!"

"Is Jeremiah Cole in jail?" it was asked.

"Yes."

"Did you interview him?"

"No. The sheriff would not permit it. No one has been able to see him, not even loved ones or members of the clergy."

"What is the state of Tierra Amarilla?"

"There is much anxiety. Many Mexicans in that village fear reprisal from the powerful Senator Cole if his son is hanged. Others believe riders from the senator's ranch will ride into Tierra Amarilla in an attempt to rescue his young son from the hangman's noose. Yet Sheriff Murphey dismisses such trepidation as the terrors of children."

The sheriff, Mr. Fox reported, pointed out the fact that dozens of buffalo soldiers from the 9th Cavalry, stationed at Fort Lewis, Colorado, remain in Tierra Amarilla and Chama as a result of the recent flight of some Apache males from the Jicarilla reserve, and that he and his deputies have managed to keep the peace in the county "no matter what your newspaper keeps on writing."

Peace will be maintained, the sheriff tells Mr. Fox, and the execution will proceed as prescribed.

An inquiry about the delivery of the condemned killer led R. Fox to the *cantina* known as Pedro's Place about ten doors down from the courthouse in Tierra Amarilla. A buckboard was found in front of the dingy dram shop, and Mr. Fox went inside, finding Colonel Zechariah Stone alone, leaning on the bar alongside his crutches.

The gray-haired colonel, it is not needed to report, has been a fixture in this territory for decades, having helped bring in killers of all kinds—white men, red savages, bears, mountain lions, and Confederate Rebels from the malevolent state of Texas.

R. Fox reports the interview with Colonel Stone as follows:

Fox: "Colonel, I am a correspondent for the *Northwest New Mexican.*"

Stone: "I'm drinking. Alone."

Fox: "Well, you're not alone. I see a dog at your feet, sir."

The dog, as if responding unfavorably to the joke, growled. So did Colonel Stone.

Fox: "Sheriff Murphey tells me that you brought in Jeremiah Cole."

Stone: "That's what people say."

Fox: "Where did you find him? How did you find him?"

Stone: "Get out."

Fox: "Sir, you are a testament to courage. You are one of the most notable figures in the territory alongside Pat Garrett, slayer of Billy the Kid, and Kit Carson, the great scout and soldier. What you have done ranks alongside the heroics of Odysseus, Samson, David, George Washington, and General Grant. People had lost hope, no longer believed in the law, but now, thanks to you, when Jeremiah Cole atones for his sins in the morning. . . ."

Stone: "I'm going to drink this scamper juice."

Colonel Stone held up a tumbler about half filled with the smelly liquid.

Stone: "When I finish it, if there's anyone in this whoop-up except my dog, me, and Pedro yonder, that person is going to get his *** ripped off by Ol' Griz, his ears pinned back by me, and his ***, or what's left of it, kicked all the way to Antonito."

The German shepherd rose to its feet, hair raised, revealing canine teeth that would chill all mortal men.

Stone: "And you best be forewarned that I drink real fast."

The interview ended, R. Fox left the saloon before the tequila was consumed. He attempted once more to land an interview with the condemned killer, but, denied a final time, he mounted his mare, and galloped back to Chama.

Fortified by coffee, we surmise that Colonel Stone, an old compatriot of Senator Cole, was saddened by this job, having to choose between justice and friendship.

Colonel Stone, we hereby declare your choice was the right one, the moral one, the only one, and we will request that the governor honor you for your devotion to duty.

There is no need to remind readers of the callous crime for which Jeremiah Cole must pay with his life. No one will ever forget what transpired at Los Pinos, and no one should. But this chapter will finally close.

Now, the citizens of Río Arriba County and seekers of justice await the promise of tomorrow, and wait for these orders from our Supreme Court to be carried out:

"On Friday, the 13$^{th}$ day of May, 1898, between the hours of 8 in the forenoon and noon of said day, within an enclosure secured from public view, in the presence of a sufficient number of witnesses to attest the execution of the judgment, in an area near the jail and courthouse in the village of Tierra Amarilla in the County of Río Arriba and the Territory of New Mexico, the said plaintiff, named Jeremiah Cole, shall be taken by the sheriff of said county, or other designated peace officers, and by him be hanged by the neck until he is dead, dead, dead."

It is customary to add "May God have mercy on his soul." Due to the circumstances of the criminal, unholy act, however, we will abstain from this custom.

# Chapter Twenty-Four

What, he wondered, must Britton Wade think of him now?

Wade would have faced death the way he faced life, calmly, stubbornly, but Clint Paden didn't have that kind of guts. He kicked, bit, fought, yelled in the Tierra Amarilla jail when the sheriff and his deputies came for him. He wasn't about to trade places with a condemned man. He wasn't about to be the pawn of some insane rancher and politician. They threw him to the ground. He cursed, spit, roared. Someone grabbed a handful of hair, jerked his head off the floor, slammed it into the stones. Again. Again. Until Paden couldn't fight them off any more.

The deputies—he had lost count of how many, maybe a half dozen—pinned his arms behind his back. The metal handcuffs were cold against his skin, and his assailants tightened the bracelets until the iron bit into his skin. A rolled bandanna slipped into his mouth, was jerked back, almost breaking his front teeth. The knot someone tied pulled his hair. Finding strength from somewhere inside him, Paden fought the gag as a horse might struggle against a bit, until he gagged. Once they hoisted him to his feet, someone threw a burlap bag over his head.

He was sweating. Could barely breathe.

"Let's get moving, me lads." He recognized the Irish accent of the county sheriff. A Cole man.

"Hell, it ain't but six-fifteen. The hanging ain't. . . ."

"Don't be a damned fool. We go now!"

The door opened. He heard it *squeak,* felt the coolness of the morning air. Suddenly he pulled away from those holding him, stumbled blindly, wanting to scream. Heading for the breeze. Something slammed into his side—a man—and rammed him against the adobe wall. His nose bled freely.

"Try that again, and we drag you out. Hang you while you're out cold." The sheriff was talking, his teeth clenched, the smell of whiskey permeating the hot burlap. "Criminy, lad, be a man. Don't show your Maker how yellow you are."

They shoved him again. Men holding his arms. Dragging his manacled feet. Chains *rattled* as they moved onto the streets of Tierra Amarilla.

He couldn't see through the sack, and sweat burned his eyes, yet he could hear.

"Hell's fire," the sheriff said.

"Quite the turnout," a deputy muttered.

"And more's coming."

Traces *jingled,* and hoofs sounded. A wagon passed by them, kicking up dust.

"Somebody's makin' hisself a profit in Chama," a deputy said. "Bringin' folks right off the trains and hotels in an omnibus. Yonder comes another."

"Move!" the sheriff barked. "Quickly. Let's end this before there's more people."

The metallic *click* told him that a pistol was being cocked. Then another. They kept walking. At first he heard music, singing, a guitar, maybe—could it be?—a harp, but as they moved down the dusty street, the music faded. He felt the presence of the people as he passed them. Some prayed. Some gasped. Some, he knew, just stared. He could picture their faces, see them crossing themselves as the sheriff and his men led this monster to the gallows.

"¡*Viva* Juan Vasco!" someone shouted, and the cry echoed

across the village.

He wanted to scream: *Don't you know you're being played for fools? Don't you know I'm innocent? Can't you see . . . ?*

But they couldn't see. And that bothered them.

It was a murmur at first, but it grew as they walked, grew into a steady chorus, into cries of rage. Some voices were Spanish, and he had never grasped more than a dozen or two words, but he could understand the English. Not at first. Not until his head cleared, until he summoned a modicum of courage, until he thought that maybe he had a slight chance.

"Let us see his face!"

"Remove the mask!"

"Show us Jeremiah Cole!"

"We must see his face. It is our right! Show us the face of the killer!"

They walked on, but slower.

"Sheriff . . . ," one of the deputies began.

"Keep moving."

Yet they stopped.

"Get out of me way." The sheriff spoke again. "You people are interfering with a legal hanging. Move."

He tried to breathe.

"Roberto, tell them what I said. Tell them if they don't quit blocking the gateway, I'll arrest them. Tell them those gallows can hang more than this fellow here."

He heard the translation, and the rallying cry of the people.

"Show us his face!"

"Remove the hood!"

"The lad is shamed!" the sheriff yelled, desperate. "He ain't . . . he's scared. Men have the . . . right . . . to wear a hood when they're being executed. It's . . . it's. . . ."

Spanish voices drowned out his attempts at reason.

The shotgun roared, ringing Paden's ears.

"I'm the law, damn it!" the sheriff said. "That's a warning. I'm bringing the boy to the gallows. Now step aside." He swore, muttered to one of the deputies: "Why do those nigger soldiers just stand there? Why don't they come help us out?"

Paden tried to swallow. Couldn't. Not with the gag in his mouth.

"Roberto, tell them I put the next load of buckshot in their bellies." The hammer *clicked.*

They were moving again. Someone spit. He wondered if they had been trying to hit him, or Sheriff Murphey.

"Just a few more feet," the sheriff whispered, "then up the gallows. I ain't reading no death warrant. We just put him on the door, put the noose over his head, and drop him. Curtis, you and Greg wait below. Make damned sure nobody jerks off the sack after we spring the trap."

They were inside the enclosure. Nearing the gallows. The deputies holding him gripped his arms tighter. As scared as he was.

Ten more yards, and they'd be walking up the gallows.

Roman Cole wiped clammy palms on his trousers. He spit out the cigar, tried to breathe. Those damned peasants were chanting again, demanding to see the face of the man condemned, but Luke Murphey was earning his pay.

Cole stood just in front of the cavalry troopers inside the enclosure. He wanted to look over his shoulder, see what those Army boys might plan on doing, but didn't want to give anything away. His stomach gurgled, and he felt the urge to run to the nearest privy, relieve his bowels.

Damn. He ran his hand over his stubbled jaw. Father Amado and Father Virgilio blocked the steps up the gallows. Talking to Murphey. Pointing at the prisoner.

"He's my son!" Cole hadn't wanted to scream, but the words

came out, cracking, revealing the panic. "Let him . . . die in peace." His chest felt as if someone had laid a dozen anvils on it, and he knew his plan was shot to hell.

Only . . . maybe his stricken plea had worked. He hadn't planned that, either, but those two fool priests stepped aside, and Luke Murphey moved toward the awaiting noose, the masked prisoner shoved up after him.

"Stop it! Stop it! For the love of God, that is not. . . ."

Cole whirled, felt his heart skip, saw the red-headed woman rushing through the crowd that had formed a human wall next to the ten-foot high pine palisade. He cursed Matt Denton and Big Boy Davenport for not killing the girl, but it was his own damned fault. He should have done it himself.

Only someone grabbed the woman, put a gloved hand over her mouth. At first, he thought it might be Zech Stone, but that old fool lay passed out on the floor in Pedro's Place with his cur dog. No, it was one of the sheriff's deputies, but everyone in the whole damned place stared at the man and the woman, and some idiot officer from Fort Lewis marched for the couple, followed by a sergeant and three darkies.

"Get it over with, Luke!" Cole roared. He was racing for the redhead, gripping the butt of his Remington revolver. He'd kill her if he had to.

He slid to a stop, almost fell, let his hand slide off the .44. Blinked, unbelieving. Heard the crowd gasp. Wished he were dead.

"Leave her be," Jeremiah said. "It's over, Pa."

Roman Cole's eyes shot around him, feeling all the prying looks, hearing all the whispers. The officer and his buffalo soldiers had stopped, too. Cole wet his lips. He tried to call out his son's name, only he couldn't speak.

Paden heard a Spanish prayer, followed by another voice.

"What is the meaning of this?"

He was jerked down the steps, and leathery hands tore the mask off his face, the light from the rising sun almost blinding him. The next thing Paden knew, he was on the ground, hands and feet still manacled, the gag still in his mouth.

The younger of the two priests pulled Sheriff Luke Murphey down the wooden steps, yanked the shotgun from the lawman's hand, and pitched the weapon underneath the scaffold. Then the priest spit in Murphey's face.

Another priest, much older, crossed himself, walked past Paden, straight to the man standing in the center of the enclosure. Paden feared he was dreaming. It couldn't be. Why?

Jeremiah Cole wore a fine suit of black broadcloth. His face had been shaved, his hair cut, slicked back, combed. He wore a black silk cravat, boots shining like the ace of spades in a new deck, a white shirt, and a silver cross pinned on his breast. The elderly priest stopped in front of him, turned, and, head bowed as both men prayed, they walked toward the gallows.

Someone was working on the knot, and the bandanna fell from Paden's mouth. Paden sucked in fresh air, tasting the blood from his nose, his own sweat. Rolling over, he saw Fenella. He fought back tears. She was alive!

"How?"

*"Shhhh,"* she whispered.

The boots of Jeremiah Cole and the sandals of Father Virgilio *thumped* on the wooden steps. Cole walked directly to the platform, just behind the dangling noose. Father Virgilio knelt, still praying, while Father Amado raced up the steps. He roughly pulled the noose over Jeremiah Cole's head. The kid barely blinked. After tightening the coils, the priest walked to the lever, and pointed at Senator Roman Cole, who stood like a marble statue in the center of the compound.

"Roman Cole, you are a disgrace. You have no decency. There

should be two Coles on this platform today, to fulfill the prophecy." After repeating his words in Spanish, the angry priest gripped the lever with both hands.

Softly Father Virgilio prayed.

Jeremiah Cole stared at his father.

They waited. Amado's knuckles whitened, but the lever never budged, and then the priest started backing away, color draining from his face, staring at his trembling hands, tears cascading down his cheeks, and he ran to the back of the scaffold, sobbing at first before retching, then crying harder, shamed.

Nothing happened for what seemed an eternity. No one spoke. Even the wind had stopped. There was nothing to hear except Father Virgilio's prayers, and Father Amado's sobs.

Then footsteps.

Slowly, unevenly Sheriff Luke Murphey ascended the platform, walked to the lever, and turned to the crowd. He looked straight ahead as his unsteady hands gripped the lever, but Paden doubted if the lawman saw anything.

Paden swallowed, felt Fenella's hand grip his shoulder, tighter, tighter.

A moment later, Jeremiah Cole's eyes locked on Paden.

"Hey, Paden." Cole smiled.

Paden couldn't believe how calm the boy looked.

"I'm standing on my own two feet."

The trap door sprang open.

# Epilogue

*Letter from Paden Farms, Martinez, California*
*To Sean Paden, Gadsden Hotel, Douglas, Arizona*
*Postmarked Thursday, August 17, 1939*

Dear Son:

Your letter of the 3rd came as a blessing, and I hope this overdue reply finds you in good health. You would not believe the orchards this year, especially the peaches, and I attribute our bountiful crop to your father, looking down upon us, watching over us, as he has always done, only now from the Kingdom of Heaven.

I trust you have heard from your sisters, but, if not—for I know all of my children are busy—Colleen is a mother again, but still teaching those poor Indians at the reservation, while Karen is busy with all her costumes at Paramount Studios. My dear friend Edna jokes that she can never take me to a moving picture because I get so excited that I'll scream out during the show: "That's my daughter's dress . . . on Carole Lombard!"

But you did not write me to hear about fruit, or the accomplishments of your sisters, and, so, with arthritic hand I will do my best to answer your questions.

When Clint was called away last winter, I did not know he kept a journal, but your father was always full of surprises in the forty years we had on earth together. The carefree vagabond I first met in New Mexico would have been the last man I'd ever expect to settle down and raise plums, pears, peaches, and apricots on a farm in Contra Costa County, but he did, and we've done it well, I think. I never knew of the journals until I found them after his passing. I didn't read them. I couldn't read them. Not then, not now, but maybe later. Yet I knew you would want to see them, and I think he would want you to have them.

He didn't write them when we first met. I think later, when he had settled down, when he came to accept and maybe even understand all that happened, he began to write, secretly, to try to put things in perspective. Maybe for his children to read, so they might better know their father.

Yes, your father spent time in the territorial penitentiary in New Mexico. I really don't know much about the circumstances that landed him in trouble, but I know all too well of the events leading up to the execution of Jeremiah Cole. Yes, your father rode with Britton Wade, and me—for I was that strange woman mentioned in some newspaper articles after the hanging, and the novels, trash, that were published a short time afterward.

Yet you must understand that Britton Wade was not the rough-hewn man-killer he has been made out to be in those dreadful books and that even worse movie, and your father certainly wasn't the foolish sidekick that Andy Devine made him out to be.

You father and I never talked much about what happened in New Mexico. After reading his journals, and from all your subsequent research, you know why.

How did I survive? God watched over me. He always has. Those two riders carried me into the woods, and when those rough hands lifted me out of the saddle and set me on the straw, I thought I was dead. No, I knew it was over, for me.

"All right," the cowboy said, and, when I opened my eyes, I saw he was not talking to me. He was looking at the other cowboy, a bigger man. In fact, if I remember correctly, he was called Big Boy. The younger man was Matt Denton. I do remember that, for it was he who saved my life. The big one, still mounted, had drawn a knife.

"You can put that knife back in its sheath," Matt Denton said, "because I ain't never laid a hand on a woman, and I ain't about to start now. No matter what Mister Cole wants."

The big man did as he was told, with relief.

"Ma'am." The young man swept off his big Mexican sombrero when he looked at me. "You reckon you can find your way out of these woods?"

I nodded. I guess I did. I'm not really sure, though.

"Well, you do that. Stay clear of T.A. Just get to Chama, get on the train, get as far away from here as you can. Don't let Mister Cole or none of his men catch you. They ain't . . . well, ma'am . . . I'm the one who ought to be hanging. Not that man that you was with. I'm sorry this is all I can do for you."

It was enough.

He pulled tally book and pencil from his war bag, and started writing. "You want to ride south with me?" he asked his companion.

"Reckon so."

I'll never forget the note they left tacked to the tree, before they left me, alive, in the thick of Roman Cole's forest.

*We, the UndeRsignD, do herby dEclar that we kwit Roman Cole we take horses 4 payment, & dont nobody dar come lookN 4 us*

*(Signed) M.J. Denton*

*X*

It's likely the hired hands Senator Cole had charged to make sure his son remained at his ranch house also abruptly quit, and lit out of the territory, after failing in that task. I hope they did. For their own sake.

I'm sorry to say I can't help you out much when it comes to further research about the story. Jeremiah Cole hanged, and I might add that no one ever died so bravely as that poor, troubled young man. It comes as no surprise to me that Luke Murphey resigned as sheriff of Río Arriba County shortly after the execution, since you discovered such reports in the New Mexico state archives. Undoubtedly he had no choice but to resign after his shameful complicity in trying to hang your father.

Likewise, I cannot say what became of Roman Cole. He left the Senate. I know that much, but whether it was of his own volition, I cannot say. Fifteen years ago, a man I had worked for in Chama, James Gage, who ran the mercantile there, I met by chance at the railroad station in Martinez. He was on his way to San Francisco. He told me that Roman Cole spent the rest of his life alone in his ranch house, letting it fall into disrepair. On the rare occasions that he showed his face in Chama or Tierra Amarilla, Cole never admitted that he had ever had sons. He was a bitter, old man. The lumber mills, and all his other interests, were sold shortly after Jeremiah's execution, although he stingily held onto the land he had fought so hard to take. Those were the reports of Mr. Gage, but he had never really cared for Roman Cole, although he certainly straddled the fence while in business in Chama. He had to. I don't blame him.

Who owns Cole's land now? I haven't a guess, but I suppose the Mexican settlers of New Mexico are still fighting for the return of their land grants. Alas, many, I fear, will always be losing that fight.

You write that you found Roman Cole's obituary in the October 10, 1909, edition of the Santa Fe *New Mexican,* and that it cites his cause of death as cerebral apoplexy. Was that a lie? Did the senator really hang himself? Was the curse of the *bruja* fulfilled? Well, I, for one, have never believed in curses. Maybe Cole hanged himself, perhaps he had a stroke. If you want to believe in witchcraft, you can always argue that Roman Cole died by the rope when Jeremiah died by the rope.

I think Roman Cole was dead, spiritually, when I left him with his dead son on a cool May morning in Tierra Amarilla.

No, I did not know that Zechariah Stone wrote a book about his life. No, I do not care to read it. I only met that famous scout briefly, and while he may have done many great things during his life, what happened on the road through the Tusas Mountains was vile. Let him try to wash his hands of the matter, much as he tried to forget about the evil he had done by drinking himself to near-death in that saloon. I'm sure his story is "lively reading"—lies usually are—but my reading pleasures these days are usually limited to lies—ha, ha!—from my children.

Where is Britton Wade's grave? I squeeze shut my eyes, try to picture the country, but I can't remember. I'm closing in on seventy years, you know.

Sean, if your father's journals and your subsequent investigations have revealed anything, I hope it is this. People change. There is good in the darkest of men, and evil in the best. We can only hope that we ride toward the light, and somehow manage to beat off the Devil. Your father did that. So did Britton Wade.

All of us who undertook that journey in 1898, all of us who rode up the Río Chama, changed, Son. The foolish girl who waited in the loft of the stables at the church in Santa Cruz was not the same woman who stood at the foot of the gallows crying as Jeremiah Cole was hanged.

Those were violent times. It was a savage country.

History isn't neat, Sean. It's messy. It's ugly. Often, there are no easy answers or explanations. I hope you understand this. I also hope you will forgive me for asking you not to mention what you have read in Clint's journals to your sisters, until after I am gone. Yes, of course, you may seek that truth, and maybe, just maybe, with your passion for history and for fighting injustice, you may correct all of the lies about the journey up the Río Chama, and the execution of Jeremiah Cole.

I just don't know if I have anything else to say. There is not much more that I can add.

It has been a beautiful summer here at the farm, Sean. I do take pleasure in the smell and taste of fruit, in the hills, in the forests. I do love to hear the train whistle blow at night, although that sometimes leaves me melancholy, especially these past eight lonely months. And I do so enjoy your descriptions of the desert in southern Arizona. It sounds like a wonderful, adventurous place, and maybe one day I'll let you lure me away from Paden Farms to stay in that fancy hotel where you're working. I haven't traveled far from Martinez in a long, long time.

Well, Son, it is getting late, and I am an old woman, so I will close for now. You should write Colleen if you haven't yet, and maybe you can urge that older sister of yours into finally giving me a grandson. Don't get me wrong, I love all of my granddaughters, but I'd love to have a boy to bounce on my knee.

Your loving mother,
Fenella

P.S. The train whistle from the 11:05 just blew, and I remembered something else. It's probably not important to the truth of your story, but it explains, I think, the life your father and I shared.

We were stunned after the execution. The wind began to blow. A sign of God, many said, and slowly the men, women—and children!, Lord have mercy—left the gallows. The soldiers marched away, Father Virgilio continued to pray, Father Amado continued to cry, and Sheriff Murphey, the drunk, stumbled down the steps. He saw Clint and me, knelt, unlocked the hand and feet manacles, and disappeared with the throngs.

I really don't remember what happened next. It's like piecing together a dream so many years later. I wanted to help take down Jeremiah Cole's body, but Father Virgilio and Father Amado, who had recovered enough to assist with the grim task, begged me to leave. When I turned, I saw Roman Cole standing there, just staring, unblinking. So I walked away, looking for Clint, but he was gone.

Gasping, I hurried out of the enclosure, fought my way through the crowd. I couldn't see him. I don't know what made me think of it, but I got onto a wagon that had carried the curious from the railroad to T.A., and rode it back to Chama. As I write this letter, I can smell the cinders, feel my eyes burning from the thick, black smoke, and I jumped off the wagon, and ran. Lifting my ragged skirts, I ran. The train had started to pull away, and I almost tripped on the tracks, saved by a kindly drummer who pulled me onto the smoking car.

I blessed him, then walked through the cars, swaying with the rhythm of the rails. Just when I was about to give up hope, feared I had made a foolish mistake, I saw him, sitting alone, next to the window, staring at the morning light, empty. Exhausted, I dropped into the seat beside him. He looked at me, then back out the window.

"Where are you going?" I asked him.

He didn't answer for the longest time. I grabbed his right hand, locked my fingers in his, and squeezed.

"I don't know," he answered at last.

I squeezed harder. He kept looking out that window.

"That," I said, "sounds just right to me."

I kept squeezing his hand, and did not stop, until, finally, I felt him squeeze back.

# AUTHOR'S NOTE

Although many places in this novel (Elephant Rock, Holy Cross Catholic Church, Echo Amphitheater, and, of course, the Chama River) may be real, or based on actual sites, *Río Chama* is a work of fiction. Britton Wade, Clint Paden, Fenella Magauran, Jeremiah Cole, and the rest are all figments of my imagination. The only two legal hangings in Río Arriba County history occurred in 1896 when Perfecto Padilla and Robert Torres were executed for separate murders.

Helpful literary sources included *The Tierra Amarilla Grant: A History of Chicanery* by Malcom Ebright (Center for Land Grant Studies, 1980); *Death on the Gallows: The Story of Legal Hangings in New Mexico, 1847–1923* by West Gilbreath (High Lonesome Books, 2002); and *La Tierra Amarilla: Its History, Architecture, and Cultural Landscape* by Chris Wilson and David Kammer (Museum of New Mexico Press, 1989).

Thanks also to the staffs at the Billy the Kid Museum in Fort Sumner, New Mexico; Chama Valley Chamber of Commerce; Cumbres & Toltec Scenic Railroad; El Rancho de las Golondrinas; Jicarilla Apache Reservation; Santa Fe Public Library; Vista Grande Public Library; and Santa Fe State Records Center & Archives; to Dennis and Lisa Hall of Fayetteville, North Carolina, for some tricky Spanish questions; and to my wife and son, for traveling with me into the Chama River wilderness for some on-site research for this novel.

Special thanks to Colleen and Ray Milligan of Milligan Brand

Outfitters in Chama, and the Glisson family—Bill, Rhonda, Cody and Dillon—at The Timbers of Chama for all their hospitality, help, support, and encouragement.

Johnny D. Boggs
Santa Fe, New Mexico

# ABOUT THE AUTHOR

**Johnny D. Boggs** has worked cattle, shot rapids in a canoe, hiked across mountains and deserts, traipsed around ghost towns, and spent hours poring over microfilm in library archives—all in the name of finding a good story. He's also one of the few Western writers to have won three Spur Awards from Western Writers of America (for his novels, *Camp Ford,* in 2006 and *Doubtful Cañon,* in 2008, and his short story, "A Piano at Dead Man's Crossing," in 2002) and the Western Heritage Wrangler Award from the National Cowboy and Western Heritage Museum (for his novel, *Spark on the Prairie: The Trial of the Kiowa Chiefs,* in 2004). A native of South Carolina, Boggs spent almost fifteen years in Texas as a journalist at the *Dallas Times Herald* and *Fort Worth Star-Telegram* before moving to New Mexico in 1998 to concentrate full time on his novels. Author of more than thirty published short stories, he has also written for more than fifty newspapers and magazines, and is a frequent contributor to *Boys' Life, New Mexico Magazine, Persimmon Hill,* and *True West.* His Western novels cover a wide range. *The Lonesome Chisholm Trail* (Five Star Westerns, 2000) is an authentic cattle-drive story, while *Lonely Trumpet* (Five Star Westerns, 2002) is an historical novel about the first black graduate of West Point. *The Despoilers* (Five Star Westerns, 2002) and *Ghost Legion* (Five Star Westerns, 2005) are set in the Carolina backcountry during the Revolutionary War. *The Big Fifty* (Five Star Westerns, 2003) chronicles the slaughter of buffalo on the southern plains in the 1870s, while *East of the Border* (Five Star Westerns, 2004) is a comedy about the theatrical offerings of Buffalo Bill Cody, Wild Bill Hickok, and Texas Jack Omohundro, and *Camp Ford* (Five Star Westerns, 2005) tells about a Civil War baseball game between Union prisoners of war and Confederate guards. "Boggs's narrative voice captures the old-fashioned style of the past," *Publishers Weekly* said, and *Booklist* called him "among the best Western writers at work today." Boggs lives with his wife Lisa and son Jack in Santa Fe. His website is www.johnnydboggs.com. His next Five Star Western will be *Hard Winter.*